MW01413917

# TRANSFORMATIONS
## the next step.

# TRANSFORMATIONS
## the next step.

A NOVEL BY

**JOHN NELSON**

*Author of* **STARBORN**

THE
DONNING COMPANY
PUBLISHERS
NORFOLK / VIRGINIA BEACH

*For Robert Friedman,*
*friend and editor,*
*without whose support and encouragement*
*this book would never have been written.*



The Donning Company/Publishers
5659 Virginia Beach Boulevard
Norfolk, Virginia 23502

Edited by Robert S. Friedman and Richard A. Horwege

**Library of Congress Cataloging-in-Publication Data:**

Nelson, John, 1947-
Transformations.
I. Title.
PS3564.E465T7 1988 813'.54 88-7142
ISBN 0-89865-634-6
ISBN 0-89865-549-8 (pbk.)

**Printed in the United States of America**

# CONTENTS

*If the round shining objects [flying saucers] that appear in the sky be regarded as visions, we can hardly avoid interpreting them as archetypal images....Anyone with the requisite historical and psychological knowledge knows that circular symbols have played an important role in every age; in our own sphere of culture, for instance, they were not only soul symbols but "God-images." There is an old saying that "God is a circle whose centre is everywhere and the circumference nowhere." God in his omniscience, omnipotence, and omnipresence is a totality symbol par excellence, something round, complete, and perfect. Epiphanies of this sort are, in the tradition, often associated with fire and light. On the antique level, therefore, the Ufos could easily be conceived as "gods." They are impressive manifestations of totality whose simple, round form portrays the archetype of the self, which as we know from experience plays the chief role in uniting apparently irreconcilable opposites and is therefore best suited to compensate the split-mindedness of our age. It has a particularly important role to play among the other archetypes in that it is primarily the regulator and orderer of chaotic states, giving the personality the greatest possible unity and wholeness. It creates the image of the divine-human personality, the Primordial Man or Anthropos....an Elijah who calls down fire from heaven, rises up to heaven in a fiery chariot, and is a forerunner of the Messiah....*

*Flying Saucers: A Modern Myth*
C. G. Jung

# PROLOGUE

## Roykenvik, Norway
## June 25

The flowers lining the side of the dirt road stood straight and tall in the breeze stirred up by the passing car. On either side fields of wild flowers stretched to the horizon. At the front of the dust storm, the Volvo slowed down, and the driver cracked open the window only to roll it back up a moment later. The moving air outside the car offered little relief from the stifling heat. The man turned and looked at his elderly passenger with some concern. Dr. Max Kellgren's long gangly figure was hunched up in the bucket seat of the small sedan. He patted his forehead dry with a handkerchief, then ran his fingers through the remaining strands of steel-gray hair.

Johan Amundsen reached over and tapped the air conditioner. The motor raced faster, hitting both of them with another burst of warm air. "Sorry, professor, but this car wasn't built for hot weather."

"Maybe I should postpone my visit until winter."

"Believe me, you'll want to see this today."

"I only hope," Kellgren said with mock impatience, "that this time you have more to show me than black roses."

"That was child's play in comparison."

There was an intriguing note in the young man's voice that Kellgren could not immediately identify. He turned and studied Amundsen's outward appearance for a clue to this barely perceived change in his former student. He looked much the same as he had when they had met six months earlier in Stockholm to discuss his latest crossbreeding experiment. Amundsen had been flushed with excitement over the creation of this new hybrid. And like many scientists of his generation, the man's mastery over nature had led to an overestimation of his position in the grand scale of things. At least he could joke about it, as he had that day at lunch, giving nature credit for supplying him with such marvelous raw materials. Kellgren now realized that what he had detected was a note of humility in his young colleague, and he wondered what new mystery had inspired this curious respect.

They drove through the gate to the experimental plant station, past the outlying buildings that housed the laboratories, and stopped at the main greenhouse. There was a caravan of trucks and vans parked out front with white-coated technicians busily moving their hi-tech equipment inside. Amundsen now reached into his coat pocket and took out a guest pass. He peeled off the back and stuck the tag to Dr. Kellgren's jacket. "This will get you inside, but stay close. And please don't take any shavings. I'll see what I can get later."

The two of them walked up to the entrance and stood aside while an impressive array of photographic lights were wheeled into the greenhouse. With the door clear, they stepped up to a young security guard who recognized Amundsen and waved them through

Dr. Kellgren had begun to question the need for such security measures, when he spotted out of the corner of his eye the odd-shaped corolla of a bellflower hanging overhead. The huge white flower bending its long slender stalk drooped down to eye level where Kellgren stepped over to examine it. The outer rim of petals had been re-formed to flare out at the bottom in a girdle that perfected its shape. This formation indicated engineering skills that localized genetic tampering to an extent unknown to him. It was indeed an exciting breakthrough, but before he could congratulate his colleague, Kellgren looked out to discover a greenhouse packed with even more startling creations. He decided to investigate further before awarding any credit.

He walked down the center aisle followed by Amundsen and inspected the plants and flowers of this botanical wonderland. There were lavender roses, short-stemmed bearded irises, six-petaled orchids, violets with three-lobed leaves, bellflowers with girdles of various sizes, and shootingstars, their normally inverted petals hanging down. And while Kellgren examined each specimen, others were photographing them, taking soil and water samples, as well as testing the air for radiation levels. All of the technicians were lost in their measurements; only Dr. Kellgren saw what was actually there.

He stooped over to pick up a potted flower, and Amundsen explained, "One day we planted seeds for a more insect-resistant white tulip, and the next day we came in and found a fully mature plant with candy-striped petals." Kellgren smiled as he ran his finger up and down the perfectly formed tulip petal. "Overnight, something...some force re-formed mature, adult plants while accelerating the development of seedlings a thousandfold. Tell me, professor. What could do such a thing?"

Kellgren had hoped that the mystery locked away in his colleague's greenhouse would help nature reclaim lost ground in its battle with modern science. He would have loved to see one last show of force before he passed on to whatever awaited him on the other side of death. But, as he studied this marvelous oddity, he knew that once again nature had only supplied the raw materials. It was obvious that these plants had been transformed by a science far in advance of their own. Now, faced with his own personal unknown, he found the unthinkable almost plausible.

Amundsen looked up at his old mentor in hope that some pronouncement would unravel this mystery and restore order to his world. Dr. Kellgren's answer was to hold up the potted flower for both of them to contemplate in silence for a long moment.

"I don't know, Johan. But whatever it is, at least it has a sense of humor," he said.

Looking at the ludicrous stripe, Amundsen shook his head in agreement before the personified "it" of this seemingly innocent statement began to bother him. While he thought about it, a bee landed on one of the outside petals of the tulip and slowly edged its way down into the heart of the flower. Gathering the nectar and inadvertently the flower's pollen, the bee flew away to spread its load abroad.

CHAPTER ONE

# TRANSDUCTION

*The movement of genes*
*from a donor to a recipient*
*using a phage (virus)*
*as the vector.*

# PART I

## San Martin, California
## September 6

Clouds of fog rolling in off the ocean swept across the highway. A young hitchhiker stepped out onto the road and looked up the highway for any oncoming traffic. He waited for a moment, and when no cars appeared, he slung his backpack over his shoulder and began to walk. Carl Owens was in his early twenties, medium height, with broad shoulders from years of manual labor. His dark hair was cut short to hide the curl a longer style would bring out. He had a ready smile but was just as quick to anger, and for that reason, along with his vagabond spirit, Carl never held a job very long. Like steady work, the same surroundings also had a way of closing in on him. Some would call him a fickle young man, others would say he was unstable, and a few would label him as rebellious. What none would have guessed was that Carl Owens was a very serious person. He had discovered early in his life an inviolable part of himself that he refused to compromise. The first sign of any such infringement would drive him away.

Suddenly, as he walked along, two headlights popped up behind him. Carl with his trained ears heard the engine sound just in time to jump out of the way. The car whizzed past him and pulled off the road skidding to a stop in the loose gravel. With his backpack bobbing up and down, he ran fifty yards through sand and gravel to reach the car and chide this reckless driver. Carl stuck his head through the open window, but he paused long enough for the driver to disarm him with his apologetic smile.

"Sorry, son. But this last patch of fog snuck up on me," the driver said. The man was in his early forties, wearing a tan suit stained under the arms, and from his appearance and from the box of advertising premiums on the front seat, Carl assumed that he was a traveling salesman.

"Then you should be driving a little slower," Carl finally added.

"You're right, and I will," he replied. Again he flashed that smile, and Carl could feel his hostility slowly draining away. "If you need a lift, why don't you hop in."

The man's voice was flat with none of the tell-tale eagerness that signaled a potential problem for a hitch-hiker. Carl gave him another quick look but concluded that the only price for this ride would be an earful of talk. He opened the door and slid inside. "Sure, why not. It beats walking."

The driver slowly drove back onto the highway as an eighteen-wheeler came barreling out of the fog blowing its horn. He floored the accelerator; slick back tires spun on the wet road before finally gaining traction and pulling away from the oncoming behemoth. In a moment, after checking the rear view mirror, he was able to slow down to a safe speed. He now looked over at Carl who was shaking his head in disbelief.

"Maybe walking isn't such a bad idea after all," Carl said.

"It's the fog; I've never seen it so bad."

"You have if you've driven this road for very long." Carl wondered if this were merely a bad driver's excuse, or whether the man was new to the territory and was lying about it.

"Oh, so you're from around here then?"

Was he ignoring his query, or was this a spontaneous response? Carl assumed the latter and turned off his normally suspicious mind. He looked out the windshield through a clearing in the fog to the ocean churning below.

"Yeah, well I was born here all right, but I was never from around here, if you know what I mean."

The driver nodded his head in recognition, apparently familiar with this subtle distinction. "Been away very long?"

"Not long enough for some, I'm sure," Carl said.

"Well, the worse they can do is run you out of town, and you've already left once."

Carl turned back to the driver annoyed by this unsolicited advice. "Now that's reassuring."

The driver threw his hands up in the air. "Can't say I didn't try." The car edged its way across the center line and into the next lane, where an oncoming car had to swerve around them. The driver now grabbed hold of the steering wheel and pulled back into his lane. He looked over at Carl to apologize but could see it would take more than a killer smile to pacify that anxious look. In self-defense he hunched over the wheel with an air of exaggerated conscientiousness that proved irresistible.

Carl sat back in his seat, laughed it off, and added in the spirit of the moment, "Thing is, I was hoping to tie up a few loose ends. Who knows when I'll be back this way again." The driver nodded his head, and his mask of sweet joviality dropped briefly to reveal a look of profound understanding more suited to a Dalai Lama than a traveling salesman.

They drove on in silence as the fog cleared and the coast road turned inland. A small town soon came into view, sandwiched between the ocean on one side and the mountains on the other. Although it was too small for an active tourist industry, San Martin had a wide range of motels and shops that made it an ideal stopover for a night's rest and an early swim before heading north to the Bay Area or south to the beach resorts. There was just enough year-round commerce to satisfy the shopkeepers and to provide the tax base that kept longtime residents who opposed more development in control. So far San Martin had avoided the type of commercialization that had plagued many towns along the coastal highway. With its predominantly Spanish architecture, it retained an old-fashioned charm somewhat out of step with the rest of the modern world. Most young people could not wait to leave, but in time a few would return to lead healthier, more productive lives. They would also have a better chance of one day joining the local octogenarian club.

The driver drove into town as the coast road became Alameda, and the traffic slowed down as teen-agers just out of school freely crossed from one side of the street to the other. Finally, the car in front of them beeped its horn, and the road cleared. Carl had been absently staring out the window when the loud noise brought him back. He looked up to see Park's Cinema and knew he had arrived.

"You can let me off anywhere along here," Carl said.

"So this is home, then."

"Yeah, I guess you could say that, but don't hold me to it."

Seeing the local diner, the salesman turned at the next corner, drove up and parked in front. "Well, I don't know about you, but I haven't eaten all day. The food any good in there?"

"Everything but the chili."

"Then I'm in luck. Can't stand the stuff," he said. "How about you. . . hungry?"

"I could probably do with a cup of coffee before I head out to the farm."

The two men stepped out of the car and walked up the sidewalk to the diner. The salesman opened the front door, and the two of them went inside. However, Carl stopped short and stared at the waitress behind the lunch counter. He now turned and went back outside. The salesman followed after him.

"I think I'll pass on the coffee," Carl said.

"Then it's goodbye and good luck," the salesman said. He stepped over to Carl, shoved a ballpoint pen into his coat pocket, and grabbed his hand in a two-handed hand shake of legendary proportions. Carl's eyes popped wide open from the pressure before he pulled his hand out of the vise grip.

"That's one hell of a handshake, mister."

"I like to be remembered," the salesman said with a strange intensity that would linger in Carl's mind long after the momentary discomfort had passed.

Carl backed away from this awkward moment, turned and walked up the street as the salesman went into the diner. At the next corner the coast road intersected the main inland highway heading east to the farmland on this side of the coastal mountains. Carl went over and stood at the bus stop. He knew if he thumbed a ride anywhere in town he would be greeted with unwelcomed questions. Also, his return would be a well-known fact by the next morning. The few old friends he looked forward to seeing could wait for his call, and the others would know soon enough.

Carl was not avoiding anyone in particular, although the waitress at the diner, Jennifer Barnak, an old girlfriend, was someone he needed to approach with great care. They had gone through high school together and had planned to attend the same college, or at least that had been Jennifer's plans. Carl acceded almost by default. He was certainly bright enough to attend college, and his college boards were considerably higher than anyone had expected. Yet, when he thought about a course of study, there was nothing that appealed to him. He could not see himself in any of the standard professions although, while growing up on the farm, he had considered becoming a veterinarian. When trying to decide about his future the summer after graduation, Carl had a strong premonition that his life would take a strange turn. His path would veer away from the more conventional avenues pursued by his fellow classmates into uncharted territory. Carl did not know exactly where it would lead him, but he knew the starting place was not a college campus. When he decided not to attend school that fall, Jennifer was unconcerned. She could not imagine him staying behind very long, working at jobs way beneath his abilities and hanging around old friends with little or no ambition for themselves. She was right in that regard, but what Jennifer never expected was for Carl to leave town and walk out of her life for five years.

They spent Christmas together when she was home on vacation that first year, and he came down to UC Santa Barbara for spring break. Their relationship, despite the separation, remained much the same. Carl would ground her with his quiet depth, and she would draw him into the world with her outgoing personality. But, almost from the day she left, Jennifer could detect in his letters a strange remoteness, as if in her absence he were withdrawing further within himself. She did not become alarmed until she saw him during spring break, and by then it was too late. Jennifer had hoped Carl could hold out until summer vacation, but when she returned home from school, he had already left town. Although he sent postcards from New England, Canada, and Mexico, it was a one-way communication with the ghost of someone she had once loved.

The bus drove up. Following a line of Mexican farm workers, Carl got on and took a seat. He did not recognize the driver; old Charlie Hatcher must have retired, but he suspected the worst. He wondered what else had changed in the five years while he was away. Carl expected that San Martin was much the same as he had left it. The people who ran this town liked it that way. Old California money was just as conservative as old New England money; the only difference was that the bankers here wore knit shirts with little polo players embroidered on them. The bus had left town and was driving past the outlying suburban developments with their rich-sounding Spanish names. Here was where the new landed gentry had built their modern haciendas. Soon the bus left the well tended lawns behind for the wide expanse of open land, and for the first time since he had returned, Carl looked upon a welcome sight.

When he left town, it had been to pursue a destiny, not to flee any unresolved conflicts with the local establishment. He had inherited his father's side in a long-standing feud with big business interests in town that sought to buy out the small farmers and farm the entire coastal valley under one corporate banner. If he had stayed and worked the farm, he would no doubt have become involved in the dispute. This had been his father's wish, but it was not the life he would choose for himself. Certain local factions were glad to see him go, because every strong son that left weakened the farmers' position, but it was neither his reason for leaving nor for his return.

In the year after high school, while Jennifer attended college and he stayed home left on his own, Carl was seized by a great discontent. His restlessness had little to do with this area and these people but with the strange new life welling up within him that found no connection to them. He had always been in touch with those secret places. His vivid dreams and almost total recall of them had astonished family and friends since his childhood. Now the dreams had become too compelling, and the images were popping up in his waking life. Carl was driven by a great inner necessity to discover the meaning of such activity. It would take him on a strange outward journey that had now come full circle.

The bus stopped at the long dirt road leading to his family's farm. Carl got off and found himself walking over to the box, as he had done for many years, to pick up the day's mail. He now slung his backpack over his shoulder and headed down the road. He had written his parents saying he would stop by on his way to Oregon for the logging season. Carl did not know what to expect, but he knew it was time, with his father getting on in age, for them to settle their differences.

**2.**

When Jennifer Barnak came to work that morning, she felt her best since withdrawing her application to chiropractic college two weeks earlier. She had worked at this job every summer while attending the University of California, and with the tourist business added to the local trade, Jennifer had been able to save enough money to pay all expenses for the coming year. That was mainly due to low tuition rates for state residents. However, the cost of attending the chiropractic college in San Francisco was considerably higher. She had planned to pay her tuition and then work on the side for living expenses, but the school did not allow their students to hold outside jobs. Her counselor suggested she continue working until she could afford one full year, and when she had completed it in good standing, they would help arrange student loans for the remaining three. Jennifer agreed that was the most sensible approach, but wondered if she could handle a waitress job for more than three months at a time.

There was very little early business that morning. Since labor day the tourist trade had dwindled to nothing, leaving them with their lunch trade, a regular dinner crowd and the stragglers that moseyed in at odd hours. At eleven o'clock, businessmen trying to avoid the crowd came in for an early lunch. By noon the diner was packed, and she found herself buried under a load of orders with no time for self-pity. This was how she liked working this job, the busier the better. It was after the crunch that afternoon, while Jennifer was standing at the counter serving a customer, that she looked up and saw Carl walking down the sidewalk. After five years, it took great self-restraint for her not to run outside and call to him.

She placed the plate in front of her customer and then went back to an empty table for a coffee break. The thrill of seeing her ex-boyfriend had quickly passed. He had treated her in a shabby manner that no personal problems could excuse. And to keep writing, maintaining the fiction by a one-way communication that theirs was an on-going relationship, was an insult. Although Jennifer felt that way, she had still had her parents forward the cards to her at school. She suspected that beneath the hurt, in the place where she had buried her first love, lay long dormant feelings for him better left undisturbed. Jennifer had carefully arranged the course of her future life, which included four more years of school, and there was no room in it for a free-spirited vagabond.

She was soon back on the floor finishing her shift, anxious to get home and sort out her feelings about Carl's return. A customer now came in and sat down at the counter. He was in his forties, short and balding, and was no doubt a salesman. Jennifer walked up and handed him the menu.

"Cup of coffee while you're waiting?"

"Gives me acid stomach. How about a cup of tea instead, with lemon."

Jennifer had thrown out a routine question, but when she received such a charming reply in return, she was forced to look at the man more closely. She could see that a genuine person with real feelings resided under that rumpled exterior, and she would treat him accordingly.

"I know what you mean. Coffee is my last remaining vice."

"Hey Jenny, pick up," said Herb, the short-order cook, calling out from the kitchen. She continued to stare at him, caught in the web of that dazzling smile, as she backed up toward the swinging doors. Jennifer now heard footsteps approaching from the other side; she stepped forward and ducked as a waitress came charging through the doors with a full tray of food sailing overhead. With the way clear, she looked up to see the salesman, his hands pressed together, bowing his head in mock thanksgiving over her close call.

Jennifer reckoned that her salesman had showed up just in time to ease her through the dreaded afternoon lull. He certainly looked like an interesting character, and she was hoping that he had some amusing stories to tell. But, when she picked up her order and came back through the swinging doors, Jennifer stopped short and stared at a counter with four new customers. She quickly went to work passing out menus, laying down silverware, filling and dispensing glasses of water. In between trips to the kitchen, she was able to take the salesman's order.

"These friends of yours?" Jennifer asked.

"I thought you could do with a little business," he said.

"Well, don't do me any favors, will you."

Freak runs happened occasionally, but if they caught you between shifts and shorthanded, they could turn nasty. This was a particularly mean run. Nothing seemed to be going right. The customers were impossible, ordering meals not on the menu or rearranging it with substitutions. Everything needed to be cooked with elaborate instructions. Fortunately, when it became too heated, Jennifer could stop in front of her salesman and solicit some needed sympathy. She also was able to tell him her life story in short snippets, and learned a little if not much about him.

It now looked as though Jennifer had made it through the worst part of the rush. The salesman had finished his meal and was waiting on a check. All but one of her other customers were eating, and that man was drumming his fingers on the counter and giving her nasty looks. Jennifer went back into the kitchen to see what was holding up his order. She came through the doors a minute later with his plate, and she laid it down in front of him. He took one bite out of his omelet and pushed it toward her.

"Hey lady, the thing's cold. Take it back and do somethin' with it," he said.

Jennifer picked up the plate and brought it back to the cook. He wanted to reheat the omelet in the microwave, but she insisted that he throw it out and prepare another one. A few minutes later, with the customer making more disgruntled noises, she brought it out to him. He ate a piece, shook his head in disgust, and stood up.

"It's the wrong damn order, you imbecile." The man threw his napkin down and walked out of the restaurant without paying.

Everybody else at the counter checked their orders to see if they had been switched. Jennifer stepped back from the counter, her eyes flashing with anger. A strand of sandy-blond hair, pinned in a bun at the back of her head, had come loose and now fell across her face. Jennifer closed her eyes while she fastened it. This job had brought her close to tears several times, and she had talked back to more than one customer in her summers there. It came with the territory, and it usually happened when she was weakened by some emotional upset. Jennifer was determined, especially today, not to let this incident defeat her. When pressed, as an old trooper had once said, pour coffee. She grabbed the pot and went down the line refilling everybody's cup.

When she reached the salesman, he was leaning back on his

stool observing her. His sudden intensity seemed out of character, and she assumed that he had become impatient with the long delay. Jennifer flipped through her wad of checks, found his and laid it down on the counter. When she looked up, he was smiling again.

"Thanks, you're a real life saver. Don't think I could've made it without you."

"You were doing just fine," he said.

"Well, I know you're just passing through, but if you ever come in again, please ask for me."

"Why, next time I'm in town I'll be coming to you with my sore back."

"It's nice of you to say so, but I still have an awfully long way to go yet," Jennifer said.

"You'd be surprised how fast time can fly," he said with a sparkle in his eyes. He left the money for the check on the counter, and as he stood up to leave, the salesman handed her a dollar tip. When she reached for it, he took her hand and placed it between both of his and shook it gently. For Jennifer it felt like holding hands with a hot radiator, and then he walked out the door. She watched him stand out front observing the sidewalk crowd for a moment, but one of her customers ordered dessert, and by the time she finished serving it, she saw that he had gone.

The salesman was in a good mood when he came out of the diner. So far he was ahead of schedule and had high hopes of locating the necessary candidates in time. The fact that the first two contactees were bound by strong emotional ties was an added bonus. Although there was no optimum number, too few would be ineffective and too many might provoke an over reaction that could terminate the experiment before it had barely begun. Two dozen prime candidates capable of making the transition would be enough to trigger the process. But whatever the harvest, he had until Sunday night before he would have to vacate the contactee's body.

He stopped in front of the diner and looked up and down the

street at the passing townspeople. Coming out of a grocery store was a well-dressed matron followed by a dark-skinned woman carrying bags of food. A spot check indicated the first woman was totally unsuited to their needs, although the second woman, despite a low energy level, had the required emotional resourcefulness. He would keep her in mind as an alternate. The man now driving up and parking in front of the hardware store looked like an interesting subject. He was an outdoor type, robust and energetic in good physical condition. No doubt his body could withstand the rigors of total change-over.

The salesman had begun to cross the street to initiate contact, when he felt coming toward him, too far away for a visual reading, an extremely potent life field. He stepped back on the sidewalk to await their arrival. Within a few minutes, a school teacher escorting a line of young children came into view. A quick check confirmed his earlier impression: she was a primary candidate undergoing a personal growth cycle, which accounted for the high readings. All her body systems were already set to regenerate themselves, and although theirs would be a thousand times more drastic, it was basically the same process.

The salesman could not believe his good luck. If it continued, he might even finish early and could vacate this body before the appointed time. After only a three-hour habitation, it had become extremely confining. It might be suitable for life in this density, but one day, sooner for some than others, they would hopefully discard these puny vehicles in favor of ones capable of travel among the stars. Humankind had arrived at a critical juncture, a fork in the road, between an evolutionary path that led to the stars and one that ended elsewhere. He hoped his brothers would listen carefully and choose wisely.

The woman and her students were now a block away. All that remained was for him to stage an impromptu stress test to gather additional readings. As she walked along, a passing driver suddenly lost control of his car. It pulled right, heading for the line of children stretched across an intersection. The schoolteacher jumped in the vehicle's path and yanked two of her students out of the way. The car now veered off, missing her by only a few feet. There was a brief moment of pandemonium with scared children crying and running loose. The woman quickly cleared everybody off the street, calmed them down, and had another line formed within minutes. She hesitated for a long moment, trying to decide whether to continue, but then she headed for the park at the far end of town, just as he had hoped.

The salesman was satisfied but would wait to contact her at the park. He did not want to lose track of his other candidate, and he now walked across the street and went into the hardware store. He spotted the man across the aisle and watched him collect a basketful of small items. His overall readings were good if not great, but there was only one way to find out. A bale of heavy duty wire now fell from a second floor loft and landed precariously close to him. Startled, the man dropped his basket on the floor and angrily looked up at the young man leaning over the outside row of bales.

"What're you trying to do, kill me?" the farmer yelled. The boy just stared at the bale in disbelief. He could not imagine how it rolled off. The manager now hurried over.

"What's the problem, Hank?"

"Your young friend up there is using me for target practice."

The manager grabbed hold of the heavy bale and moved it out of the aisle. He now called up to his part-time helper, "Arnold, what the hell happened here?"

"I don't know, Mr. Kline. The damn thing just rolled off on its own."

"That's highly unlikely," he said. The manager looked over at his irate customer before deciding on disciplinary action. "Come on down here, and get your things. Can't take a chance of you killing off my best customers."

The farmer nodded his head in agreement before bending over to pick up the loose items on the floor. The manager turned to wait on his new customer, but the man was halfway out the door and was leaving in a hurry.

## 3.

Linda Boyer had returned to San Martin early that year after living in San Francisco for the last five years. After she had separated from her husband and left her real estate job, she felt a change of scenery might help her gain a much needed perspective on the faltering course of her life. She had not come home merely to recuperate but hopefully to start over again in the last place she could remember being truly content. Of course, when looking back, much of that supposed happiness might now be attributed to the delusions of youth. Linda thought otherwise. And so she returned, if not to a life already lived, to the potential it had once offered.

She rented a small one-bedroom apartment in the beach district, and after turning down offers from influential friends of her father, Linda decided that a year of teaching school might be a perfect interim job. She assumed the profession had not changed much in the years since she had last taught school. It was the same in some ways but different in others, an old colleague told her on her first day back. A week later, as Linda prepared to take her first grade class on a field trip to the park, she had begun to understand that distinction. At first she thought it was the new curriculum, but now she realized it was her students. They were brighter and better prepared than any past class she could remember. Most of them were six going on sixty.

This afternoon it had taken five minutes to quiet her class and have everybody lined up against the side wall. Any further delays might cause a cancellation. Linda had knelt down to zip up a little girl's windbreaker, when the principal stepped into the room. Paul Jordan, only a year away from retirement, had been Linda's first grade teacher. He had fond memories of a little girl always in too much of a hurry. Now, standing in the doorway, he watched her with great affection and concern. He still had doubts about her teaching the first grade after such a long layoff.

"Sure you don't want Coach Roberts to go along with you?"

Linda zipped the jacket close, stood up and placed the girl

back in line. "Thanks, Paul. But I can manage it."

"You know these kids today aren't the same as you were at their age. It's the video games, it warps their minds."

"Tell me about it," Linda said.

Jordan suspiciously looked down the line of first graders. "Why, it wouldn't surprise me if one of these little 'persons' had a nuclear device on them."

A boy coming back from the bathroom snuck up behind the principal and stuck a toy gun to his leg. Jordan jumped back, and then seeing the pint-sized gangster, he grabbed the gun from him and threw it to the ground. It went off, shooting a plastic bullet that hit Jordan in the leg. The children giggled their approval.

Linda gave them a look stern enough to quiet their laughter. She now knelt down, picked up the toy gun, and handed it to her student. "Jason, when you point a gun at somebody, it hurts their feelings. Did you want to do that?"

This was entirely more serious than he had expected. The boy shook his head no and tried to break for the line, but Linda caught him. "Don't you think we owe somebody an apology?"

"Sorry," Jason blurted out, and then jumped back in line.

Jordan was impressed with how Linda had handled the young boy. She now had them close rank and marched everybody out of the classroom and down the hall. Jordan followed as far as the front door but could see that she had the class under control. He watched from the window as they turned the corner and headed downtown, and then he returned to his office somewhat relieved.

When he was out of sight, Linda loosened her tight grip on the children and let them spread out along the line. This was not basic training but an excursion, and she wanted everybody to enjoy themselves. She had sensed Paul's concern and wanted to allay his fears, but Linda had enough trouble containing her own anxiety without assuming his load. This included a vague suspicion that with this teaching assignment she had once again undertaken more than she could handle. She wondered if today's field trip were an attempt to prove that to herself.

Linda now noticed that the children at the front of the line were crossing an intersection without her, and then, out of the corner of her eye, she saw a car coming toward them. It was a purely instinctive reaction that propelled her into the path of the car to retrieve the two exposed students. A moment later the driver swerved out of the way, and everybody was safe. Linda stood in the middle of the intersection shaking. It would have been her fault if anybody were injured. How did she let this happen? Her mind had drifted off the job at hand and once again had become caught up in a tape of her own personal concerns. Maybe she was too self-centered, as her husband had always claimed, to be a mother or, for that matter, a good teacher.

With great effort Linda stuck her head out of this emotional morass to discover her students scattering in panic. Again drawing on hidden resources, she quickly responded to the emergency and gathered them together. She had to decide whether to return to the classroom, admitting defeat and possibly resigning her position, or to proceed with greater caution to the park. Linda knew that if she allowed her self-doubt to cripple her, she would never be able to reach beyond herself back into the greater world again. She turned her children around and marched them up the sidewalk toward the park at the far end of town.

At the park, the ducks had just come into the pond for their afternoon feeding. The children gathered around the guardrail, and Linda passed out freezer bags filled with stale bread. They hurriedly ripped them open and tossed pieces of bread out on the water where the ducks glided over and devoured them. Still shaken, Linda retreated to the shade of a nearby park bench to gather herself. Watching them she thought how quickly they had recovered from the nearly tragic incident in the streets only moments earlier. She only wished she were so resilient, but soon the merry sound of their laughter soothed her jagged nerves.

One of her children, Randy Carter, now broke away from the others and ran up to the bench. "Mrs. Boyer, I ran out of bread. You got more?"

Linda reached into her satchel for another bag of bread. "I think there's one left." She found it and went to hand it to him, but Randy was looking past her to the trees behind the bench. Linda turned around to see a man step out of the shadows and walk up to them.

"You come to feed the ducks?" Randy asked.

The man squatted down to the young boy's level. "Yes, little one. I have."

Randy looked at him with a puzzled expression. "Where's your bread?"

The man nodded at the bag Linda held in her hand. "Well, I was hoping you'd share yours with me."

Randy gave this careful consideration, turned and looked around at the others waiting on him. "Okay, but hurry." He took the bag of bread from his teacher, yet his eyes never left the stranger. Suddenly, he stepped over and gave him a hug. The man hesitated before running his hand through the young boy's hair. Randy now ran back to the pond.

"Do you have this effect on all children?" Linda asked.

The man stood up and looked down at her. "That one's pretty special."

"I'd say. You should see his drawings."

The salesman came over to the bench, and without hesitation, Linda moved her satchel over to give him room to sit down. The two of them watched the children divide up the bread and toss it out to the ducks.

"You know every time I get down on 'people,' I try to remember that they were once children themselves, innocent and loving, who lost it somewhere along the way," he said.

"Well, they can also lose their temper and throw a mean fit."

"But they don't hold onto it. Here one moment, like a summer storm, and gone the next, leaving clear skies behind."

Linda considered this observation for a moment. "You know, you're right; they don't." Seeing it for the first time, she nodded her head and said, speaking to herself, "But I do." She paused and thought about it for a moment. "And maybe that's why I've come back here, why I'm teaching again. To learn how. . . ." She groped for the answer just out of her reach.

"How to let go," he said.

Linda turned and stared at the stranger. How did he know? The man extended his hand to her. "I'm Charlie Bonner, salesman extraordinaire."

The last thing she remembered after shaking his hand was looking into eyes that seemed to go on forever, and then she fainted.

## 4.

When she woke up in the park after fainting, the salesman had gone and it seemed that she had slept for hours. However, the children were still feeding the ducks, and she suspected only minutes had elapsed. That was when the first hunger pangs struck. She was famished! Each throbbing beat sent a pulse running through her entire body. It was an empty ache that cried for nourishment. Linda was soon rummaging through her satchel for crumbs of bread, and within minutes she had gathered the children for an early return. After school she had several errands to run, with grocery shopping the last but by now the most important.

When she finally arrived home that night, Linda broke open her groceries, put away the eggs, milk, and butter and left the rest for later. She then fixed a quick meal of scrambled eggs and toast. She was too hungry to sit down and eat at a table, where manners taught by her mother always seemed to prevail. To wolf down her food, she needed to be on her feet. Linda took the plate of eggs and walked out of the kitchen into the living room. Some would find her apartment too small, and it was, for more than two people at a time. There were only three large rooms and a bath. It was the type of apartment that did not encourage friends to stop by without calling; finding anybody else there meant a full house. For now she needed to be alone, and this was an ideal hideaway.

On the wall in the living room, there were photos of Linda shot at various times in the last fifteen years. She had taken them out of storage and put them up without thinking about the order. Linda now walked over and looked at the pictures, studying first the most recent of them. It showed her accepting an award given by her real estate firm for most sales by a first-year agent. In fact, she was best overall that year but was ineligible for that award because of her freshman status. When she protested, Linda became the target for a few diehards who resented women agents in general and ones who outsold them in particular. At first it did not bother her, because she spent most of her time on the road meeting clients and showing them properties. She had gone into the real estate business to get away from paperwork and office politics. In the end, although she stayed another two years, that combination finally beat her.

Next was a picture of her marriage to Tom Boyer in San Francisco three years ago at the age of thirty. She was, as her mother had said after too much champagne, the oldest bride in family history but still the prettiest. He was an investment agent for a nationally-prominent brokerage firm. They had met while Linda was showing him commercial properties for several of his overseas' investors. The deal went through, and they both made a substantial commission. Looking at this couple, Linda thought that if they had only gone into business together and not gotten married, they might still be friends. But, as lovers, and not just as sex partners, there was not enough depth to their relationship to sustain it. Neither seemed connected to the other's secret self.

Linda had to look closely to spot herself in the back row of her graduation picture from the University of California at Berkeley. She was one of the older graduates that year, and the expression on her face questioned if it had been worth the grind. She still wondered. It seemed more of a test in sheer fortitude, as if she had to prove herself, than a course of action with a tangible goal. Afterwards she turned down several lucrative job offers and got a teaching certificate instead. To understand Berkeley, she had to come to grips with the years spent between high school and college.

Linda moved along the line to a picture that still sent chills up her spine. It was taken on a plateau high in the French Alps; surrounded by snow-covered mountains were a small group of devotees meditating with their aged Sufi master. They were wearing only thin muslin robes in the cool air, but their intense withdrawal into this other world was enough to keep the natural elements at bay. That weekend had been the culmination of long years of meditation and study, of practicing yoga until her body was a wet noodle. It had brought Linda face to face with the cold, dark infinite emptiness within her. And she could not surrender herself to it. To lose herself, she had realized, she would have to first find that self. Six weeks later Linda was back in California taking a refresher course before entering the fall semester at Berkeley.

And finally, as she finished her meal, Linda came to her favorite photo. She was fourteen and had run away from home to spend the summer in San Francisco. Here she posed with a motley group of street people outside a communal kitchen in Haight-Ashbury. Charged with an idealistic fervor, she had come to join hands with other flower children as the vanguard of a new revolution. Soon their protests had escalated into riots, group meetings were marred by bitter infighting, free love became promiscuous sex, and communal property realigned the wealth for the greedy few. To build a new society, Linda had decided at some point, would require a new type of person. By summer's end she had taken too many drugs in search of that self and blown the ballast out of an already fragile psyche.

Now, looking over these photos, Linda could see a pattern emerging at first vaguely suggested by the reverse chronological order of the layout. It appeared that establishing herself in the world had been the end of a cycle. The line pointed back to its start and the promise offered, and it showed that the entrance to a new beginning lay hidden there. Understanding the meaning of this last photo was the key.

Linda went back to the kitchen to clean up and put away the rest of the groceries. She had never liked kitchen work and wondered if it were why she had resisted having children. Cooking for Tom, who could not boil an egg, had been enough trouble, but a family would have tied her to an oven for years. Linda was finishing up when she had a sudden hot flash. She sat down on the bar stool and put a wet rag to her burning forehead. It hit again with more force, temporarily blinding her. She had a sick woozy feeling all over and began to tremble. Popping her eyes open, she saw the room as if from a great distance, as through the reverse end of a telescope. Linda could feel some part of herself rapidly slipping away, and she struggled to bring it back. Linda tried to get up off the stool. Her legs were wobbly, all the muscle tension in her body had gone slack. She fell to her knees, but, holding onto the counter, was able to pull herself back up. Linda stood in place for a moment to regain her balance, and then she slowly edged her way down the row of stools to the hallway.

In the bedroom she flopped down on the bed and rolled over on her back looking up at the ceiling. Here she saw a swirling pattern of bright light in which an image slowly began to form, or that was what Linda thought she saw. Something in her grasped it before she did, causing a vague feeling of knowing what was coming next but without knowing how. And then, unmistakably, there appeared a most distinct set of eyes staring down at her from on high. The image stopped growing at this point with a hint of other features lurking in the background. More lifelike details might suggest an actual face, but she knew it was only a facade, a mask, to soften the harsh realities beneath. Linda found herself irresistibly drawn into those bottomless caverns and knew she could easily lose herself in them forever. She closed her eyes and turned her head away, and the image disappeared. Opening them, Linda wondered if she were dreaming when she saw those same eyes reflected back from her vanity mirror.

The next morning sunlight streaming through the side window struck Linda's face, and she moved her head out of the light before it triggered the alarm clock in her brain. She fell back into a deeper sleep right before the phone rang from the next room. Burying her head under the pillow muffled the noise but did not silence it. Finally, Linda sat up in bed, still fully clothed from last night. Lifting her eyelids felt like pumping weights. And she was sure somebody had blow-dried the inside of her head: every membrane was raw. When she tried to slide out of bed, she followed through with the motion but her body stayed behind. Only with great effort was she able to coordinate the movement. Standing up Linda now looked into the vanity mirror to check if she was totally there.

In the kitchen she picked up the ringing phone and carried it over to the counter. As she lifted the receiver, she threw away the three-day-old grounds from her instant coffeemaker.

"Yeah, who's there?" she asked in a deep voice and then cleared her throat. Linda reached for a new coffee filter.

"Linda, is that you?" Pam asked.

"Well, this feels like my headache all right." She filled the filter with fresh coffee and turned on the coffeemaker.

There was a long pause on the other end of the line. "You sound funny. Are you all right?"

"I'll survive. Hold on for a second." The coffee had started to drip, and Linda replaced the pot with her cup for a quick fix. She now looked up at the wall clock but could not read it in the dark kitchen. "What time is it anyway?"

"Nine-thirty," Pam said. "You didn't forget about today, did you? We were having lunch together?"

"Oh yeah, where?"

"Paco's. Where else?" Pam asked impatiently.

"Well, just point me in the right direction," Linda said.

While Pam was giving her directions, Linda finally remembered the luncheon date, the restaurant and its location. How could she forget Paco's? The two of them had eaten there at least once a week since her return. What she could not remember was what had caused this epic hangover. And then she started feeling sick. After she hung up the phone, Linda went to the bathroom and leaned over the sink waiting to vomit.

## 5.

The light reflected off the azure blue sea was blinding. From shore two wind-surfers gliding across its surface looked like skaters on ice. And the race was on. The two daredevils attacked the course with a reckless disregard to the dangers of a high-speed spill. It was head-to-head for the longest time, and they came perilously close to a collision on two occasions. And then one of them hit a wave and soared into the air. The board got lost in the light, suspending time momentarily, and when it emerged with its sail flapping wildly, it looked like a winged creature taking flight. Then it fell tumbling end-over-end in slow motion. Viewers from shore almost expected to hear a loud crash when it hit the water, but both man and board silently sank beneath the surface. A moment later the sailor popped back up and waved his hands overhead.

Sitting at their oceanfront table, Linda had watched the race while Pam was away chasing after their waitress. She now came back and sat down in triumph.

"I had her change the order to Pina Coladas. Hopefully she'll get here before you expire," Pam said.

"Thanks for the vote of confidence."

"I believe you, I'm your friend . . . remember. But you do look like a candidate for AA."

Linda reached into her purse, took out her sunglasses and put them on. "Is that any better?"

"Barely."

Looking out at the ocean, she realized that the bright light had bothered her more than usual. "You know right after you called, I had, from all appearances, the worst case of morning sickness on record."

"Whose is it?" Pam asked half-seriously, knowing her friend too well.

"Well, unless Roy took advantage of me when I slept on your sofa last month, there aren't any candidates," Linda said, keeping up the pretense.

"And you haven't seen Tom since when?"

"Not since June, and nothing happened. But I did talk to him on the phone last week."

Pam shook her head in mock dismay. "You never were very good at biology."

"Yeah, tell me about it." The waitress now came over and set down their drinks. It was getting hot on the open patio, and Linda looked forward to something cold and, in her condition, mildly alcoholic. Pam played with her fruit-stick for a moment and finally separated the orange slice from its pick.

"You're still such an innocent," Pam resumed, "and after all you've been through. It's amazing."

"But you're saying it's not entirely admirable."

"Oh, you would've been a hit way back when, but if you intend to get by in today's world, you have to look out for your own interests." She waited to see if Linda was listening. "Which brings up the subject of your divorce settlement."

"What divorce."

"Yours, and you know it. And if you don't act now, he'll liquidate his assets and you'll end up with a nickel on the dollar."

"As long as I get the silverware," Linda said smiling.

"Oh, so you don't mind living in a one-bedroom apartment, while he entertains his lady friends in your highrise condo in San Rafael?"

"I'm sure if it comes to a settlement, I'll be treated fairly."

Pam knew it was useless to argue with her any further. Hopefully, she would think it over and decide to take action on her own. She had learned over the years that you could not force Linda to do anything against her will. She might appear passive to some, but she was actually as intractable as a brick wall. Pam had known her since grade school, and even back then she was more interested in the cause-at-hand, finding homes for stray cats and dogs, writing pen pals in Africa, than in the latest schoolgirl craze. Linda was always out of step with the others, and when they did not share her passion for truth, or justice, or whatever the current catchword, she went looking for those who did. Pam found herself in the role of an older sister giving a wayward youngster advice, but that did not prevent her from admiring her friend's shining spirit.

The waitress now brought their lunch platters, and the two of them settled down to eat while keeping the conversation on a neutral subject. School was one such topic. Pam had planned to ask Linda's help in her campaign to petition the school board for some innovative new teaching aids. She started to read down her list, but after only a few key items, Pam could see her friend was barely listening and decided to drop the matter until later. Since school and community played such a big part in her life, Pam would definitely badger Linda, as she did with everybody else, until she had at least heard her proposal. Although only a small-town girl, and one still in awe of her big-city friend, Pam liked to think of herself as a modern woman and a progressive educator. She felt that keeping San Martin small and manageable did not necessarily mean keeping the town and its school system in the Middle Ages. Some changes, she felt, if laid on a solid foundation, were for the best. The challenge was knowing how to integrate them into the established order. It was a task Pam had assumed for her corner of the known world.

Halfway through her meal, Linda started having cramps and had to stop eating. She told the waitress to put the sandwich in a take out bag, but Pam asked if she could finish it. While she waited, Linda went through her list of symptoms and wondered if she had caught the flu. It looked as if she had, but since it was not as prevalent in this climate as elsewhere, she could not readily assume that. Since Linda refused to see a doctor this soon, she would treat it as the flu and hope for the best. She planned to stop by the pharmacy on the way home if she could pull Pam away from the table.

"Pam, why don't I just run along," Linda finally said.

"Just one last bite and I'll walk you out."

Pam took two, and they stood up and left. In the parking lot Linda felt sick again and helplessly looked back to the restaurant a good fifty yards away. She would never make it in time. The wave of nausea soon passed, and reaching her car she leaned against the door and fanned herself with the new sample menu.

"If I'd known you felt this bad, we could've called it off," Pam said, feeling just a little guilty.

"No, really. Getting out helped; I just need more rest."

Pam looked at her friend's sickly pallor and seriously doubted that prognosis. She now turned away, looking for her car, when she saw the salesman coming out of the barber shop across the street.

"Do you know who that is?" Pam asked, nodding her head in the man's direction.

Linda put the menu up to shade her eyes and saw the salesman talking with Joe, the town's barber. "Some kind of traveling salesman. Sat next to me at the park yesterday."

"Looks like a real character. Does he pass through here often?"

"Don't know. Didn't say much about himself," Linda said.

"I think I'll just walk on over and introduce myself."

Seeing him talking with the barber, Linda remembered shaking the man's hand and noticing how hot they were, and she also remembered how his eyes had shone at that moment. "Well," Linda said, feeling sick again, "whatever you do, don't shake his hand."

Pam had already started across the street when she heard this curious warning from her friend. She looked back over her shoulder, momentarily puzzled, and then passed it off as another one of Linda's oddball statements and walked on.

Linda got into her car, and as she drove out of the parking lot, she saw Pam talking with the salesman in her rearview mirror. And then he turned and waved at her, and she wondered how he knew she was watching. Linda drove up from the oceanfront and turned onto Alameda. Two blocks down, she pulled into Clarke's Grocery. Inside, she walked straight to the pharmacy section and searched the shelves, reading the back of a dozen boxes for a remedy that would offset some of her flu symptoms. Linda had never been keen on drugs, and she had taken no more than two dozen aspirin in her entire life. And yet a growing uneasiness was creeping through her body triggering biological alarms and sending her into the enemy's camp.

Finally, Linda settled on aspirin, the brand her mother popped like bonbon balls. At the check-out counter, she laid the bottle down and took out her wallet for the money. Suddenly, she had another hot flash and dropped it on the floor. Linda grabbed hold of the steel counter to steady herself. In an instant she recalled last night's episode; she now exerted her will, feeling her stomach muscles tense up, and forcefully pushed the feeling away.

"Are you all right, Miss?" the cashier asked. The bag boy had knelt down to pick up her wallet, and he now held it out to her. When Linda opened her eyes, the wallet waving in her face looked threatening, and she stepped back.

"I'm sorry," Linda said and took it from him. She tried to open it but was all fingers. She now handed the wallet to the cashier. "Please, take out thc right amount for me."

The owner, Hugh Clarke, who had been watching from the next register, stepped over. "Go ahead, Nancy. The lady trusts us." He came around to Linda. "Should I call somebody, Linda?"

"Oh no, I'll be all right. Just give me a second." The cashier put the bottle in a bag along with her wallet and laid it on the counter.

"Okay, but let one of my boys drive you home."

Linda picked up her purchase. "Thanks, but really. I'm fine now." She walked slowly and steadily out the door and waved to him from the other side.

Driving back home took an eternity at ten miles an hour, but she was afraid of going any faster. She could have parked and called her father, but she did not want to alarm her parents. Finally, when arriving safely on her doorstep, Linda had another hot flash. Holding her key steady with both hands, she unlocked the door and used her body to push it open. She dropped the bottle of aspirin on the floor and stumbled down the darkened hallway toward the sunlit bedroom at the end. Linda collapsed on the bed in relief. Looking up at a swirling pattern of lights, she passed out.

## 6.

Carl's reception went much as he had expected: his father was happy to see the added muscle on him and hoped he would stay to work the farm; his mother was glad to have someone to talk with again. For his part he was relieved to find both of them healthy. If either were infirm and the other in need of his help, Carl would have been forced to stay on longer than he had planned. He did not have a job waiting for him up the road with a fixed starting date, but after he paid his respects and went over his father's books, it would be time for him to leave or put on his gloves and dig post holes. Carl would not have minded the work if it were not unceasing. He preferred jobs with short intense spurts of activity with plenty of spare time. It was during these periods that he turned within himself and did the only work that really mattered to him. A farm was no place to find yourself, and that was why he had left.

It was on his first night home, before he had even unpacked his duffel bag, while sitting at the dinner table, that his father had first pressed him to stay on and help with the farm.

"You've been out and about long enough, son. Never knew why you left, but now that you're here, why don't you stick around and try your hand at it again."

"I could, but it wouldn't last long," Carl said and then shrugged his shoulders. "I'm just not cut out for it."

"But you're cut out for the road, is that it?" Matt Owens asked in a peevish tone.

"For now, but when they let you off in the middle of nowhere, and it's raining like crazy, you start to have your doubts."

His father could only shake his head. "Don't sound all that great to me."

"What's great about it is packing up after a good bit of work, saying your goodbyes and then moving on with nothing holding you back."

"By 'nothing' I take it you mean people, don't you?"

Carl thought about it for a moment. "Yeah, I guess so."

"Well son, if you don't give a damn about people, you'll never be worth a damn yourself," Matt said. "And that's a sure fact."

"Just because I don't want to get tied down," Carl said, hurt by the implications of his father's remark, "it doesn't mean I don't care."

Matt cleared his throat and turned away in embarrassment from his son's open display of emotion. The dried-out, blotched skin of his cheeks, dotted with brown spots, were momentarily flushed with color. Matt looked down at his half-eaten plate of ham, mashed potatoes, and black-eyed peas and finished his meal in silence.

Afterwards, when his father had gone out to the porch to smoke a cigarette and read the evening paper, Carl helped his mother clear the table and wash the dishes. And in only a few minutes, the last five years were wiped away, and their relationship settled back into the easygoing familiarity of Carl's teen years.

Wilma now handed her son a plate, but when he tried to take it from her, she held on to it. Carl looked up at his mother. "Tell me," she asked, "has it been that hard for you?"

"No, not really. Hitching rides is only part of it. What I do is ride into a town, take a liking to it, find work and stay around until I get bored."

"And what happens if you can't find work and you run out of money?" Wilma asked with some concern.

"It's never happened," Carl lied, "but if it did, I'd find the nearest Red Cross blood bank and sell a few pints." Wilma let go of the plate and allowed her son to dry it, and she turned back to a sink filled with more dirty dishes. It was best she did not probe too deeply, afraid of what she might discover, and even worse what he might try to keep from her. He was an able-bodied young man with a strong character and a good upbringing, and if that could not see him through this self-imposed ordeal, there was little else she could do about it. Although Wilma would love for her son to stay, working the farm and raising a family here, Carl would have to choose that course for himself. She was not about to blackmail him with family obligations and keep him here against his will.

"And what about Jennifer," Wilma asked tentatively, "are you going to look her up before you leave?"

"How's she been?"

"Well, we haven't seen much of her these last few years. At first she'd come by on her visits home, asking for word about you, but that stopped soon enough, so I guess she gave up on it. Got a graduation notice from her last summer, and I heard she was going to some kind of medical school this fall." Finished, Wilma drained the sink, wiping the sides clean, and hung up her washcloth. She now untied her apron, folded it and put it back in the bottom kitchen drawer. Leaning against the counter, she watched Carl dry the last plate and put it away. "If you're interested, I hear she stayed on at the diner, saving money for school, but I don't know how much longer she'll be there."

"I just might stop by later in the week," Carl said, hanging the towel back on its hook, and then he turned to his mother. "But tell me, how've you been?"

"Thought you'd never ask," Wilma said, as she reached over and opened the liquor cabinet, taking out a bottle of peach brandy and pouring the two of them a drink.

Later that night, just before sunset, Carl went out and took a walk around the farm. The first thing he noticed was that only half the crops had been harvested this year; the rest were plowed under. Most of the equipment was run down: the tractor in total disrepair. And the farm animals were not any better. But, what really alarmed him was the condition of the outbuildings. They were practically falling apart. He knew his father now had little use for them, but if kept in good condition, they would add a great deal to the market value of the farm if he should ever decide to sell it. Of course he never considered that possibility, and at this point he appeared satisfied bringing in enough crop to feed them and pay the mortgage.

While Carl was in the stable looking over the horses, he had his first hot flash. He fell to his knees on the straw floor and grabbed hold of a bridle hanging from a nearby post. Looking up he saw a circle of diffused light; he blinked his eyes in disbelief as a distinct pair of eyes formed. Carl pulled himself up and stumbled out of the stable. He staggered along the dirt path that ran past the pigpen and led back to the house. He tried to focus on the porch light like a beacon in a raging storm, but his bobbing head kept losing it behind the fenceposts. Looking back, ahead, wherever he turned, Carl saw those same eyes pressing down on him from above. Turning the corner, he now headed across the backyard to the porch some fifty yards away. Carl tripped on a clump of crabgrass and fell to the ground. He crawled another ten feet before giving up. Lying there, he thought of Jennifer and hoped they would have a chance to settle their differences before it was too late. And then he passed out.

They met two days later and had a picnic at a secluded spot up the coast. The place had sentimental value, and Jennifer hesitated when Carl suggested they drive out to it. Anybody else would have picked it for that reason, but one look at Carl told her he was innocent of such maneuvering. He had always liked the view there, and that was his sole consideration. And he was lucky she would go anywhere with him. Her first reaction had been to say no, why open old wounds, but she needed to look him in the face just one time and ask him how, after all they had meant to each other, he could walk out on her without saying a word. On the ride out, Jennifer had been polite but distant, asking all the right questions about his travels. After twenty minutes of strained conversation, Carl turned off the highway and parked behind a clump of bushes. It took a few minutes to walk down the path to the overhang, but after laying out the spread and setting everything up, they sat in silence across from each other. Jennifer now asked that question of him.

"Well, you saw the shape I was in at Easter that year. I don't think I could've made a whole lot of sense out of it."

"You could've tried. You owed me that much."

"I guess I did," Carl said. For the first time, he could see the pain he had caused her and was truly sorry. "But I was afraid, if I remember correctly, that you would try to talk me out of it."

"I would've," Jennifer said, and Carl nodded his head as if that proved him right. "The point is not whether I would've talked you out of leaving, but if it would've been in your best interest to stay." She paused and studied him for a long moment. "I mean, what did it get you, but a few saddle sores?"

Carl turned away and looked out at the ocean, letting the memory of these last five years sweep over him. "No, that's where you're wrong. I was right to go, because I met in my outward journey a whole undiscovered part of myself never encountered here." Carl now turned back to see if Jennifer was really listening to him. "It wasn't the best of me, but certainly part of me, and something I had to meet and if not overcome, at least come to terms with. Although there's a lot of open farmland around here, it's still pretty tame. And if you're still wild, it's no place for you. It's easy to get fixed here, become part of the scenery and let it turn you into a walking fence post. Out there it's different. Just about anything in you can find a port of call, and believe me, I've been to some real hellholes, caught in some unbelievable situations, all because of what I am and chose not to hide from myself."

Jennifer found this explanation a little unnerving. It covered an area that made her uncomfortable, and one she could hardly pass judgement on. She now wondered if this were the same boy she had grown up with. The one she had eventually come to love. If this change in him indicated real growth and proved that he had made the right choice in leaving, it might open the way for a reconciliation between them.

"So tell me," Jennifer asked tentatively, "just how bad is the worst of you?"

"Not somebody you'd invite to a college mixer, but not really all that bad."

"And you're coming to terms with it?"

"I'm trying."

"How much longer is this going to take?" Jennifer asked.

"Well, it's probably something I'll be working on all my life."

Jennifer studied him and could now clearly see the man her boy had become. "Maybe you did have to leave," she finally conceded, "but from what I see, you're through the worst of it. So why not stay and work it out here among family and friends?"

"Maybe some day, but not now. I'm not strong enough yet," Carl said. "You see people, old friends in particular, relatives, even enemies all have a way of fixing you in their minds. It's not so much who you really are, but what you trigger in them. And if you listen to them, like we all do, whole parts of yourself get submerged, lost in the shuffle. And that's the part I have to keep looking for out there."

Jennifer could only nod her head in agreement. She could see that he was slowly winning her over and that disturbed her. But, before she could fight it, Jennifer had a hot flash. Those mysterious eyes formed overhead, and when she finally pulled away and looked at Carl in desperation, she could see the great resemblance between the disembodied eyes that would soon engulf her and the ones coolly staring back at her now.

## 7.

Sitting in this man-made cathedral, after three long days confined to a corporeal body, the salesman now had only hours to count off until his departure. He had come not only to select their candidates and inoculate them, but to reevaluate humankind before the impact of their experiment changed this race forever. And now, as he looked around the congregation, he sensed the great gulf that existed between each individual and how all of them were further subdivided within themselves. At this stage the split between mind, body, and spirit produced divisions ad infinitum. But, as he well knew, this was the engine of evolution. It drove a species toward more complex structures capable of greater integration. In his natural state, he was pure energy at one with himself and with the universe. But he had once traveled this lonely path and knew its great dangers. He had returned to point the way, but as always the choice was theirs.

Finally, the service concluded and his fellow worshipers rose to leave. The salesman looked around and spotted Linda across the way; he scooted down the pew to exit in the center aisle and followed her out. At the door she stopped to talk with the minister, a Reverend Taylor. They exchanged a few words, and he heard her mention having the flu and watched the minister step back to avoid close contact. Linda walked on, and the salesman tried to slip by unnoticed, but Reverend Taylor, always on the lookout for strangers, saw him and came over.

"I don't believe we've met," he said and extended his hand.

The salesman had read him earlier while he was giving his sermon and was unimpressed with the man's numbers. He now took the minister by the forearm and swept him along as he walked down three steps to ground level.

"Sure is a nice church you have here, Reverend. Kind of reminds me of ours back home."

"Oh, so you're just passing through?"

"Aren't we all," he said with a mischievous smile.

"Well, you're welcome anytime," Reverend Taylor said with genuine warmth.

The salesman did a double take and read him again, but just when the minister was showing real promise, he saw Linda walking down the sidewalk, getting away from him. "Well, thanks for the hospitality. It's appreciated, but I do have to go." The salesman lingered a moment longer, then turned and walked off, waving back at Taylor over his shoulder. He hoped that he had not missed this one, but then there was always the possibility of a spontaneous conversion later, if all went well.

Crossing the lawn, he finally caught up with her at the end of the block. She stopped to greet him, but despite all his personal charm, there was something in her that withdrew from him.

"Feeling any better?"

Linda looked at him suspiciously. How did he know?

"Sorry," he said, "I'm being nosey. Occupational hazard. It's just that Reverend Taylor said you weren't feeling well, and I was concerned."

That might explain this situation, but it did little to assuage the growing feeling that this man's arrival in town, their contact, and the onset of her illness were all somehow connected. "Well, don't worry," Linda said coolly, studying his reaction. "I'm sure it's just the flu."

"Are you sure it isn't more serious than that?" the salesman asked with an edge to his voice.

He watched her shrink back from him even further. Her inner center was developing rapidly now and could read him well. The salesman was using this confrontation to test its strength, and he was satisfied that the process had taken hold.

"Look, I have to go. It's a long way to my next stop," he said. "But, if I were you, I'd see a doctor real soon."

The salesman turned and walked across the street, then up the sidewalk for another half block. He got into a late model Ford Granada and drove away. In town he picked up the coastal highway and headed north. The day was clear with a slight breeze, and the bay was dotted with bright sails, and up the coast one could see broken strings of hardy beachgoers edging their way along narrow paths down rock cliffs to the ocean below. And he drove on through this beautiful sunlit landscape on the last leg of his journey home.

He left behind in this small seaside community seeds of a new life that had taken hold and would soon grow strong and vigorous. They could nurture this growth and transform themselves, or they could fight it and die. One beckoned the future only at great risk. From the beginning humankind had shown the inclination to reach beyond itself, and one could only hope it had not lost that knack. When archaic *Homo sapiens* began burying their dead on beds of flowers with tools for use in the afterlife, the awareness of spirit, of a soul, an essence that survived death, had been awakened. From there came belief in the supernatural, to rituals and strategies to placate or harness these mysterious forces. Acknowledging a force greater than the self had set them on a unique evolutionary path toward the development of group consciousness and the formation of a distinctly human culture. At its root was another singular value uncovered in graves containing the remains of those evidently cared for after they were too old or infirm to hunt or gather: conscience.

At the next town, the salesman stopped for gas and to have the windshield cleaned. He wanted to leave the car in the same condition he had gotten it. While the attendant filled the tank, he walked out to the sidewalk to look around and gather one last impression. It was late afternoon and droves of beachgoers were now returning from their day in the sun. Life for them was far removed from the gruelling struggles of their ancestors. They had earned this brief reprieve from harsh natural elements, and in the last thousand years, this race had blossomed and fulfilled the promise of their youth. And yet, buried within them, there lay a far greater potential. One that when triggered could change them and their planet forever.

The salesman returned to his car and paid the attendant. The man had been watching him and figured the salesman was checking out the sky for signs of changing weather.

"Hear it's gonna be clear tonight," he said.

The salesman looked up at him and smiled. "From what I hear there's going to be a meteor shower."

"Oh yeah. I'll have to watch for it."

"About nine o'clock look north," the salesman said and drove off.

The attendant mulled over this advice for a long moment, and then he shook his head. You can't predict a meteor shower, he said to himself, turned and went back to work.

Charlie Bonner lay stretched out on the front seat of a car parked on a deserted stretch of the coastal highway. It was dark, and as he began to wake up, he rolled over on his back. A brief flash of light from a passing car hit the ceiling and shone in his face. Bonner closed his eyes tight; it felt like he had been sitting in a dark theater for a week. He now looked around but could not see anything; he tried to sit up but his arms collapsed under him, and he fell back on the seat. That was when he heard the radio. The D.J. was talking excitedly, and he strained to hear him.

"Got a special treat," the radio blared, "for all you night-watchers. That's the stargazing variety, and not the peeping Toms. Right now, in the northern sky, there's a spectacular meteor shower. Hurry and take a look, before they burn out; like a certain D.J. we all know and love."

Bonner finally pulled himself up and sat there looking out the window at this unfamiliar stretch of road. Where was he and how did he get here, he asked himself? The last thing he remembered was driving up the coast in the fog. But, if he had pulled off the road and took a nap, which he would not have done under those conditions, the fog had certainly cleared fast. It was either that or he had slept for twelve hours. The night air blowing in through the window was slowly reviving him. Bonner now thought to look at his watch. He brought it up to his face and clicked on the digital readout: SUN, SEPT 08, 8:55 pm.

"Sunday? Sunday?" he asked himself in utter amazement. "What the hell happened to the weekend?"

The radio now blared out. "The news at the hour is brought to you by Hardley Dodge in Sausalito where, 'We've never had an unhappy customer,' or one," the D.J. added, "who's lived to tell about it."

"Sausalito? But I was supposed to stop off in San Martin today..., or on Friday, or...what the hell is going on here?"

The meteor shower had now begun, and shooting streaks of light raced across the night sky in every direction. It caught Bonner's eye, and he stuck his head out the car window to look up at this natural fireworks display. One by one the shooting stars, after a brief but spectacular life, arced downward to burn up in the upper atmosphere. He was looking at another sector of the sky when, out of the corner of his eye, he spotted something peculiar and turned to examine it more closely. One of the meteors seemed to be rising heavenward, not falling to a fiery death. He watched it for a long moment and could clearly see that it was heading straight up. And then, when it was almost out of sight, it did a curlicue and disappeared. Bonner shook his head in disbelief. That settled it. Next week he was definitely going to take the cure.

# CHAPTER TWO
# ISOLATION

*To separate an element,*
*such as a gene,*
*from the substance, the cell's DNA,*
*in which it is combined or mixed.*

## San Martin, California
## September 16

On Monday morning, after another restless night, Linda took the morning off from school and went in to see her family doctor. His office was still located in the same dilapidated old building two blocks from the ocean. Unlike most of his colleagues, Dr. Bonhard had not moved to one of the new high-rise office buildings on the outskirts of town. And over the years he had lost most of his affluent clients, including Linda's parents, who had long since moved on to more exclusive neighborhoods.

Inside Linda was surprised to find a waiting room full of people. So it must be the flu after all, she thought, and took a seat alongside little Randy Carter. His mother looked up from her magazine long enough to acknowledge Linda's presence. And Randy, reading his own storybook, reached over and patted her hand. This would have been comforting if it were not so unnervingly precocious. Suddenly the boy smiled with mocking eyes that dared her to share some ghastly secret. Linda pulled her hand away and looked around at the others, but nobody seemed to have noticed it. Maybe it was just her imagination? Yet they were so preoccupied behind drawn faces and long-distance looks that nothing less than major mayhem would have grabbed their attention.

Linda knew most of the people in the waiting room. She had become reacquainted with some of them since her return, while the others were older versions of townspeople she had known as a child. Few had aged greatly; time did run slower in San Martin, but apparently all these long faces were still subject to gravity. No doubt they had grown intolerant of even minor ailments. There was one new face that nevertheless did look vaguely familiar. The boy in his early twenties sitting next to the wall was much too young for Linda to have known while growing up. And if his roughhewn appearance was any clue, he was probably a farmer making contact between them even more remote. Linda kept sneaking a look at him while thumbing through her magazine, but she could not place him. Finally, as if in answer to her silent inquiry, he turned and looked her way, and she knew in that moment that her supposed recollection of a past acquaintance was actually the portent of one to come.

Linda averted his stare and those inquiring eyes now alive with recognition. When the nurse called his name, he reluctantly stood up and followed her down the hall into the doctor's office, while looking back over his shoulder at Linda. For her part she tried to bury herself in the new *Reader's Digest*, but the words on the page would not stick in her mind. Who was this boy, she asked herself, and what was their shared future? And why did this encounter stir up such an awful sense of foreboding? A door opened at the end of the hall, and heavy footsteps trudged across the padded carpet toward her. Linda resisted a strong temptation to look up and search in the broad contours of that young face for some clue to her present distress. When the office door closed behind him and the distance between them widened, she felt greatly relieved. The nurse now called out her name, and Linda hurried into the doctor's office anxious to put this business behind her.

Dr. David Bonhard was a short, portly man in his mid-sixties with a conspicuous strand of grey hair draped across a totally bald pate. He was scheduled to retire at the end of the year, due more to the rising cost of liability insurance than any great desire to exchange his stethoscope for a putter. Over the years Bonhard had come to accept the fact that as a general practitioner, a field forced on him by the financial demands of a large family, he would never produce any of the great medical breakthroughs he had envisioned for himself as a student set on a career in pure research. He had few regrets now and could see how the years of caring human contact had made a better man of him. And yet as he filled the days remaining to him with the normal run of cases, Bonhard was on the alert for some peculiar unidentified new ailment to garner for himself some small piece of medical immortality.

Sitting on the examination table, while the nurse took a blood sample, Linda read Dr. Bonhard the same list of symptoms he had been hearing all morning long. The flu season had officially begun this past weekend in San Martin. Yet, each new patient added to this list some new complaint usually not associated with influenza. Although it could weaken the defense mechanism and leave the body, especially the respiratory tract, open to secondary bacterial infections such as pneumonia, influenza rarely spread to the blood and deeper body tissues. This could be another type of virus all together, and one with an alarmingly invasive capability.

"This may be nothing, but I'm having a problem with my bladder this morning," Linda said, while flexing her arm and holding a cotton ball to the puncture hole left by the nurse's needle.

"Well, Linda, it's been a while since I've seen you on a regular basis," Bonhard said, picking up her chart and making a notation. "Are you often bothered by bladder infections?"

"No, not really. I've had my share, especially while I was living in Europe, but nothing recently."

"Okay. I'm going to put you on Furadantin, but if there's no change in your condition by the end of the week, come back in and see me." Bonhard decided to treat her bladder infection with the customary antibiotics, which if they proved ineffective could help in determining the presence of this new viral agent. "Now for your flu symptoms, I think you know the routine."

"You mean the miracle cure: liquids, aspirin and rest?" Linda said mischievously.

After Linda, Bonhard saw three more patients before the office closed for lunch. He usually brought a sandwich from home, since restaurant food was often too rich for his sour stomach, and he ate by himself in the back office while catching up on his reading. Today he brought along the charts of all those patients with symptoms of the flu. While eating his sandwich and sipping a cup of tomato soup, Bonhard spread the charts open across his desk and began to arrange them by their extraneous complaints. It soon had six different categories ranging from Linda's bladder problem to Mrs. Casey's inflamed liver. He was almost certain that his patients were suffering from a viral infection other than influenza, but viruses rarely invaded more than one type of body cell. If some exotic new viral strain was in fact responsible for all these secondary infections, it could be a major medical discovery, and it was one Bonhard would not let the other doctors in town, swamped with similar cases, beat him to. He called Juan Ortega, a pre-med student who did lab work for him on the weekends, and told him to come in that evening prepared for a long session.

At school Linda was hurrying down the hall to her homeroom when the eleven o'clock bell rang. Students poured out of doors on either side of her, and Linda was swept along in the mad surge of bodies past her classroom, finally ending up in the gym at the far end of the hall. She decided to wait until after lunch to relieve the substitute teacher handling her class, and she walked two doors down to the teacher's lounge. It was practically empty this time of the morning, except for a few teachers smoking a quick cigarette between classes. Linda went into the ladies' room to repair a face already showing signs of wear; that morning it was her haggard looks as much as her aching body that had sent her to the doctor. Now, looking into the mirror,

Linda could not believe the face staring back at her, and she hurriedly went to work softening the harsh lines and deep furrows that had appeared practically overnight.

In the cafeteria later, none of the food looked very appetizing. Although she had taken aspirin earlier to relieve a pounding headache, her stomach was still queasy and she was not about to upset it any further. The chicken soup looked safe enough, and along with a load of crackers it would have to do for now.

Carrying her tray, she looked for an empty table and then spotted Pam across the room. From a distance Linda could sense something different about her friend. When she walked up to her, and after Pam had looked up with those big watery eyes, Linda could see that she had the flu as well.

"You guessed it, and thanks a whole lot," Pam said half-seriously.

"Sorry, if you caught it from me," Linda said, as she sat down at the table. "But, if I'm not mistaken, you're the one who wanted to finish my sandwich."

Pam knew she was being unfair, and she twitched her nose which always made Linda laugh. "And let it go to waste? Well, if anything, I've learned a good lesson: don't eat sick people's food, unless you're already sick yourself."

"So have you gone to the doctor yet?" Linda asked.

"No. What did yours say?"

"That it's just the flu, but he did seem a little concerned about it."

"I guess so, with everybody coming down with it," Pam said.

Linda gave this some thought, and a picture of the traveling salesman whom she had met at the park last Friday immediately came to mind. "I wonder if that salesman, the one who was hanging around town all weekend, was the carrier."

"You know you might be right. And I just bet he's the one I caught it from." Pam looked over and smiled at Linda. "That means double apologies to you."

"Maybe we ought to tell somebody before he spreads it

halfway across the state?"

"I'm going in to see Dr. Barrows this afternoon, so I'll go ahead and tell him."

After lunch Linda went back to her homeroom, and while her class was at recess, she worked on her afternoon schedule. The first grade required less preparation than the upper ones, but these students also demanded more personal attention and needed more discipline than the older children. In return they gave back more of themselves. This had been something of a revelation to her. Linda had taught fifth and sixth graders after college, but by then she was dealing with hardened cases. She had never really been exposed to young children, with their great vulnerability and helpless dependency. They were like walking wounds, and she was their Band-Aid. It was a healing process that cured the doctor as well as the patient.

At one o'clock Sally, her substitute, marched her children back into the classroom. They looked as if they had all survived the morning intact, and her report included only one aggravated assault with a Tonka toy. Talking with her, Linda could see just how seriously she took this job. She was no mere baby sitter. Sally had taught school here for several years and was now trying to make a living writing children's books. Pam had told Linda to ask for her whenever she needed a substitute; her former colleagues wanted to help her out. And now Linda would pass that recommendation on to other new teachers who asked.

After Linda had set her class to work drawing capital Cs, she sat back in her chair and watched them for a moment. Row after row of intent faces were pressed close to their desktops, and you could hear the squeaky sound of crayons running across slick paper. She now turned back to her lesson plans, but after a few minutes, their continued silence soon made her look up. There was not a head out of place. The sight of all these young children in single-minded focus was truly awe-inspiring. They appeared in the grip of an overriding will that drove them to draw perfect Cs. Linda finally had to turn away before she took up pen and paper and started doing letters herself.

But the scene had left in her a lingering aftereffect that was hard to shake off. And this disquieting feeling grew more intense the more she tried to ignore it. Soon it had flooded her mind and seeped down into the depths of her being until it found its point of correspondence. There an insidious bulb of foreign matter had rooted itself. Linda could sense purpose here, a will at work, but she could probe no deeper. She knew, however, although at an unconscious level, that she was no match for its awful strength.

## 2.

When Jennifer returned home from the doctor's, she took two aspirin and went straight to bed. After working a full shift at the diner and feeling progressively worse as the day dragged on, she had dropped in on her doctor after work only to find a waiting room full of people. She set up an appointment for the next day and would now get the recommended bed rest. Jennifer only slept for three hours; it was a restless sleep. In it she dreamed of a tribe of archaic humans who lived on an endless savannah under a scorching sun. Relying on her knowledge of anthropology, Jennifer could see from their complex social structure and their advanced speech, that they were on the verge of making the leap to modern man. The setting now switched to a moonlit night where the creatures had gathered in a semicircle kneeling before an image carved on the side of a boulder. It was a deep imprint and, with no metal tools, far beyond their meager capabilities. And as Jennifer's dreaming self came in for a closer look, the creatures detected her presence and they turned and prostrated themselves before her. The image now seen was the haunting visage of her waking nightmare.

Jennifer awoke like a shot and sat up in bed trembling. It took a moment to reorient herself in the darkened room. As a reaction to the vividness of her dream, she now laid her hand on an exposed thigh to see if she was really awake. She felt goose bumps and ran her hand across their scratchy surface until they were smooth to her touch. Jennifer now reached across the bed for the lamp on the nightstand, groping in the dark until she hit the shade, and then patted her way down to the switch. Light brought the external world back into being, and it cast out the tribesmen in her dream as their heavy-browed stares faded to black.

Jennifer had never been as conversant with her dreams as Carl. In fact, during their school years, his daily recital in minute detail of his previous night's dreams had often driven her to distraction. At times she felt as if she was competing with another person for her young lover's attention. And later, after he had left to pursue his Holy Grail, she rebelled against the forces that had stolen him from her by closing herself off to them. If she did have dreams, she no longer remembered them. This new intrusion into both her waking and sleeping states was no doubt triggered by Carl's reappearance. If there was more to it, as she vaguely suspected, she could at least stop the dreams by shutting Carl out of her life.

Jennifer slid out of bed, put on a pair of jeans and an old sweater, and headed for the kitchen to fix a cup of coffee. She was still in a daze when she stubbed her toe on a box of books in the living room, and she was forced to hop the rest of the way on one foot. In the kitchen, she pulled a chair out from the table, sat down and massaged her jammed toe. She had planned to unpack the rest of her things this past weekend, but when she became ill, Jennifer decided to put it off until she felt better. To prevent another accident, she would do it tomorrow.

She now got up, went over and turned on the stove to boil water for a cup of coffee. While waiting, she went back into the living room and switched on the overhead light for another look at the boxes stacked around the room. She had already unpacked most of her clothes and all of her kitchenware; what remained was her much-cherished library of books. Although she had read most of them, Jennifer would not think of selling, loaning, or giving any of them away. And so she ended up dragging her books from one apartment to the next, from home to college and back. Some boxes had remained unpacked from the last two moves, but this time all the books would be coming out and going up to line the walls of her apartment and help keep out the encroaching darkness.

The pan of water was boiling on the stove, and she stepped into the kitchen and fixed a cup of instant coffee. Jennifer now went out to the balcony and stood at the railing, sipping hot coffee and looking at the moon rising over the ocean. She had always wanted to live this close to the beach, but apartments here were too expensive in the summer, and she was always away at college in the winter when the rents came down. When her plans changed this year and she stayed on at the diner, Jennifer decided to take a place at the beach to fortify herself for the long stretch of work that lay ahead. The ocean had always had a soothing effect on her, and she could walk its shores for miles at a time. And the mere sight of it on this beautiful moonlit night was enough to dispel the gloom.

Since her picnic with Carl on Sunday, she had been in a bad mood. It had gone better than expected, and, despite long years of resentment, she had accepted his apology for leaving her so abruptly. But something still bothered her. She had promised herself that, whatever happened at their reunion, she would walk away from it and never see Carl again. But she was not prepared for the change in him or for her own overwhelming attraction for him. And that disturbed her. Jennifer wanted to be free of Carl, to bury her past with him. Yet, in his presence, this resolve was quickly shaken. If it were merely a physical attraction, she would have little trouble finding a sexual surrogate to replace him. It was more than that. The first time she saw Carl in the sixth grade, after her family had moved here from Oakland, she had recognized in him a reflection of herself, a deep-seated part then struggling for emergence. And she had been married to that image ever since. At college she had dated other men, slept with a few, but loved none of them. She had hoped that her rendezvous on Sunday would put an end to it, but it only revealed the depth of their bond, one that had survived great time and distance, growing without her consent, as if it had a life of its own, until she was once again firmly in its grasp.

Looking out to sea, Jennifer saw the silhouette of a freighter passing in the night on its journey south. She watched until losing sight of it in the moonlight's shimmering reflection. She wondered if she should not run out the next day and book passage to parts unknown. Of course Carl had planned to leave soon and that would effectively end the siege, but she sensed he would be staying on for now. She did not know how she knew, but she did. And Jennifer was beginning to sense other things as well. Things about the future she had no wish to know. They crowded in on her, pressed their hideous faces to the window of her mind and clamored for entry. She could not push them away much longer. And when they spilled in on her, they would wash away her past and replace it with a future full of terror. This she knew for certain.

### 3.

For the past three days, Dr. Bonhard had been trying to identify the virus sweeping through the town like wildfire. He faced several major obstacles that confronted even the most modern viral laboratory. Since viruses propagate only in living host cells, they could not be grown like bacteria on an artificial culture medium. Also, they were too small to be seen through an optical microscope. The procedure, which Bonhard followed, was to grow several cell cultures seeded with embryonated egg tissue in vitro. The cells multiplied and adhered to the glass surface forming a monolayer. Next he placed the live virus taken from a patient's blood serum onto cells infecting them. Each virus displayed a distinct pattern of cell destruction, the cytopathic effect, which was one way of identifying it.

This effect could be viewed through an optical microscope, and early Thursday night Bonhard and Ortega were able to confirm that this virus's cytopathic effect was totally unique, or at least not listed in any current reference book. Ortega had already lost three days of studying, and although he was happy to make the extra money and was excited by Bonhard's discovery, he needed to get back to his school work. He felt they had enough evidence to support the doctor's claim, but there was one more detection test they could run, and Bonhard insisted he stay and help out.

Ortega had little choice but to stay. In pre-med at the University of California, his partial scholarship covered tuition and books, but he had to house and feed himself. Living in a dormitory, he kept his expenses down, but since he was only an average student, if a highly driven one, his studies required most of his time. Working at Dr. Bonhard's laboratory on the weekends supplied him with much-needed income. And if he could only confine his lab work to the simple tests usually generated by a general practitioner, this would be the ideal student job. But Bonhard had him doing all kinds of crazy side-work. Study time was important to Ortega, but what was even more important, if he intended to apply to medical school, was the best recommendation slave labor could buy him.

For this next test, they used a fresh cell culture and infected it with the live virus. Viruses in general redirect the host cell's replicative mechanism to reproduce themselves. The result is the rapid degradation of the cellular components and destruction of the cell itself. This process takes fifteen minutes for some viruses, and up to several hours for others. During the process, characteristic aggregates of viral material called inclusion bodies collect in the cell. Each virus has its own pattern, and this can serve as a useful diagnostic aid. The problem was getting a clear picture of this minute cellular debris with even the best optical microscope.

Bonhard and Ortega worked into the early hours of the morning preparing one slide sample after another, and what they found was quite puzzling. Each batch of cells had many different inclusion patterns. At this stage the embryonated eggs would have several developing cell types, and so the virus was apparently mutating itself to infect more than one type. The picture forming from this discovery sent Bonhard pacing back and forth across the small laboratory, while Ortega continued to view each new slide with alarm.

"I was right all along," Bonhard said, stabbing the air with his finger to make the point. "As I suspected, the virus is responsible for all the secondary infections as well."

"Or at least its second cousins," Ortega added to be more accurate, when the absurdity of his statement made him laugh nervously. He looked up from the microscope, his eyes red from strain, and he rubbed them with the heel of his palms. Ortega now reached over, picked up a slide he had put aside for further study and anxiously slid it into place.

"I can only guess at the mechanism involved, but the results seem to be, and correct me, Juan, if you see an error in my thinking," Bonhard said, "that our virus has some kind of variable genetic mechanism that homes in on receptor sites for each cell type and produces a different viral capsid to fit them and gain entry."

"Agreed," Ortega said absently, as he studied this slide with growing excitement.

"Okay, and if that's not startling enough, one can't help but wonder what else this little monster has in store for us."

"This should answer your question, Dr. Bonhard," Ortega said as he made one final adjustment and stepped back from the microscope.

"And what do we have here?" Bonhard asked, while trying to read Ortega's expression. The fear he saw in the young man's eyes was unsettling, and he hurried over to view the slide.

"When I first viewed this cell sample and noticed the absence of any inclusion pattern, I figured that the release of interferon from adjacent cells had made it resistant to infection. So I put it aside and almost forgot about it. When I looked at it just now, the original cell had already divided two times and, as you can see, is about to divide again."

As Bonhard watched the four-cell colony in the early stage

of mitosis, he was too absorbed with the implications of this discovery to respond.

"It would appear this cell was a target for one of the offshoot viruses resulting in a cancerous growth. And one can only speculate, Dr. Bonhard, whether other infected cell types will be affected in a like manner."

"My God," Bonhard said, as he looked up from the microscope. "If this virus causes cancer, and it's able to infect a wide variety of cell types. . . ." He stopped short when the obvious suddenly became dreadfully apparent.

"And if it's infectious, which the case histories seem to support," Ortega said resignedly, looking over at Bonhard as if the two of them were dead men. "And we've been exposed to it for three days."

Dr. Bonhard practically jumped back from the microscope before he gained control of himself. "I think we'd better call somebody in Sacramento."

"Sure, and while you're at it, call the city morgue and order two body bags." Ortega pulled off his apron, threw it on the counter and walked out of the laboratory in disgust.

As Bonhard reached for the phone and dialed the operator, it suddenly dawned on him that, since neither of them had become ill after three days of exposure, the virus might not be as infectious as they had assumed. Or, its route of transmission had bypassed them. Many viruses, especially those that infect the upper respiratory tract, were spread through the air while others relied on direct contact with carriers or with contaminated materials. As the operator came on the line and he placed a call to the state's 24-hour emergency hotline, Dr. Bonhard tried to remember if he had shaken hands with any of his patients.

## 4.

Barry Hamilton from the State Department of Health Services sat amid the flasks and beakers in an overcrowded laboratory watching an animated film of a virus invading a cell. He was visiting the University of California in San Francisco, whose virologists in the last decade had done pioneering research into animal tumor viruses and were among the first to identify viral oncogenes (cancer-causing) and later prove that all vertebrates, including man, had similar genes in their genomes. When his office received Dr. Bonhard's report, samples were immediately sent here and to the Centers for Disease Control in Atlanta. And now Hamilton had come to hear their findings.

"What you're seeing is a single-stranded RNA retrovirus invade a cell and, using its reverse transcriptase enzyme, convert its RNA to double-stranded DNA and insert this alien gene into the host cell's chromosome. It's this process in other retroviruses, like the human T-cell lymphotropic virus, HTLV-1, that induces the cellular transformation known as cancer, and in that case, a particularly virulent form of adult leukemia. Some of the viruses turn on an existing oncogene in the host cell by interfering with its activity level or actually mutating it, but this route is pretty chancy at best. Others, including this nasty bugger, ferry in oncogenes already in an outlaw mode, and instantly transform a high percentage of the cells they infect."

The film ended and a grainy black-and-white photograph, transferred to 16mm, now appeared on the screen. "This is a scanning electron micrograph of the virus and, given the minute size of these organisms, it's the best we can do."

They both stared at it for nearly thirty seconds before Dr. Louis Hodges, growing tired of his presentation, took off his glasses and rubbed his bloodshot eyes. "If you've seen enough of this, I can turn it off anytime."

"Go ahead," Hamilton said in relief. "I get the general picture."

Hodges turned off the projector's lamp, leaving the fan on, then stepped over to the wall and flipped on the overhead lights. "The boys in the front office wanted to show off a micrograph of this little bugger. Guess they figure shots of it are going to be a hot item."

"Well, we really don't want word of this to get out yet," Hamilton said nervously.

"Oh, I agree. It's your show all the way, but when you need any shots. . . ," Hodges said halfheartedly, then shook his head in disgust. "The crap you've got to put up with to keep a grant around here is amazing."

Hamilton could only sympathize with the beleaguered scientist. "Yeah, tell me about it."

There was a moment's pause as Hodges pulled a chair over and sat down, and the two men looked at each other with a shared sense of camaraderie. "Well, I can relieve your mind about one thing up front. I've just talked with the boys at CDC, and their preliminary tests show the virus is not highly contagious. And in fact it has a surprisingly short life cycle. But retroviruses, once their genome has been inserted into the host cell's DNA, can lie dormant for years before becoming active. As an example, domestic cats carry a latent viral gene picked up from ancestral baboons ten million years ago and passed on through each succeeding generation."

"So there's no chance the infection will spread, and no need to quarantine the area?" Hamilton asked.

"Let's just say that with such low blood serum levels further infection would be unlikely, if not impossible."

Hamilton looked at Dr. Hodges and smiled. "In other words, I can't pass the buck to you."

"Wish I could be more definite, but we're dealing with one of the most bizarre organisms in the annals of science, and we need to study it in more detail before we can answer all your questions."

"So where do we go from here?" Hamilton asked, caught between the need to act and the lack of information to act on.

"We know how it works, or how it infects other cell types, but what we need to know is why it works this way," Hodges said, looking over at Hamilton to see if he understood this point. "You see, most viruses live to propagate themselves, but this guy acts more like a messenger for Federal Express covering every major highway and body byway."

"And you're saying it's not an elaborate way to avoid eradication?"

"Apparently not, since the virus dies out after a few days," Hodges said. He now stood up and walked over to the projection screen and rolled it up. "There must be a very compelling reason for it to infiltrate all these different cell types. Now the receptor sites on cells are designed to bind to hormones and other vital substances that trigger internal metabolic processes. Over time viruses have evolved into shapes that can bind to these sites, and penetrate the cellular membrane to gain entry and wreak its havoc. But this virus can mutate itself to fit any number of different sites. It must have a highly variable env gene complex, probably just bits and pieces of genetic material that can be rearranged to match up with any receptor site it contacts. And I just bet it's similar to the mechanism that allows B lymphocytes to churn out an endless array of antibodies from a limited number of white blood cells."

"But I thought they'd already discovered viruses that infect more than one cell?" Hamilton asked.

"Yes, but with less sophisticated methods, and with less invasive results," Dr. Hodges said. "Scientists at MIT and elsewhere have tamed some of these retroviruses, stripped away their infectious components and are using the vectors to home in on specific tissue cells and deposit their gene load. The problem is not getting a gene into a host cell's DNA; it's getting it to work properly, or at all."

"But I thought this oncogene was already turned on, and capable of transforming any cell the virus infects," Hamilton asked.

"Precisely, and that is why I'm beginning to suspect that here cancer is the byproduct of a far more drastic process," Hodges said, and waited for this statement to sink in. "We've done a cytological analysis of some of the cancer cells' chromosomes, and believe me, there are a lot of funny things going on. Now, the translocation of segments during cell division from one chromosome to another has been associated with several cancers,

Burkitt's lymphoma in particular, and many feel that eventually chromosome defects will be detected in all cancers. But the abnormalities we're seeing here are truly astounding, and they get progressively worse with each generation of cells. There's something very strange at work here, and frankly it scares the living hell out of me."

Hamilton appreciated the scientist's honesty, but he could not help but wonder whether Dr. Hodges was being overdramatic or was appropriately alarmed by his findings. His gut feeling was to trust the man's instincts. "That means those infected need immediate treatment," Barry said and looked over at Dr. Hodges.

"And the only man you want to consider is Guy Joyner at the Sloane Institute in San Diego. He's not only the best geneticist around, but a specialist in the new bio-tech treatment of cancer."

"And do you think it's too late to help them?"

"It could be, but if this thing should ever reappear in a more infectious form, what we learn now might save the rest of us later."

## 5.

When her mother called Saturday and asked if she wanted to have lunch and go shopping, Linda first checked her early-morning response time by getting out of bed and walking to the bathroom, discovered it was better than expected, and went ahead and accepted the invitation. She was surprised her mother had called this soon after their last squabble. Her separation from Tom had caused a rift between Linda and her parents, and they had fought about it constantly since her return. At dinner recently, she had told them there was no chance of a reconciliation, only to bring her mother to tears and have her father walk out in a huff.

"Linda," Millie said contritely, after she had set up a meeting place and time. "Your father and I are really sorry about last Sunday. But we just hate to see you make such a big mistake."

"Well, I don't think I am, but can we talk about it at lunch, I'm still a little groggy."

"Oh, sure, but please, Linda, try to keep an open mind about this."

"Mother, I'll see you at one o'clock," Linda said and gently hung up the phone. This was the only way to end a phone conversation with her mother when she was obsessed with an issue. And, despite a recent show of hostility on Tom's part, her parents were still very fond of their son-in-law.

This conflict with her parents had pushed Tom to the forefront of her mind lately. Although they had been officially separated for only three months, they had not been close for over a year. And the move back to San Martin was meant, among other things, to help widen that emotional distance by putting a few miles between them.

Tom was very handsome, a hunk as the girls at the office would say, but what she found most attractive about him was his remoteness. He seemed capable of resisting any influence he chose to exclude from his life. When he was able to resist her charms at first, knowing she wanted him to ask her out but waiting until the time pleased him, Linda became intrigued and began to study him more closely. Wherever she saw him, at lunch with clients, with a date at a favorite nightspot or with friends at a bar, he was always in total control. For someone ruled by her impulses, that was almost a God-like attribute. She wanted to know his secret and use it to beat back the forces that always threatened to overwhelm her. But, to her great astonishment, once she got close to him, and never with any intention of becoming serious, she discovered that he was driven to such control by those selfsame forces. Her response was to confuse compassion with love and marry him.

Linda thought she knew Tom, or at least understood his defensive mechanism, and with patience she would break through to him. Here she would discover a wealth of buried feelings waiting to embrace her. After a year she had given up in desperation. Tom was too distant from his feelings, which frightened him to death, to allow her to ever become really intimate with him. And although their sex life was satisfying enough, it was never more than a physical release. She wondered if anything could ever touch him or move him beyond his self-centered focus. She was not about to stay and find out.

When Linda arrived at the restaurant, she was ten minutes late, and her mother had already ordered for both of them.

"Hope you don't mind," Millie said testily. She was looking at Linda over the top of her glasses expecting an argument. "But I ordered you the veal."

"No, I haven't had red meat in a while. It'll be good for me."

"You could definitely use it. Are you eating all right? You look terrible."

"Well, I haven't had much of an appetite recently," Linda said in her defense.

Millie examined her daughter more closely. There was something odd about her, but she could not explain it. "You still have the flu?"

"A touch of it, but I'm getting better."

"You know, Linda. You should really pay more attention to your appearance, especially when you're not feeling well. I wouldn't be caught dead looking like you do today."

"Well, mother, I'll be sure to wear clean underwear when they take me away," Linda said angrily, after promising herself to stay calm, and then she had another epic coughing fit.

When Linda began spitting up wads of phlegm into her handkerchief, Millie squirmed in her seat self-consciously until the attack was over. "Linda, if you're not feeling any better at the end of the week, I want you to go in and see Dr. Hoffler."

Linda began to protest, but she did not have the energy to resist such a minor foray and ended up nodding her head in agreement. When the waiter stepped up to the table and set down their luncheon platters, Linda used the interruption to force a break in their conversation. The two women ate in silence for a few minutes. Finally, when she could not wait any longer, Millie posed the question uppermost on her mind. "And have you talked with Tom this week?"

"He called again on Wednesday and wanted to come down for the weekend," Linda said, and she assumed without saying that her reply was obvious.

"What harm would it have done?"

"I don't see the point of dragging this out. It's over, and the sooner he accepts that fact, the sooner we can both get on with our lives."

"How can you be that sure after only three months?" Millie asked.

"We haven't been getting along for a year now."

"But you stayed together and worked on it. You didn't give up."

"We stayed together and hit on each other," Linda said.

"So what are you going to do? You think finding somebody else at your age will be easy?"

"I'm not really worried about it, mother."

"I guess you figure while you still have your looks you have time?"

"I don't think my looks have anything to do with it."

"Oh, do you really? Well, take it from somebody who has lost hers, it does," Millie said with a catch in her voice.

Linda heard this curious note and looked over at her mother. The whole cast of her tense, tight body indicated that there was more to this last statement than was immediately apparent. And then, while she studied her mother more closely, she saw in a flash that her father had been unfaithful. She did not know how she knew—only that she knew.

"Linda, are you all right? You're white as a sheet," Millie said.

"I have to excuse myself." Linda stood up, and, feeling a little shaky, grabbed hold of the back of her chair.

"Well, if you're done, I'll just finish up here and meet you out front."

Linda hesitated for a moment, wanting to reach out and comfort her mother, but she did not know the words that would heal such a deep wound, and she hurried off.

After she finished her dessert, Millie walked out to the hotel lobby to wait for Linda. She was quite concerned about her daughter's strange appearance and the severity of this flu bug. Millie decided to force Linda to see Dr. Hoffler soon, and she walked down the hall to the pay phones and placed a call to his office. Although they did not have an opening for several weeks, Millie used her influence to have her daughter squeezed in the following afternoon.

When Millie returned to the lobby and Linda was not there, she went looking for her daughter. Millie tried the ladies' room first, but the door was jammed. She knocked, then called out to Linda, but there was no answer. Alarmed, she stopped a passing bellhop who forced open the door. They found Linda lying up against the door passed out. Millie bent over her daughter and found that she was still breathing. The two of them sat her up against the wall. While Millie tried to revive Linda with a wet cloth, the bellhop hurried back to the front desk and called for an ambulance.

## San Diego, California
## October 2

### 6.

The mouse came around the last corner of the maze to the opening directly in front of it, and ran through it headlong into the back wall. Dr. Guy Joyner pressed the stem of his stopwatch and looked down at where the second hand had stopped, nodding his head in approval. His assistant, Bob Howell, reached over and turned up the dimmer switch on the overhead lights. The two men looked at each other, and for the hundredth time they smiled at their strange headgear and then removed the infrared goggles. Joyner studied his reflection in the tinted glass for a moment before carefully patting his blond hair back into place. This tall, loose-limbed young man looked more like an overage surfer than one of the world's premier scientists. The two men now squinted their eyes until they had adjusted to the bright light. Howell took the mouse, nicknamed Dark Vader, and placed him back into his darkened carrier box. It was only a short trip down the hall to "Night City," the laboratory where they kept the mutant strain of light-sensitive mice, but even a brief exposure at this stage could be harmful.

"Do you want to run anybody else today?" Howell asked as he picked up the box.

"No, I have my hands full. Let's give the others the day off."

"Okay, then I'll go ahead and put Vader to bed." Bob Howell walked out the door holding the carrier steady since the mice, possibly as a consequence of their newly acquired trait, were easily disoriented when moved about.

Joyner walked back to his office at the far end of the laboratory and chalked in Vader's latest time on the blackboard graph listing all the fifth-generation mice. It was consistent with the mouse's other times and close to those recorded by the other mice who had also activated the latent gene. The mice who had failed this test could barely make it around the first corner, and they were forced to rely on a highly developed sense of smell to survive in "Night City." Few would live past their first birthday. Joyner sat on the edge of his desk and stared at the graph, wondering why some of the mice could utilize this gene and survive and why others could not and were doomed to an early death. If the laws of genetics were mysterious, the laws governing evolution could only be characterized as inscrutable. This experiment was the first to bridge the two and would no doubt win Joyner a Nobel Prize before his fortieth birthday.

Guy Joyner and his breed of night-seeing mice were already national celebrities. In July *Time* magazine had done a cover story on him, running a photo of Joyner holding up Vader, who was wearing a drawn-on pair of oversized sunglasses. Some of his colleagues did not appreciate the attention that Joyner's grandstanding brought to their field. Although they were aware of the grant-generating ability of publicity, it was his overoptimistic views on the future of their field that made them nervous. He saw science not only curing many of today's genetic diseases but also discovering the genetic basis of some of the species' more unsavory character traits and modifying them. It was not a position that endeared him to ethicists, clergymen, and politicians. Although others had made even more outlandish claims, like creating mutant men with gills for life in the ocean or with prehensile feet for life in the low gravity of the moon, Joyner had backed up his claims with one success after another. This latest experiment showed the real promise in his research and held out the prospect for greater gains later.

The two-part problem facing Joyner and his colleagues bent on gene therapy was how to place foreign genes into a cell and make them work properly. Scientists had developed several techniques, including viral vectors and the microinjection of eggs, that placed a workable percentage of the genes into the host cell's DNA. Unfortunately, the genes were rarely expressed, and if at all it was usually at low levels in the wrong tissue. As a first step they learned how to trick cells into producing large quantities of a protein product with very dramatic results. The protein metallothionein, or MT, is switched on in animals in response to high levels of certain heavy metals. Scientists spliced together the control signal, the turn-on switch, for the MT gene and a rat growth-hormone gene, and then they microinjected it into mouse eggs. The diet of those mice who had absorbed the combination was supplemented with zinc. This turned on the MT gene's signal, and it began pumping out high levels of the growth hormone. Within three months the mice were twice the size of their littermates. And the gene combination was passed on to the next generation with the same results: a new breed of super large mice.

Although this was a major breakthrough, it still fell far short of the desired goal: to turn the genes on in their proper place at optimum levels. That was when Joyner began to rethink the problem. Eventually he came to see how the broader application of the basic genetic process of selection, used in a classic experiment of the seventies, could force an animal to take up and properly use a foreign gene to survive a harsh change of environment. Using DNA transformation techniques, scientists had exposed mutant mouse cells that lacked the ability to make the enzyme HGPRT to hamster chromosomes with the missing gene. They next placed the cells into a dish filled with the nutrient called the HAT medium. Only those cells that had taken up the missing gene and were now producing HGPRT could survive in this otherwise hostile medium.

Now, on the large scale of evolution, this process becomes natural selection which works to keep a species adapted to its environment. It was Joyner's genius to figure how to speed up this process and make it work for him at the molecular level. He isolated the complex of mouse genes for sight and spliced in the gene that gave owls their remarkable night vision. Using microinjection he implanted thousands of copies of the gene complex into mouse eggs, and as expected a number of the mice absorbed this chain instead of similar parental genes and passed on the complex to the next generation. He isolated these mice and began to subject them to increasingly lower levels of light over a span of several generations. Eventually, the owl gene became highly adaptive and began to express itself, and by now it had become the dominant gene for this locus.

Joyner had undertaken this experiment to study the effects of a perfectly integrated gene substitution in hopes that success at this end would shed light on their failure at the delivery end. What he had not anticipated were the secondary mutations that were now cropping up as the mice rapidly adapted to their new environment. It was far faster than Darwinian evolution would have predicted. It seemed that their tampering had somehow thrown the organism into an accelerated evolutionary spiral. If the rate continued, they would soon qualify as a new species. It now appeared that under certain circumstances, probably requiring environmental stress, that gene substitution could speed up evolution. Before they proceeded with gene therapy, assuming they would develop the necessary techniques, they needed to know more about this relationship. Although this finding intimidated some of Joyner's colleagues and set off more alarms in his opponents' camps, it only showed him his goal of profound transformative change was within his reach.

Joyner's intercom squeaked on, and his secretary Janet called out to him. "Guy, are you there?"

He leaned backwards over his desk and punched the voice button. "Yes, Janet."

"They're ready for you on Ward D."

"Tell them I'll just be a minute." The intercom went dead, and Joyner stood up to leave. He was scheduled to administer an antibody treatment to one of his terminal cancer patients. Guy Joyner was one of the leaders in the bio-tech treatment of cancer. This latest method, using antibodies containing a toxic cancer drug to home in on a tumor and kill off only the desired cells, showed great promise. But, for most of these patients, it was too late for effective therapy of any kind. Many of his colleagues wondered why Joyner did not stick with pure research where they felt his true talent lay, but they really did not know the man. It appeared he had inherited from his father, a country doctor in Nebraska, a keen desire to have a direct beneficial effect on people's lives. And besides cancer research was, in his view, the first step on the road to true gene therapy, and that its eventual cure would lie in that realm. To his opponents this made him doubly dangerous: there was nothing worse than a skilled idealist with the talent and the means to fulfill his awful vision.

## 7.

In the microbiology lab, Dr. Andrea Hunter was operating a microsequenator, snipping off the amino acids in the unidentified protein product taken from Linda Boyer's bladder. Next her assistant, Ken Olson, ran it through the mass spectrometer to identify the string of amino acids in the sample. After sequencing the amino acids in a particular protein, her team could work backwards and determine the order of the nucleotide bases in the gene that coded for it. With this code, a "gene machine" would artificially duplicate the gene, and they would use that copy as a probe to locate the original gene among the one hundred thousand in a mammal's genome.

Olson now turned to Deborah Bronsky, the computer operator, sitting nearby at her terminal. "And the last one is alanine."

Bronsky entered the three-letter genetic code for this amino acid, GCU, into the computer and hit the button for a batch run.

Dr. Hunter walked over and anxiously awaited the results. In her mid-thirties, Andrea Hunter wore her lush brown hair short, because a longer style softened her otherwise sharp features and made her much too pretty. Since she worked around men most of the time, she wanted them to treat her as a colleague first and a woman second. Joyner had pirated her away from a pharmaceutical company with promises of Nobel glory. So far the work had been mainly routine. That would end today.

The terminal screen now began to fill with row after row of letters, each representing one of the four nucleotide bases that made up DNA. In thirty seconds the entire six thousand bases of the mysterious gene had been deciphered. Olson was standing by with his code book, and he now set it down under the screen and quickly thumbed through the blue binder. When he found the desired page, he took out the plastic sheet with its sequence of letters and laid it over the screen. After a long moment, Olson looked up at Dr. Hunter. "It's not even close."

Hunter gave away her disappointment with wrinkled brow and pursed lips. Earlier she had used another method in an attempt to detect the oncogene in the foreign growth, but she had failed to discover the transformative agent. She had hoped that it was a failure in execution and it would turn out to be the oncogene Harvey ras, identified with bladder cancer, but she was badly mistaken.

"Okay, Deborah, send the gene sequence along to Genbank and the Cell Repository in Camden for identification, and see if the people in Washington at the Bio-medical Foundation can match up the protein."

Hunter walked away, heading for the cafeteria for a cup of coffee, and then she would move on to a quiet place in order to think over the problem. Olson stayed behind staring at the screen. There was something vaguely familiar about a long sequence of bases within this gene, but he could not place where he had seen it.

"Deborah, give me a hard copy of this gene breakdown." Olson closed the blue binder, walked over and placed it back on the bookshelf.

"Why don't you just memorize it," Bronsky said, teasing Olson about his supposed photographic recall.

"I need a copy for my written report, smart ass." Olson looked down at the pretty computer operator while she fed the machine a print signal, and he decided his report would require plenty of terminal time.

Dr. Hunter opened the door and stepped out onto the fourth-floor balcony. She walked over and stood at the railing and looked out at the ocean over rows of palm trees and beach bungalows. This was her little hideaway, where she would hole up on warm days for some serious thinking. When the Department of Health Services first contacted them, and after reviewing Louis Hodges's report from UC/San Francisco, they concluded the virus must carry an oncogene that was responsible for the cancerous growths now appearing in the infected patients. The fact each one had a different type was attributed to random chance. Most viruses, unlike this one, were cell-specific; but the normal counterpart of oncogenes appeared in all cells. And these sequences have been found in other mammals, and so they must have existed millions of years ago before the diverse groups separated.

This theory gained further credence when they were able to view cell samples from the patients. The cells had several chromosome translocations; they produced an unusual protein product; there were large amounts of the protein. Each by itself was a sign of cancer; all three together seemed to be overwhelming proof. When they next examined the viral genes and failed to locate a known oncogene among them, or even one with a family resemblance, they next assumed the virus was causing a normal proto-oncogene to turn renegade. This happened in the human oncogene Harvey ras, when one out of six thousand nucleotide bases was changed by a simple mutation.

The next step was to locate this oncogene in the mass of bladder cells from Linda Boyer. They followed a classic procedure where the host cell's DNA was fragmented into ten segments.

Each segment was then introduced into normal cells. When one of the cells turned malignant, they would know which segment contained the oncogene and would repeat the procedure with that fragment until they had isolated it. But they were unable to transform additional cells with the DNA fragments. Other techniques were used but with the same negative results. Whatever the agent involved, oncogene or not, it must have changed its mode of expression and was intent on a goal other than wild uncontrollable growth.

The balcony door opened, and Olson stuck his head out. "Good, I thought you might be here." He shut the door behind himself and walked over to the rail. The two of them stood there in silence for a moment and looked out at the ocean. "I think I might've stumbled onto a piece of the puzzle," he said.

Hunter turned and looked at him. She liked Ken Olson. He had just enough enthusiasm to handle difficult problems, but not enough for him to become obsessed with impossible ones. "Do you really?"

"You know developmental genetics was my specialty in school, and when I first saw the breakdown on this gene, there was something familiar about it. And so I started comparing it to known homeotic gene sequences, and. . . ."

Olson handed her two computer readouts stapled together. She lifted them up against the bright sky to see the comparative outline more clearly.

"It's not a direct match with the Homeo Box sequence but close enough to suggest we're dealing with a homeotic gene."

Hunter lowered the paper and stared at it for a long moment, unsure of the implications of this development. She now reviewed what she knew about this recent discovery. The "Homeo Box" was first identified in fruit flies and later in a wide variety of invertebrate and vertebrate organisms from worms to frogs, and from birds to humans. This sequence of only 180 pairs of nucleotide bases was believed to code for a regulatory protein that switched on other genes and initiated development of diversified tissues during the early stages of a mammal's growth. It appeared to be an ancestral gene so successful in orchestrating such activity that it was appropriated by nature for widespread use.

"Well, a lot of oncogenes have regulatory functions that go haywire and cause cancer, and this just might be a new variety."

"I've never heard of an oncogene with a Homeo Box sequence," Olson insisted.

"Look," Hunter replied impatiently, "whatever its normal function this gene has been triggered inappropriately and is pumping out large quantities of a strange protein." She lowered her voice. "Now doesn't that sound like a mutant gene gone wild to you?"

"Yes, I guess so," Olson reluctantly agreed, intimidated by Dr. Hunter's outburst.

"What else could it be? It's certainly not orchestrating embryonic tissue development in a thirty-three-year-old woman."

When Olson hesitated, giving this option serious consideration, before responding with an incredulous smile, Hunter began to wonder if her confidence in Olson were not misplaced. She finally decided it was the long hours taking its toll.

"Why don't we go down and see if Deborah has found anything."

When Hunter and Olson walked into the laboratory, everybody stopped for a moment and gave them the kind of inquisitive looks reserved for the holders of arcane knowledge. The two of them walked over to the computer terminal where Deborah Bronksy continued to work correlating her research findings.

"Anything turn up?" Hunter asked.

Bronsky rolled her chair back from the terminal and looked up at her boss. "Nothing on the gene, but the protein seems to be related, though somewhat different, to a family of embryonic enzymes." Bronsky reached over, tore off the computer readout, and handed it to Dr. Hunter. She watched her for a moment before asking, "Is this lady having a baby?"

## 8.

Guy Joyner stepped back from the wall and chewed on the end of his pen, while he studied the row of photographs. The chromosomes from each cell were neatly arranged in twenty-three pairs, and had been blown up several times to reveal hundreds of stained bands. The size and position of these bands are constant for each chromosome in any given species, and they can serve as genetic markers for certain types of cancers. But, as Joyner studied the photographs, he did not detect any of the more than thirty chromosomal abnormalities associated with cancer. Since there were over two hundred types of cancer, this might indicate a new type with its own signature, but he was not certain about that.

There was something very odd about the karyo type, the chromosome complement, of Linda Boyer's cancer cells, if they were indeed that. Comparing them with normal bladder cells revealed an extraordinary amount of abnormalities. It would take further testing to identify all the specific deletions, inversions, and translocations between chromosomes; but Joyner had already marked off at least a half-dozen.

When Dr. Hunter walked into his office, Joyner was marking up the last photograph. She did not want to interrupt him, and so she went down to the other end and began to read each photograph working her way back to his position. Here she saw for the first time an overall view of some of the abnormalities she was discovering on a daily basis in her laboratory work. Following the trail left by Joyner's pen, a pattern emerged that seemed to fit the puzzling results of this latest test. Starting over and walking through them again only confirmed that impression. Dr. Hunter was so lost in her analysis that she lost sight of Joyner until she turned and found him studying her.

"So what do you see?" Joyner asked.

"Looks like a regular Mexican jumping bean contest to me."

Joyner threw his head back and laughed. "Doesn't it though!" He gave both of them a moment to calm down. "I was watching you, and you did see something."

"Well, for what it's worth, we've determined that a complex of these viral genes gets spliced into the host cell's DNA, and then starts jumping about from one generation to the next. And they're involved in some of the chromosome swaps you've marked up here."

"And you're saying they're acting like transposons?" Joyner asked.

"Maybe. And they're not just moving about, they're replicating themselves from one location to the next."

"And what about repeat sequences?"

"They're there too," Hunter said.

Dr. Joyner reviewed what he knew about transposable elements, or jumping genes, as they are sometimes called. Although they are most active in bacteria and found in fruit flies, their existence in higher life forms has yet to be determined. But retroviruses, such as Rous sarcoma, have been known to act like transposons. When they land in the middle of a structural gene (one that codes for a protein), they can inactivate it and all downstream production. Some, when they excise themselves, return the gene to normal function. Current research indicated that most spontaneous mutations and chromosomal rearrangements in fruit flies are caused by these elements. Since such a system could play an important role in evolution, scientists awaited discovery of its widespread appearance in other organisms. Hunter's findings seemed to confirm that.

"But what's really surprising," she added, "is we've discovered the location of the gene pumping out this strange protein, and it's not involved in any of the chromosome swaps. Now, what we expected, was an oncogene that got shuffled off and landed on one of the hyperactive areas, let's say on chromosome fourteen or twenty-two, that code for antibodies, and was turned on."

Joyner was not at all surprised. It was becoming increasingly apparent they were dealing with something far more complex than they had at first assumed. "What exactly do we know about this virus?"

"Well, it's the fourth retrovirus known to infect man. It has a pol gene for its characteristic enzymes, a gag gene for its internal structure, and an env gene for its viral coat, and I agree with Hodges that the env gene is probably hypervariable."

"And a line of open reading frames that could contain as many as eight additional genes."

"Some of which must code for the transposon effect."

Dr. Hunter studied her colleague for a moment. "So you don't believe an oncogene is involved at all?"

"So far nothing points in that direction."

"But they are almost always present in viral-induced cancers?"

"And you're so sure that we're dealing with cancer here?" Joyner watched frown lines form on Hunter's brow. Her mind did not take as readily to uncharted waters as his. "Tell me," Joyner asked, "have you tried to grow these cells in vitro?"

Hunter reluctantly nodded her head. "Yes, but they eventually died."

"Cancer cells grow indefinitely when cultured," Joyner added.

"Okay, if it's not cancer, then what is it?"

"As unlikely as it may seem, it appears to be newly differentiated normal tissue growth of an unknown type. Of course, it will take further tests to confirm it, but that's my guess."

"Normal tissue growth?" Hunter asked incredulously.

"Come on, Andrea. It's not that hard to accept. I mean from one fertilized egg we develop into an organism of one hundred trillion cells divided into two hundred different types. That mechanism remains intact; you just need the right key to turn it back on."

"But fully mature organisms don't suddenly sprout new toes, or another ear to replace one that's been lost."

Joyner walked over to where Hunter was standing next to the photographs. "Take a good look at this chromosomal architecture. Have you ever seen anything this drastic before? I've seen cells from aborted fetuses that look normal in comparison."

"And that's what I mean. They're mutant cells only capable of wild growth."

"Or the type of new growth we see during speciation."

Janet now walked into the room, much to Hunter's great relief. "I'm sorry to interrupt you, but Barry Hamilton keeps calling, and I can't put him off much longer."

"Okay. Tell him I'll call in my report within the hour." Janet left shaking her head, and Joyner turned back to Dr. Hunter. She was strictly a laboratory-based microbiologist and sometimes had trouble following Joyner's more speculative theories. "Look, all I'm saying, is that we have to see what is actually here, if we hope to deal with it and help our patients."

"Well, cancerous or not, if it continues to grow and becomes invasive, it could pose the same problem."

"And we'll just have to find some way of killing it off," Joyner said.

Hunter found this prospect reassuring. "So what are you going to tell Hamilton?"

"He's heard from Hodges that the virus is not highly contagious, and I'm going to add that it doesn't induce any known cancer in the samples we studied."

"So you're not recommending a quarantine?"

He shook his head. "But, since I'm not offering any guarantees until we've had a chance to examine more samples, who knows what they'll do."

Hunter looked at him and read the bad news in his sheepish expression. "Don't tell me we have to move up there?"

"I'm afraid so, and within the week. And tell your people it's on a strictly volunteer basis. Who knows what we're getting ourselves into."

## 9.

Wearing a blue terrycloth robe, Linda sat with a half-dozen patients outside the examination room waiting for her next antibody treatment. The group as a whole was subdued this morning; it was becoming apparent to all that they were seriously ill. The recent arrival of the famous Dr. Joyner only underscored that point. So far they had not been told very much about this strange malady, but now they could only assume the worst. What added to their anxiety was the innocuous appearance of their bio-tech treatment. They had expected sessions with exotic equipment but receive a twice-daily shot in the hip instead.

When they called out the next patient's name, the last woman in the row stood up and went inside. A moment later the nurse came out, and she motioned for Linda to move down a place. When Linda ignored her, she walked down the line saying, "We've got a place open at the front if anybody's tired of waiting." Finally, a teen-aged girl, frightened by this old bulldog, took the seat. When the nurse went back inside, Linda turned to Jennifer, who was sitting next to her. "Looks like we've got a long wait."

"Can you believe her. We're suffering from God knows what, broken up and beaten down by it, and we have to put up with this shit."

"'Cheerful attention to detail' is how the brochure reads. Should we give her high marks for that?" Linda asked.

Jennifer laughed. "Yeah, that was a real four-star performance all right."

The two of them had met earlier in the week in the therapy room, and found they both shared a distaste for hospital food, regulations, and personnel. And they had led the patient protest over being held at the hospital under court order without being told the nature of their illness.

"Don't say anything to the others yet," Linda confided in whispers, "but they're going to let us go today."

"Where did you hear that?"

"Well, it's not exactly an unimpeachable source,"Linda said, shrugging her shoulders. "My mother heard two nurses talking in the bathroom."

"There's no question about it then," Jennifer said in mock seriousness.

Linda's name was called out, and she stood up and gave Jennifer a conspiratorial smile, then marched into the doctor's office ahead of her replacement. Seeing the mix-up, the nurse tried to intervene and switch her patients, but the resident administering the treatment, fearing his own mix-up, told the nurse to stick to the listed order. Linda came in and sat on the examination table. Dr. Mathers carefully compared the code on the bottle's label with Linda's name tag before drawing out the serum. Linda opened her robe, and the doctor gave her the shot.

Afterwards, Linda walked back down the hallway to her room at the far end. She was trying to keep a positive attitude, especially around the other patients, and even now she nodded her head and said hello to people passing by, but she had to struggle with her own mounting fears. From the beginning, the day after she met that strange man in the park and after her first hallucination, Linda sensed there was more to her illness than a mere viral infection. To have that confirmed now was of little comfort. But at least, given its apparent seriousness, the doctors could tell them more. Upon his arrival Dr. Joyner had addressed the group, and he managed to enlist their cooperation without actually telling them very much about their affliction or his treatment. This only added to her apprehension. If she only had a name to identify it, even one as dreaded as cancer, it would be easier on her. Now all she knew was what her deepest fears told her, and that was worse than any scourge.

When Dr. Joyner came around the corner, the two of them looked up and spotted each other at the same time. There was a moment's hesitation; both of them considered ducking out, but the longer they waited the more inevitable the confrontation became. Finally, he walked over.

"So Linda, how are you feeling this morning?"

"Oh, about the same as yesterday," Linda said curtly.

Joyner could feel the woman's pent-up anger and decided it was not very therapeutic to feed it more fuel. "Well, then how did you feel yesterday?"

This took Linda by surprise, but she was quick to respond.

"Actually, not much better than the day before."

The two of them just stood there in silence for a moment while they became reacquainted. Dr. Joyner now took Linda by the arm and walked her down the hall. "So tell me, what would you like to know?"

"Well, for starters, I assume this isn't the flu?"

"We're not really sure what it is," he conceded, "and that's one reason why we weren't saying anything."

Linda did not find this very reassuring. "You must know something?"

"We know the virus triggers what appears to be a cancerous growth, but which is in fact healthy new tissue if of an unknown nature."

"And that's bad?" Linda asked.

"If it continues to grow and becomes invasive, it will crowd out the surrounding tissue and interfere with organ functions. But so far none of them have undergone metastasis, where shredded cells cause secondary growths, which is what kills most cancer patients."

"Can you treat it?"

"The growths all appear to be immunogenic, unlike most tumors. And at this stage, they're very treatable."

Linda took a deep breath and let it out with a burst of relief. "Then why the high-powered treatment?"

"I can explain it to you, but it's fairly technical," Joyner warned her.

The two of them had now walked as far as the first floor nurse's station, the halfway mark back to Linda's room. "No, go ahead, I'd like to hear it."

Joyner explained that to attack and destroy this new growth required a recently developed technique used here on patients for the first time. Monoclonal antibodies, or clones of one specific antibody, aimed at a particular antigen, had been touted as the long-awaited "magic bullet" in cancer treatment. Unfortunately, it worked better in laboratory tests than on actual patients. To increase their potency, scientists were now attaching cell-killing drugs or radioactive material to them. Although suited for Joyner's purposes in some ways, they had one major drawback: it was difficult to produce them in humans for a wide variety of antigens.

To solve this problem, he used a new hybrid antibody constructed from both human and mouse cells. By immunizing mice with the antigens, he was able to produce the needed antibodies. Next he attached the variable region, the target-seeking part, of the mouse antibody with the constant region of a human antibody to minimize an immune reaction to the foreign mouse part. Then he cloned the hybrid in the time-honored fashion. The finished product when attached to a cytotoxic drug was a guided missile with a warhead aimed at the new tissue growth in each of his patients.

"It's early yet," Joyner added. "But we feel very confident we can kill it off with this treatment."

Although Linda was thankful for this prognosis, she was not thrilled that they had injected her with foreign mouse cells to achieve it. She assumed that was why they had withheld information about the treatment from them. The whole idea was repugnant to her. It evoked deep-seated prohibitions from mankind's racial memory about the mixing of the species. She had been reading almost daily about new discoveries in genetics and their application in biotechnology, but she never realized how far they had progressed.

Linda walked on in silence until they had reached the door to her room. She now turned to Dr. Joyner. "I know you're trying to save my life, but I'm not sure about this treatment of yours."

"We thought some of you might have reservations," he said hesitantly, looking down at the floor and shuffling his feet.

"Oh, did you really," Linda said in a mocking tone. She waited until Joyner lifted his head. "We should've been consulted, and you know it." With that she turned, walked into her room and closed the door in his face.

## 10.

Walking back to the laboratory, Joyner thought about Linda's rebuke. All along he had considered this the best treatment for his patients. The fact that this medical emergency would allow him to bypass at least a year of animal testing was only a bonus. When he presented his case to the FDA in Washington, Joyner had overstated his appeal by claiming it was the only treatment worth considering. Time was a big factor, and he wanted quick approval. Some standard cancer therapies, including radiation, might have been as effective in the first stages of their treatment. But, if complications developed, like new offshoot growths, antibody therapy would definitely be more effective. Of course its success here would put Joyner at the forefront in his field. He did not want to think he was at all influenced by such considerations, but he had enough doubt to make him feel guilty.

When Joyner walked through the main lobby, he heard his name spoken, and he turned to the stranger walking over to him. In his early thirties, dressed very conservatively, the man had the mark of a bureaucrat.

"Dr. Joyner," the man called out to him. "I'm Barry Hamilton from the Department of Health Services." The two men shook hands.

"You've come just in time," Joyner said without further introduction. He now walked off, and Hamilton hurried to catch up with him. "We've got a little problem brewing you might be able to help with."

"I know. That's why I'm here. Sheriff Howser called us yesterday."

"Did he really?" Joyner shook his head in astonishment. "So just tell the Sheriff it's my call and get him off my back."

"Are you sure about this?" Hamilton asked.

Joyner looked askance at the man. "You read the report from the Center for Disease Control. The virus is contained. And by allowing my patients to resume a normal routine, we hope to lower their stress level and enhance their immune response."

"If I may correct you," Hamilton insisted. "It said no further threat could be ascertained at this time, and that's a big difference."

"The sheriff's concerned that the virus, instead of dying off, has just become inactive, and might still spring back to life and infect everybody else. But, since I'm taking blood samples twice a week, I'll know in time to ward off further contagion."

Hamilton could hardly dispute this claim. Although it had since been discounted, the specter of an infectious cancer virus still made him overly cautious. The two men walked on in silence for a moment. "I'll tell the sheriff we concur with your decision, but I still insist, and I'm sure the governor will back me up, that the patients be restricted from traveling out of town."

"Oh, I agree. This treatment is their only hope; to leave at this point would be tantamount to suicide."

Hamilton looked over at the scientist and shook his head. He had never met such a self-assured, arrogant bastard in his life. "Okay, but you will inform us of any change in their condition, and let us evaluate its threat to the community."

"Agreed," he said as they walked into the laboratory.

"Mind if I look around?"

"Sure. Just don't touch anything." Joyner walked away leaving Hamilton to fend for himself.

He wandered up and down the aisles watching the lab technicians at work. Although he was somewhat more familiar with microbiology than the general public, he had the same general misconception that the techniques of biotechnology chopping and splicing pieces of DNA, inserting and excising them from microorganisms involved surgery-like procedures. In fact most of the chopping was done in flasks by biochemical agents called "restriction enzymes," and the different fragments spliced together by glues called "ligases." He even saw one technician using shake-and-bake plastic bags to "cook" raw DNA with a radioactive probe to search out its complement in a sample gene pool.

Hamilton's tour was cut short when he noticed Dr. Joyner and one of his assistants huddled together at the far end of the laboratory. Joyner had a report in his hand and was reading it with heightened concern written all over his face. Hamilton decided that he would not wait to be informed, and he walked over to them but stopped a safe distance away.

"And you're sure it's not an offshoot growth," Joyner asked Dr. Hunter.

"It's not. We've compared cells from both growths in the same patient, and they don't match up. But what's really curious is that this pancreatic growth does match up with a similar growth in Betty Howard."

Dr. Joyner considered this strange anomaly. Tumor cells were so specific that they even expressed different antigens for tumors induced by the same carcinogen. That was why tumor cells could not be used for immunization, whereas immunity from an oncogenic virus did offer protection from others of its kind. This was further proof they were not dealing with cancer. But how could cells from two different people form such a close match? Tissue typing did allow for successful organ grafts, but only identical twins would match up this closely. Fortunately, as a consolation, the treatment for one type of growth should work with the same growth in another patient.

"I don't like this at all," Joyner said. Dr. Hunter nodded her head in agreement.

Finally, Hamilton stepped over. "Anything I should know about?"

Joyner looked at this intrusive bureaucrat and shook his head. "No, not really." He now turned his back on Hamilton and looked up at the chart hanging on the wall, showing an anterior view of the human torso. One of the technicians was placing a red acetate overlay over the pancreas.

Andrea Hunter stepped over and introduced herself. "You'll have to forgive him," she said. "He's not always this charming."

Hamilton threw his head back and laughed. He liked this woman. "He seems concerned. Is this a serious turnabout?"

"Not unless we start seeing a whole slew of these secondary growths."

"Could the new one have been caused by a reactivated virus?" Hamilton asked gingerly.

"We considered that possibility and checked, but there's no sign of viral activity. No, this is just a delayed reaction."

"But it does indicate that their condition is still very unpredictable."

Hunter nodded her head in agreement. The phone rang, and Olson picked it up. After listening to the caller, he turned to Dr. Joyner. "It's the sheriff. They've caught Carl Owens trying to thumb out of town, and want to know if they should bring him?"

Hamilton looked at Dr. Hunter. "He's one of the locals who's refused treatment," she said.

"And he's out and about on his own?" Hamilton turned and asked Joyner.

"We had him confined to his farm," Joyner replied."But since we're letting the others out of the hospital, he's free to go unless we take further legal action."

Hamilton considered this possibility and quickly decided on a course of action. He now stepped over and picked up the phone. "Sheriff, this is Barry Hamilton. Go ahead and bring the boy in."

## 11.

Carl Owens came down the stairs with his duffel bag slung over his shoulder. His father was sitting at the kitchen table reading the paper and drinking his morning cup of coffee. He looked over at his son, took note of the bag, and went back to his paper without saying a word. Wilma was standing at the stove cooking breakfast, and she had to turn away to hide the tears welling up in her eyes. Carl sat the bag next to the back door and took his place at the table. He waited, but when his father continued to hide behind the newspaper, Carl took a section and started to read it.

Wilma came over and set down plates of ham and eggs. Matt Owens was now forced to put his paper aside, but he replaced this barrier with a hostile glare. Wilma sat down and started eating, but she could only take so much of the silent treatment.

"I assume that . . . ," she said, nodding toward her son's bag, "that's not your laundry?"

"I wouldn't do that to you," Carl said with great affection.

This statement greatly perturbed his father. "No, but you'd worry her to death by running off sick as hell without a thought about yourself or anybody else." Matt pushed his chair back from the table, stood up and threw his napkin down onto a half-eaten plate of food, splattering egg yolk on the tablecloth. "I don't know what happened to you on the road, but you're sure the hell no son of mine."

He now turned and walked across the kitchen, pushed open the screen door and went outside. The door's wooden frame snapped back with a hard thud. Carl just sat there in shock, his stomach doing flip-flops, before getting up and going over to the trash can to scrape off his plate. At the stove he picked up the coffee pot and poured himself another cup.

"I don't think I've ever heard him talk like that before."

"He's concerned about you," Wilma said, and then added. "We're both concerned about your condition. There's talk it's some kind of new cancer, but you won't even let them check you out."

"It's the flu. It's run its course, and I'm feeling fine."

Wilma looked at her son and knew it was useless to argue with him. "But that's only half of it. He's hurt, we're both hurt that you don't want to stay. I think I understand, but your father, he's still kind of old-fashioned. He remembers helping his father through the Depression and figures you owe him the same. Now, if you had a profession and were doing well, he'd feel differently about it, I'm sure. But seeing you flit about like this really sticks in his craw."

"Well, maybe he's right, maybe I am pretty self-centered. I know I called and wrote and all, but five years is a long time to stay away."

"Well, I won't argue with that," Wilma said.

Carl walked over and stood at the back door looking out to the barn and the fields beyond. There must be something here that had driven him away and kept him from coming back for so long. It certainly was not his parents, despite his conflict with his father. He loved them both deeply and missed them greatly. It had more to do with Jennifer than with anybody else, or at least what she represented. Thinking of her, while he watched the farm and its inhabitants waking up to a new day, he started to see what she had in common with this land he could not abide. She would ground him, bind him to herself, and in her as in this land he would be brought into contact with the innermost part of his being. And this was what had sent him scurrying across the face of the earth. He was running away from the very thing he sought, peering into a thousand different faces for some sign of it, when all along the image abided in him.

Carl turned back to his mother sitting at the table with infinite patience, waiting on him as she had waited on both him and his father these many years. When would they come to appreciate this woman, Carl thought, come to understand that she held in her quiet strength the better part of themselves. Carl took a seat at the table across from his mother, and they talked. They had always had an easy familiarity with each other, but now a new intimacy opened between them. Subjects heretofore off-limits were brought up and delved into without hesitation. Wilma was able to ask questions about Carl's life on the road she had shied away from earlier. She was curious about the type of people he met in his travels, the friendships he formed, even the women he slept with. Who were these rootless people, where did they come from, where were they going, and what would become of them? They talked through the morning, and Carl could see a wanderlust in his mother stifled all these years by duty and obligation, but most of all by love. Carl had never known a love that would sublimate its own needs and desires for another. Such a concept was totally alien to him. He had always been so self-absorbed that other people were only of marginal interest to him.

He was as he would now have to admit: a child. But one who had just seen a glimpse of the adult to be.

By late morning, with a hundred miles of road ahead of him until his next stop, Carl had to leave or end up camping out. He had friends in San Francisco he would stay with on this first leg of his journey north. Two years earlier he had worked as a lumberjack in Oregon, and he felt in need of hard physical labor to work the stiffness out of his psyche. He knew it would be his last outward journey, that he was coming to terms with himself. Soon he sensed he would be able to commit himself to a life grounded in a piece of this man's earth that he would carve out for himself. But for now the road beckoned. He said a long lingering goodbye to his mother. He went out into the barnyard looking for his father, but as Carl had expected, he was nowhere to be found.

By noon Carl had walked down their mile-long dirt driveway to the main road heading into town. Here he would pick up the coastal highway going north. It was a good day for thumbing, and he picked up his first ride within minutes. It was an old friend of his father's, Bernie Hall, a cranky old coot, who ran on about the current water shortage until they reached town. Carl was glad the man was not going any further. He walked past the hospital but decided against tempting fate by visiting Jennifer. They had met once since their rendezvous, right before she was confined to the hospital and he to his farm, but their meeting left more unresolved feelings than it cleared up. The time for a full reconciliation was still in the future, and since he planned on returning within the year, he would wait until then.

If Carl gave in to the current hysteria, he would be more concerned about Jennifer's illness and the possibility of her death. He did not disagree with the doctor's diagnosis; he just viewed this malady in a different light. From the start it had been accompanied by this strange vision, and he sensed this was its greater part. From his experience a change in consciousness was always accompanied by an illness as the body realigned itself. The fact that the virus appeared so virulent to the medical profession only attested to the potency of consciousness intruding on them. He would not fight it and was going off into the wilderness to align himself with it.

When he had reached the outskirts of town, with the ocean on one side and the coastal mountains on the other, Carl began to feel that wild exhilaration only the road brought out in him. He was unbounded like a cloud drifting heedlessly across an open expanse of sky. For now he could not put enough space between himself and those earthbound forces that would tie him down. He knew his days on the road were numbered, but that only added a sense of urgency. This trip, his last, would be something special. He would push himself to experience all the road had to offer, and he would savor it for a lifetime. A car approached, and Carl stuck out his thumb. By now he could tell a car's speed at a quarter of a mile. This one was coming very fast, and then it started to slow down even faster. An alarm went off in Carl's mind, but before he could act, the unmarked police car had pulled off the road. Carl knew, as the two officers rushed toward him, that this trip was over before it had begun.

# CHAPTER THREE
# PENETRANCE

*When the outward expression of a gene*
*is dependent on other factors such as:*
*the presence of modifiers, epistatic genes,*
*suppressors in the rest of the genome,*
*or the modifying effect of some unknown influence.*

## Ankara, Turkey
## October 27

The jeep wound its way up a twisting mountain road that was still hidden in the early-morning shadows. The driver and his two passengers were wearing local headdresses and goggles to protect them from the wind-blown dirt. The swirling dust cloud stirred up by their passage, coupled with near darkness, lowered visibility to a few feet. Yet Gamal, a local herdsman, drove the jeep at breakneck speed with one hand on the wheel while he smoked a cigarette with the other. He now turned to Mehmed Edib in the back seat and began telling him a dirty joke in the local dialect. Gamal took the man's anxious expression as a sign of rapt attention, when in fact Edib fully expected them to plunge to their death at any moment. The driver continued with his story. Suddenly, they drove out from under the shadows into open sunlight. Gamal slammed on the brakes as the jeep skidded to a stop in the loose gravel at the top of the mountain, only a foot away from a three-thousand-foot drop to the valley floor. He now leaned over to check his turning radius and indicated with his hands a foot apart how close to the edge they had come. He told Edib that but for the grace of Allah they would now all be dead. Looking into the driver's maniacal smile,

Edib had to agree with him. Gamal now jammed the gearshift into first and spun the jeep around, his right back wheel suspended in mid-air, and then they careened down the mountain road.

Edib, a minor government official in charge of the investigation, had taken this perilous trip too many times. He knew his luck was running out, and if he did not solve this mystery soon and was forced to bring in more experts, one of these crazy herdsmen was bound to drive him off the side of this mountain. He did not need a fortune teller to predict his future. It was written in wrecked jeeps on the floor of this valley. Edib now turned to Max Kellgren to brief him and keep occupied in hope the driver would not continue with his story.

"Dr. Kellgren, you must see how grave the situation has become. In this herd alone, half of the year's drop of 'kids' have been aborted."

Kellgren lowered the fold of cloth over his mouth. "And only the herds in this valley are affected?"

"Yes, but these have always been our most productive ranches," Edib said. "And if, whatever it is, should spread to the other herds." Mehmed shook his head in despair. "We are a poor country, Dr. Kellgren. The Angora goat and its wool, the world's only true mohair, is a national treasure. If this breed is wiped out by disease, the damage to our economy would be inestimable."

Kellgren nodded his head in agreement, although he was uncertain if he could be of any direct help. Actually, he was there more out of curiosity than to be of assistance. A team of scientists had gone in two months earlier and discovered a very strange genetic anomaly. The tissue from these aborted goat fetuses was made up of a mosaic of normal diploid (two chromosome sets) cells and polyploid cells with four sets. There was no doubt that this was the cause of the abortions, as was the case with all polyploids in higher animals. What was less certain was the cause. Spontaneous duplications of this nature did occur, if rarely, in plants; however, it was far rarer in animals and it could hardly account for anything this pervasive. This was when Dr. Kellgren was called in, and since he saw in these tissue samples similarities with the polyploid plants in Roykenvik, he decided to make the long arduous journey to collect more samples for himself. If his hunch was right, he might indeed know the cause, but he would not be able to share such a discovery with his colleagues, or at least not yet.

The jeep raced through the open log gate and drove into the ranch, scattering a mother hen and her chicks crossing the road. The driver drove up in the middle of the courtyard, jumped out and wandered off. The two men took off their headdresses and waited in the jeep for someone to approach them. Edib knew the routine well. If you showed the least bit of impatience, they would make you wait for hours. In fifteen minutes, Abdul Kemal, the owner, a big rough-looking brute, stepped out of the ranch house onto the porch. He stood there and made a sweeping survey of his domain, looking straight through the outsiders. He now lit a cigarette and smoked it while ignoring them. Finally, it was time to dispense with these fools and their useless science. Kemal jumped off the porch and headed for the barn waving them over.

Inside the barn Kemal reached into a barrel of ice and pulled out a plastic bag, containing a badly deformed goat fetus. He now tried to hand the bag to Edib, practically shoving it in the man's face, but he stepped back gagging from the sight. Kemal began to laugh when Kellgren grabbed the bag from him and lifted it up against the sky for a better look. This startled the herdsman, who could not decide whether to be angry over the affront or just curious. When the scientist took the bag over to a nearby workbench, slit it open and took out the fetus, Kemal watched him closely. After setting up a battery-powered lamp, Kellgren quickly dissected the fetus and began scraping tissue samples onto a stack of glass slides. Edib hung back but soon the smell had chased him out of the barn. Kemal lasted longer, and when he was finally driven away, he looked back at the old man with respect. In his experience, a strong stomach had great practical value.

Next Dr. Kellgren set up his portable microscope and began to view the slides. He needed to check if more of the polyploid cells, like those in his samples, had shortened or missing chromosomes. Analysis of the plants in Roykenvik had shown a doubling of the chromosome sets that at first appeared to be exact duplicates. However, Kellgren then discovered the progressive elimination during cell division of whole sections apparently due to incompatibility. He compared them and found genetic material not present on the original chromosomes that caused the disjunction. Further analysis showed these genes to be responsible for the phenomenal growth of the plants and their unique characteristics. The question was, since they were not mutations of existing genes, exactly where did they come from?

By now Dr. Kellgren had viewed a variety of the tissue samples and discovered, as expected, especially in the more developed tissue, polyploid cells with missing chromosomes. Also, given their wide dispersal, the initial duplication must have occurred as early as the blastula stage of fetal development. The fact that only a few of these founder cells were affected allowed for any growth at all. He could only imagine with great anticipation what exotic new genes would be found on the unmatched chromosomes. That they would be there he had no doubt whatsoever.

Kellgren began to sort his slides and pack them away. He could not help but look at them one last time in the light. He wondered how substantial a case he could make using these slides and comparing them to the ones gathered in Roykenvik. It was now obvious to him that this foray had been a planned genetic experiment to introduce new genes into the goat's genome. That the method failed here, after succeeding spectacularly on plants, was due in large part to an inherent mechanism in higher animals that depends on a delicate balance of chromosomes for sexual reproduction. Although polyploid organisms do exist like flat-worms and brine shrimp, they reproduce by the asexual cell division of parental cells. It was an understandable miscalculation by experimenters who seemed to be learning as they went along.

Kellgren did not want to hazard a guess as to exactly who these "beings" were. He could only assume that their interest extended beyond the animal kingdom. When they would make their next foray, Kellgren did not know. He could only hope that they would improve their methods before tackling anything as complicated as the human genome.

With a handkerchief covering his nose, Edib now edged his way back into the barn and walked over to Dr. Kellgren. "Tell me, doctor, have you discovered anything new?"

Kellgren closed the microscope case, picked it up and turned around. He paused for a moment. "From a scientific standpoint, I'm afraid nothing very conclusive." Edib was visibly disappointed, and as they walked out of the barn, Kellgren tried to cheer him up. "But, strictly as a personal opinion, I think you'll soon see the end of this."

That was definitely encouraging, and Edib looked to Dr. Kellgren for more details. "This opinion, it must be based on. . .something?" he asked. "Please, you must see my position. To tell my superiors this without facts." Edib ran a finger across his throat. "They would have my head."

As they walked out of the barn into the sunshine, Kellgren gave this some thought. "Tell them, that in my opinion, it's a totally isolated incident, possibly due to inter-species' breeding that didn't take." Edib nodded his head. This sounded reasonable enough. "And that I recommend they keep the herdsmen away from the goats while the females are in heat."

Edib was caught off guard by Dr. Kellgren's serious delivery, but then he threw his head back and laughed until tears rolled down his face. "Yes, that will do very well indeed."

The two of them walked up to the open fire where the herdsmen were gathered for their late-morning cup of coffee. The banter stopped as the outsiders approached, and all of them looked to Kemal for a key to their reception. Finally, he told them that Kellgren had the stomach of an old goat. Everybody relaxed, and conversations were resumed. One of the herdsmen handed Kellgren a thick cup of coffee, and when he pulled out the spoon, only the handle remained. Apparently this was a joke foisted on all outsiders. Dr. Kellgren lifted the cup and drank the coffee straight down. The herdsmen were impressed. Kemal, his opinion vindicated, beamed with delight.

## 2.

Jennifer had returned to work the day after her release from the hospital. Her boss, Maggie, had told her to take a week off and recuperate, but she could not afford that luxury. Although the state, because of the unknown nature of her illness and its social repercussions, was paying her hospital bill, Jennifer still had to maintain her apartment and make her monthly car payment. She could not depend on her parents to help her, since they were barely surviving themselves. Nevertheless, her mother wanted Jennifer to give up her apartment and move in with them for the duration of her treatment. What she really needed was to be by herself. Her parents, as much as she loved them, were very negative people. Their home represented everything that she was struggling to leave behind, and to return there, even under these circumstances, would be a moral defeat.

One of the hardest trials she had to face was the kindly well-wishers among her regular customers who did not have the decency to let her keep her illness a private matter. Every day somebody would ask how she felt, what were the latest test results, what did the doctors say? Finally, Maggie, seeing her predicament, told one of them it was none of his damn business. And this was what she was telling inquiring friends. She appreciated their concern, but the last thing Jennifer needed was to dwell on her illness. It would be easy to feel sorry for herself, to be consumed by self-pity. She wanted to think only positive thoughts, to imagine her recovery, to see herself leading a full productive life again. But that was difficult when somebody kept reminding her every fifteen minutes that she was deathly ill.

It was a slow afternoon; business seemed to be slacking off lately. To keep busy, Jennifer helped out with the monthly inventory and spent the rest of the day locked away in the pantry. After a couple hours, one of the other girls looked in on her, and Jennifer could not wait until she left. She had never liked being alone, but now she clung to her solitude. Jennifer told herself that she needed time alone to gather her forces together, but it definitely went beyond that. She was shrinking away from the outside world and contact with family and friends. Although the agent was external, the process of her destruction was an internal one. And she needed to focus her attention there. But, to venture inward and confront this side of herself, was a form of dying and for Jennifer as fearful a journey as death itself.

At the end of her shift, Maggie stuck her head into the pantry. "You like working here so much, why don't you just move in?"

"Yeah, and I'd be so big within a week the nurses wouldn't be able to find a vein."

"Well, unless you want to donate your time, get your ass out of here."

Jennifer ate a quick dinner, and then changed into a pair of jeans she always kept in her car. She decided to drive up the coast instead of going straight home. She could watch the sunset from her back porch, but viewing it while driving, passing in and out of the shadows cast by seaside cliffs, until the light was gone and the night had fallen and the stars shone overhead, eased the passage into the nocturnal world. The twilight hour was not her best time of the day. It was not the dark that scared her, but the changeover from day to night and the acclimation it required. Once there she could make her way about, but getting there, leaving the security of one world for the uncertainty of another, was difficult for her.

Jennifer had arrived at a similar point in her inward search for understanding. She stood in the twilight of consciousness caught between two worlds, watching the life she lived out in the light of day, with all its dreams and ambitions, give way to a secret life with its unknown designs rising to the surface from some netherworld within. Jennifer had little choice in the matter. She could either accept this new consciousness and try to salvage something of the life she knew, or deny it and watch it sweep over her and destroy all that she cherished. She knew the key was the phantom image that had first appeared with the onset of her illness. She would have to discover its secret if she wished to survive.

The twilight had faded to near darkness by the time Jennifer reached her destination. She pulled off the highway into a roadside picnic area and parked behind a huge clump of bushes. This was the spot where she had met Carl recently, where she had come over the years to sort out her problems. Now, standing at the top of this cliff, with its two-hundred-foot drop to the ocean below, as the light slowly seeped out of the world, Jennifer looked down the rocky path to the overhang halfway along and wondered if she should proceed. If she hurried, she might make it before the light was totally extinguished, but she would never find her way back up the path on this moonless night. Jennifer would be stuck on the windblown precipice until first light in the morning with only her illness for company. Before she could stop, she found herself racing down the path at breakneck speed, dodging stones left and right and arriving at the overhang shaken but unharmed.

Jennifer spread the beach towel she had brought along and sat down with her back resting up against the stone wall. It was dark with only the soft glow of city lights off in the distance and a clear sky full of stars overhead. And she sat there, letting the darkness envelope her and the wind blow around her and the sound of crashing waves sweep over her. She sought surrender. To throw herself upon the elements and let them make her over. She sensed that to grasp new meaning she would need a new self to see with. Where else could she find it? This place had always been her refuge, where she encountered her other side. Here she had first made love to Carl, here she had welcomed him back into her life. Here was where she would have to come to terms with the visage that had stalked her these past few months.

Was it the face of death, some evil spirit, some unknown God? Who was it that oversaw her destruction, whose image grew with each passing day, as if feeding on her weakened flesh? In answer to her summons the visage now arose before her out of the darkness. She waited for it to speak like some biblical

Jehovah, but it spoke not. Was it disembodied spirit, she wondered, or a projection from her own subconscious depths? She closed her eyes but the image persisted, and yet this only showed how easily it could penetrate both worlds. Either way the great unknown, whether it be inner or outer space, was one and the same. Whatever its origin it did appear cold and imperious. There was no emotion in those bottomless pits that passed as eyes. No empathetic feelings reached out to her. She sensed that it was unmoved by her plight, that her suffering had no effect on it. What it lacked was any human dimension at all. Yet she knew it was the key to all that she was and all that she might become.

What did it want of her, she asked repeatedly? What use could be made of such an insignificant life as hers? She sensed that its appearance here was part of some great drama, and that she had been drafted as one of the players. Now she pleaded for her life, asked that she be returned unharmed to the life she had known all these many years. Jennifer waited through the night for a reply, but none was forthcoming. She knew there was sentient life here, that it had heard her petition. That it chose not to respond could mean that one life was of little value in its great design, or that the only true value that life had was yet to be bestowed on it.

Linda had spent the whole week trying to catch up with her school work and had not had the time to clean her apartment. With three weeks' worth of dirt and grime, it was a real disaster. When she woke up in the morning, she hoped a summons from the outside world would call her away in time to save her from the awful task. But none came. So she went to work after breakfast dusting the furniture, washing and waxing the kitchen floor, doing the front windows. Yet the more she cleaned the more she found to clean, and soon the job had turned into an all day affair. But then halfway through the afternoon, a visitor arrived to spirit her away from the drudgery.

Linda was in the bathroom wiping down the tub when the doorbell rang. She plopped the wet rag in the sink and hurried out. From a distance, looking down the long hallway, the figure standing in the shadows of the front porch looked strangely sinister. Linda rubbed her eyes clear and saw as she cautiously approached the front door that it was only her friend Jennifer. One look at the woman's stooped figure, no doubt bent over by the concerns of their illness, explained Linda's mistaken impression.

"Oh, Jennifer, it's you," Linda said, and opened the screen door. "Come in, but hold your nose, I've been dusting up a storm."

Jennifer walked past Linda, smiling weakly at her joke, and wandered into the living room in a daze. Linda watched her friend with concern. She appeared to have slept in her clothes and to have had her hair blow-dried in a wind tunnel.

"Can I get you something to drink? A cup of coffee maybe?"

"Yeah, that would be great," Jennifer said, and added as if she just realized it, "I've been up all night stuck out on the cliffs."

"What were you doing out there?" Linda asked.

Jennifer looked at her hesitantly, unsure of her reply, then abruptly turned and walked off. Linda was alarmed by her friend's strange behavior, and she hurried off to the kitchen to fix her a much-needed cup of coffee. When she returned, Jennifer was viewing the row of photographs on the wall. Linda handed her a steaming hot cup of black coffee and watched her gulp it straight down.

Linda tried to stop her, but she was too late. "That must've really burnt. Are you all right?"

Jennifer shrugged off the question and continued down the row. When she came to the photograph of Linda at fourteen with her hippie friends, Jennifer stopped and looked at it intently. "You were a real flower child then?"

"Yeah, with poppies in my hair and nothing in my head."

Jennifer just nodded her head and moved on to the next photograph. It was the picture of Linda meditating in the French Alps, and Jennifer stared at it for the longest time. She continued studying it until she finally asked, "When you were in your spiritual trip, meditating all the time, did you ever see anything strange?"

This question took Linda completely by surprise. She knew it was a roundabout inquiry, and that Jennifer must be seeing her own disembodied image. She wondered if they were the same.

Jennifer turned to her. "And yours started the day you got sick?" She waited until she saw the answer in Linda's eyes. "And, as our illness has progressed, the eyes have become more defined, and now other features are starting to appear."

Linda was now the one in a daze, and she walked over and sat down on the sofa. Jennifer came around and sat down in the rocking chair across from her.

"Do you have any idea what is going on here?" Linda asked.

Jennifer shook her head and then added, "Well, since we're both seeing the same thing, it's not a hallucination."

That was obvious, but Linda sensed Jennifer knew more. She studied her friend for a moment. "That's what you were doing out on the cliffs, wasn't it?"

Jennifer nodded her head. "I thought if I could sustain contact long enough with it I might learn something useful."

"And did you?" Linda asked.

Jennifer shrugged her shoulders. "Well, it's alive, it has awareness, I'm sure of it. And it has designs on us."

Linda closed her eyes and tried to feel her way through these words to the heart of this puzzle, and there she discovered that the words were indeed true. But there was more, much more of this monstrous mystery left undisclosed, and they would have to probe further and deeper if they hoped to uncover its secret and the key to their survival.

"I think we'd better look into this a little further," Linda said.

"To say the least," Jennifer added, and then she smiled for the first time. "But I don't think we should tell Joyner or the others about it right now."

"Agreed. Let them conduct their research and we'll do ours."

## 3.

Linda was running up the steps to the school when she dropped one of her books. She squatted down, holding the stack of books with one hand and groping for the fallen one with the other. Paul Jordan came up from behind and picked the book up for her.

Linda stood up slowly, trying not to lose her balance, and Jordan took her arm and helped her up the steps. "That's quite a load you've got there."

"I was trying to catch up over the weekend."

"It looks that way," Jordan said. When they reached the top, he took half of her stack of books and carried them as they walked inside. "I hope you're not going to overdo it now?"

"Well, I don't want to fall behind any further."

"Please, don't worry about it. That's what we have teacher's aides for."

They had now reached Linda's homeroom, and when she struggled to get her key out, Jordan used his to open the door. Linda went over and set the books down on her desk and took Jordan's from him. When she turned back to him, he stood there shuffling his feet, wanting to say something but finding it hard to bring up the subject. He finally said, "Linda, everybody's just sick about this. And, if there's anything anybody can do, just ask."

Jordan now reached over and kissed his former pupil on the cheek, and Linda gave her old teacher a big hug with tears rolling down her cheeks. After he left, it took her a few minutes to put her books away and lay out the day's lesson plan. But, before she knew it, her students started coming in and taking their places. In ten minutes the bell rang, and Linda began teaching her first class in over a month.

Linda had to determine how well her students had learned their lessons from their substitute teacher. She started where she had left them, drawing Fs. And they slowly worked their way through the alphabet to the Ns. Linda walked up and down the aisles checking their papers and was generally pleased by their overall progress. However, most of her slow learners had fallen further behind. Apparently Judy had not taken enough time with them. And now she would have to redo these lessons. Linda reviewed other subjects covered in her absence, and again she was satisfied with their progress. It looked as if she could continue from where Judy had finished on Friday. It was much better than she had expected, and it lessened the pressure she felt on returning to work after such a long sick leave.

After lunch, Linda began teaching new material, but for the last period, as a reward for a very long day, she let them draw for an hour. Within minutes they were totally absorbed, and she was free to work on make-up lessons for her slow learners. She kept tabs on her class by listening to the background noise. After a while it became unusally quiet, and Linda looked up to find her students had stopped and were sitting there staring at her.

"Does it hurt, Mrs. Boyer?" Amy Henderson finally asked.

"No, Amy. Not yet." Linda was touched by her innocent curiosity. She looked around the class openly encouraging their questions.

"You goin' to die?" Jason asked.

This was one question even Linda had avoided asking herself. Now she felt out a reply and was not surprised by her answer. "I don't know, Jason. But it's possible."

It took her class a moment to absorb this. "Are you scared?" Amy asked.

This time Linda did not need to probe deep down for her answer. She looked over at her young cherub and nodded her head. The little girl could understand fear and nodded back in sympathy. The bell rang, and her students quietly gathered their things and walked out in a somber mood. The last one to leave was Randy Carter, who did not seem nearly as affected as the others. He now dropped off his drawing and went out.

As one of the newly released patients, this was also Randy's first day back at school. At first Linda had lavished him with extra attention, but she soon realized he was doing just fine without it. In fact, Randy seemed as healthy as ever. Linda now reached over and picked up his drawing. It was a picture of the eyes seen in her vision, yet they were even more defined with other features beginning to show. The words "TRUST ME" were written underneath. Linda was so startled she almost screamed in fright before calming herself. So the others were seeing it as well.

After school Linda went looking for Pam. She had called her several times over the weekend, and although her husband Roy had taken the messages, Pam never called back. Linda found her swimming laps in the school pool.

It took Linda a couple minutes to get her friend's attention. Pam was at the far end of the pool turning around when she saw Linda waving. She had already pushed off, and when she came up, Pam waved back at her. She did another lap before swimming over to the ladder and climbing out of the pool. Linda brought a towel over, and Pam dried herself off.

"I've been calling for two days now. Didn't Roy give you my messages?" Linda asked.

Pam walked over to the wall and sat down on the bench and wiped her legs off. When Linda came over, she looked up and told her, "He's been so busy setting up my new exercise program that he must've forgotten."

Linda found that hard to believe, but she really did not want to cross-examine her friend. "Look, I had a talk with Jennifer Barnak on Saturday about this . . . image, we've both been seeing." Linda watched Pam for any signs of recognition, and she saw her ball up her right fist. "And today, one of my students, Randy Carter, handed me this drawing." Linda gave the paper to Pam. She took one look at those eerie-looking eyes and jumped up off the bench and walked away in shock.

Linda followed after her. "Come on, Pam. We've all been seeing it." Pam had stopped, and when Linda came up to her, she could see goose bumps on her arm. "Let's talk about it."

"What's there to talk about?" Pam asked and turned back to Linda. "It's a drug-induced hallucination."

"One that we all share?"

Pam just stared back at her blank-faced, and, looking into

eyes terror had robbed of all life, Linda knew it would be useless trying to reason with her. Pam now walked around to the diving board and stepped up on it.

"Linda, I think it's best we don't see each other for now."

"Oh really," Linda said, shaking her head in astonishment. "And what brought this on?"

"I'm sorry. I don't want to hurt your feelings, but this treatment is my only hope, our only hope for survival. And yet you keep knocking it, keep fighting Dr. Joyner's brilliant efforts." Pam started bouncing up and down on the board. "And now you come in here with this crazy story about mass hallucinations. Really Linda, I think you're losing your mind, and I don't want anything else to do with you."

Pam now dove into the water, and Linda just stood there and looked down at the stream of bubbles left in her wake. Crestfallen, Linda turned around and walked through the double-doors into the hallway, and headed for the parking lot.

Pam glided through the water only two feet above the white-striped lane divider on the pool's bottom she used to keep a straight course. She had already swam half the length of the pool underwater and her lungs were about to burst. And yet she swam on. Pam would risk the danger of a watery grave to out-distance the terror staring out at her from a young boy's drawing. The far end of the pool was now in sight, and she gave it one last kick but fell short and turned upward. As she rose that self-same image formed in the bubbles above her, and Pam swam through it breaking the surface of the water and screaming at the top of her lungs.

**4.**

Guy Joyner sat back in his chair and watched the technician place another red overlay on the skeletal chart hanging on the far wall. When he finished taping it to the brain, he stepped back down the ladder and slowly exposed the remainder of the chart showing overlays on all major organs. Although Joyner had known the test results for some time, watching this ritual only added to his frustration. It was becoming increasingly clear that they were dealing with an unknown process that was consuming the body organ by organ.

By now tissue growth had slowed down to the point where cancer could be totally ruled out. This had been Joyner's prognosis from the beginning, but now even his most skeptical colleague had to concur with it. Yet nobody could determine exactly what these growths were. Although each of them corresponded to major body organs and pumped out a wide array of strange enzymes, their individual and collective function was still a mystery. This had not stopped Joyner from treating his patients, and so far he had successfully retarded several growths. The problem was that they were proliferating faster than he could kill them off. Already his less hardy patients were being overwhelmed by the antibody treatments coupled with the toxic die-off of cell tissue.

Fortunately, the new growths had not yet interfered with the body's normal functioning. Organs of elimination were working doubly hard to cleanse the body of this buildup. But, before too long, and Joyner was only now begrudgingly facing this fact, the body could not possibly withstand the massive treatments needed to kill off all the new growths. He could either destroy one or two of them completely, or treat all of them at a minimal level in hope of retarding the system long enough to understand its purpose. That it was purposive he had no doubt. For six weeks he had watched these growths pop up one after the other. In each patient it started with a different organ, usually one already weakened, and the others followed in rapid succession. If this were cancer and this wildfire spread were metastasis, it would be alarming but explainable. The fact that each growth was a separate fully differentiated tissue type, combined with the presence of the CEA antigen, pointed unmistakably to some kind of embryogenic development. That it was happening to fully mature members of the human species could only mean, as far as

Joyner was concerned, that this virus had tripped a process too drastic for normal fetal development.

Dr. Hunter now stuck her head into Joyner's cubicle. "Just got the results back on the enyzme comparisons, and you're not going to believe this."

Joyner looked up at her. "Oh, something unusual for a change?" he asked ironically. And Hunter nodded her head in beleaguered agreement. He stood up and followed her across the lab to a sink at the far end. Here Ken Olson was sorting out a row of gel tubes.

"We did a gel electrophoresis of liver, bladder, and pancreatic enzymes from all the patients," Hunter said, as Olson handed her the first row of tubes. She held them up for Joyner to see. "And there's absolutely no variation whatsoever between the different enzymes for each type."

Joyner found this news disturbing. From past experience he knew just how effective this test was for identifying variations among like proteins. It used the substitution of five ionizing amino acids that gave such proteins a detectable net charge. Substitution will alter this charge and tell the degree of variance between the genes coding for similar proteins. It is an effective tool in population genetics allowing the whole genome of a species to be scanned for genetic variations. Many species have been sampled in this manner, and the percentage of polymorphism (multiple genes for the same loci) is consistently one-third in any given population. This great variability is the raw material for evolutionary change.

Joyner closely examined the dark-staining bands for the pancreatic enzymes, and they demonstrated the same electrophoretic mobility in all the gel tracks. He now looked over at Hunter incredulously. "And the others are the same?"

"That seems to be the key word today."

Dr. Joyner gave the gel tubes back to Olson who tried to hand him the next set, but he waved him off. Joyner had seen enough. He took Dr. Hunter's arm and walked her back to his office. "This is really a little mind-boggling."

"Tell me," Hunter said.

"I know this is a statistically small sampling, but still we should be seeing some variance."

"You would think so." Hunter was about to make a point when Joyner started another one of his rambling monologues.

"And I was beginning to think that maybe, just maybe, we were seeing some kind of speciation process. I mean genetically the signs are all there. Just look at all these chromosome deletions, inversions, and translocations. That's what we would expect to see when existing functions get changed around. And I just bet we're going to discover gene mutations all over the place. That means totally new functions building on old ones. Which is what we have with all these new tissue growths. But this," Joyner said, and walked on in silence for a moment, "this destroys my theory. Genetic variation is the fuel of evolution, and yet here we have matching tissue growths pumping out perfectly matched enzymes. If it's evolution, it's the end of the road, because without variance, there's no possibility of further change."

They had now reached Dr. Joyner's cubicle, and when it appeared he had finished, Hunter asked, "But, if evolution is the adaptation to changing conditions, what are these people adapting to?"

Joyner thought about it for a moment. "That, my dear, is a very good question, and one I would like to pose to my old mentor, Max Kellgren."

**5.**

After being rebuffed by Pam, who had been her best friend, Linda could not bring herself to ask the others if they were seeing the disembodied image. Jennifer assumed the thankless task and met with the same kind of resistance. Everybody was seeing it, but nobody wanted to admit it had any importance. They had all placed their faith in Dr. Joyner's treatment, despite the fact new growths were cropping up on a weekly basis. Linda would place her faith, she decided, on her intuition, which clearly told her that the image was the key to her recovery.

Although it had first appeared with the onset of her illness and seemed somehow connected to it, Linda had come to accept it in a more positive light during this period of soul-searching. One way of looking at it, and not the only way, she realized, was to treat it as a projection from her subconscious mind. From years of self-growth therapies, Linda saw the subconscious as the matrix of life. It had sent her, she thought, an image of wholeness to help ward off the attack of this foreign intruder. It appeared sinister, especially to the others, in proportion to the threat it posed to their conscious self's autonomy.

There was another possibility she would have dismissed outright years earlier, but faced with death and its leveling effect, she found herself more open to it. Although Linda had been raised as a Christian, she had since outgrown that faith and replaced it with a concoction of Eastern beliefs and humanistic philosophies. The concept of a Zeus-like God sitting on a heavenly throne dispensing justice gave way to an all-pervading force best characterized as All-That-Is. Recently she had come to realize that both were metaphors for an unknown and probably unknowable mystery. It allowed her to take up the faith of her childhood without total allegiance to its doctrines. Caught in the grip of a life-threatening illness, Linda had now begun to wonder if, when this image appeared, she was not in fact looking into the eyes of the Godhead itself. Could it or would it appear in this manner?

The following Sunday Linda had arranged to meet Reverend Taylor after the morning service to discuss a "personal problem." She waited patiently until he had greeted the last member coming out of church, and then the two of them walked around to the garden at the back of the building.

The minister looked over at Linda, waiting for her to speak up, but she seemed reluctant and so he finally asked, "Have you ever seen my famous roses?"

They had reached the garden, and Linda cupped one of roses

in her hands. "As a child, I used to sneak back here, steal them and put them in my hair for church."

The mere thought of it made Reverend Taylor wince in pain. "Let's not call it stealing, but church beautification." Linda smiled. His good humor was having an effect on her. "Just don't do it again."

They walked down the sidewalk past the roses to the rhododendrons and on to the carnations. Reverend Taylor waited, and when Linda again failed to broach the subject on her mind, he reached into his frock and brought out a bookmark. On it was a poem entitled "Prayer For A Cancer Patient." He handed it to her. "Linda, here's a prayer a dear old friend of mine wrote before he passed away last year. I had these bookmarks made up, and would like you to have one."

She took it from him and read it while they walked on. "Thank you, Reverend. I'll say it. I believe in the power of prayer."

"I'm glad to hear you say that. Some people in your condition turn away from God, feel betrayed and abandoned, and at the very moment when His love, His comfort is most needed." Reverend Taylor looked at her and could see she was listening, that his words were having an effect. Too many of his members only listened with their heads and not with their hearts, but this young woman was different. It could be her illness; fear of death could soften the toughest heart, but it was not that. He sensed in her a unique sensitivity he found strangely compelling. "Believe me when I say miracles do happen to those who invite Him into their hearts."

Linda stopped at the end of the garden, the sidewalk exit only feet away, before she finally asked, "Reverend Taylor, have you ever had a direct, personal experience of . . . let's say: a divine presence?"

This question took the minister by total surprise, and at first he thought she must be joking, but one look at Linda convinced him she was serious. "You mean like in burning bushes?" he asked uneasily.

"I'll accept burning bushes, but only if they talk," Linda said with a smile, to Reverend Taylor's great relief.

The answer to her question was simple enough, but Reverend Taylor paused for a moment while he considered what was behind her inquiry. Finally, he said, "No, Linda. I'm afraid my personal experience in that regard is limited to four-colored illustrations of the real thing." And then, with great anticipation, he asked, "Why do you ask?"

"Well, I've been seeing an image, all the patients have, a strange eerie sight. And at least I was wondering if. . . ." Linda found it difficult to actually say the words.

The minister could well understand the woman's reticence at this point, and could complete the sentence on his own. "And you want to know how one would judge such an apparition?"

"Yes, sort of."

Here was a question, Reverend Taylor thought, and he had to smile to himself, that he did not hear every day. But, also, it was one with no pat answer. He now searched his heart for the words that would help this troubled woman deal with her unique problem. "The mind is the great deceiver," he said, tapping a newfound voice within himself, "so I would listen to my heart for a true sense of the thing." He paused to find just the right tone. "And I would remember a quote from the New Testament, 'It is a fearful thing to fall into the hands of the living God.'"

## 6.

Linda reached the knoll and looked back down the steep mountain trail and wondered how she had ever made it that far. When she turned back, Jennifer was standing on the overhang reaching out to her. Linda took her hand and pulled herself up.

"Let me help you off with this," Jennifer said, as she held her backpack, while Linda slipped off the shoulder straps. She now twitched her shoulder blades several times to work out some of the soreness.

"That was quite a hike," Linda said, as she sat down and rested in the shade of a pine tree. "Didn't look that steep from below."

"Never does." Jennifer took out her canteen, and took a swig of water and then handed it to Linda. "We'd better catch our breath here. Once we go in the caves, the air gets real thin."

Linda nodded her head in acknowledgment while she guzzled down the water. Finally, Jennifer was forced to take the canteen back from her. "You'll get a stomach ache if you drink too much too fast."

"Sorry," Linda said, wiping her mouth dry. "Guess I'm not in such great shape after all."

"With what we've been through it's understandable."

The two women rested for five minutes before picking up their packs and heading for the caves set back fifty feet from the side of the mountain. They had to pick their way through a jungle of excavation equipment left behind from last summer's big dig. The archaeologists had returned to college for the fall semester, and so they would be free to roam about without interference.

"But I thought these caves had been gone through for ages?" Linda asked as they stepped inside the outer cave.

"Six months ago," Jennifer explained, "two archeology students were up here getting high and fooling around with a sonar set, when they detected a whole network of inner chambers."

Inside they threaded their way between roped-off plots of earth under excavation to the back of the cave. Here was a four-foot high opening. Jennifer took out her oversized flashlight and shined it down the length of the tunnel that led to the inner chambers.

"I don't know how you feel about closed spaces, but this isn't nearly as bad as it looks."

Linda squatted down and peered inside. "It could fool me."

"Well, it's the only way in," Jennifer said firmly, and without further entreaty, she bent over and waddled into the tunnel. Linda waited for a moment, but as the light receded and the outer cave grew darker, she screwed up her courage and followed after her friend. When she came out at the other end, Jennifer was waiting there for her. She now handed Linda a flashlight.

"You're going to need this in here."

"I could've used it back there," Linda said and grabbed the flashlight from her.

"Sorry, but I didn't want you to turn back," Jennifer conceded.

Linda turned it on and ran it across the walls to see what Jennifer was so excited about. The cave was a perfectly squared-out room with twelve-foot-high sides. On the walls were a series of elaborate shell drawings, and Linda walked over to the far side for a closer look.

She ran her hands over one of the drawings. "This looks absolutely ancient."

"The best estimate is ten thousand years."

Linda stood there and studied one series of drawings. It depicted some sort of religious initiation ending in what appeared to be a bodily ascension. Of course she assumed it was symbolic like others in the same tradition. But the artist's style, quite pronounced despite the limitation of his material, was realistic in every other detail. Linda stepped back and viewed the drawings all together. The intent was unmistakable, and the effect on her unsettling. Jennifer now blinked her light at Linda, and when she turned around, she saw her friend disappear into the next chamber. Linda hurried after her.

"Theory has it the whole complex was a gigantic burial vault, but with one catch," Jennifer said, as she led Linda through a maze of small rooms. "Everybody was walled up in here alive, or at least that's what all the drawings seem to indicate." Linda nodded her head as if there was nothing odd about that fact. They now entered a pyramid-shaped temple at the center of the complex. Jennifer watched Linda carefully as she told her, "And yet they haven't uncovered any skeletal remains." From her puzzled expression, Linda did find that a little more curious, but it was hardly the kind of reaction Jennifer had expected. However, she was confident her next revelation would prove more shocking. Jennifer now shined her light on one of the slanting walls to reveal a drawing, some ten thousand years old, of the image the patients had been seeing.

"Oh my God!" Linda said, as she looked up into the ten-foot-wide eyes of the drawing.

"I'm sure that's what the natives thought," Jennifer replied with a triumphant note in her voice. She now shined her light on the other three walls to reveal duplicate drawings. "Now it's not unusual for the hunters of this era to have sacred caves for their religiously inspired art. But usually it's some form of hunting magic. You'll see an effigy of an animal they hoped to kill, one whose numbers they hoped to increase, or even a predator whose power they hoped to steal. But deity worship, other than of the sun and the moon, doesn't appear elsewhere for thousands of years." Jennifer gave Linda a moment to absorb her mini-lecture. "Hundreds of such caves have been discovered throughout the western United States, but this practice was apparently unique to this isolated tribe of hunters."

As Linda heard the words spoken by her friend, the images preserved here, still alive and untouched by past intruders, now appeared before her in the mist rising up from the damp cave floors. Wave after wave of these images rolled over her as the story of these ancient people unfolded before her eyes. In one scene she saw a ragged band of half-starved hunters and their tribe, driven unmercifully across the receding glacier to the top of the mountains behind this valley, look down upon this land alive with new growth and populated by fresh game and thank the God that had delivered them from their doom. She saw His visage through their leader's eyes and knew it to be her own haunting specter. Linda longed to follow them into this valley, and yet she could see no further into the future. The images that now rose before her were from their past and brought with them the lessons she most needed to learn.

For the last few thousand years, since the glaciers had begun to recede, drastic climate changes from colder-to-warmer and moister-to-dryer conditions had killed off most of the big game quarry the tribes had hunted since their migration from the Old World some fifteen thousand years earlier. Among the species that had rapidly become extinct were all the mammoths and mastodons, and all but one species of bison. Vast herds of these animals had shrunk to nothing practically overnight. And coupled with the depletion of this game was the dessication of most of the vegetation due to dryer conditions. This combination had decimated whole tribes by starvation. Those who survived did so by diversifying their food strategies. Also, decreased equability, or the lack of stable temperatures and moisture throughout the year, created drastic seasonal changes that forced tribes to constantly move about, exploiting the resources in each new area. No one area or food source could be counted on season after season.

Asawa and his tribe had been hunting small game at the eastern border of the great glacier that summer. By fall they had killed off all the rabbits in the area and had lost two hunters in a skirmish with another roving tribe. With winter approaching they now turned to gathering nuts and seeds to see them through the long months ahead. That winter was the most severe in memory, and Asawa had driven his tribe south in hope of finding more temperate weather. What they found was a snowstorm that lasted for weeks. Finally, with their way blocked and their food depleted, they sought refuge in the caves that dotted the western slopes of the Rocky Mountains. With his people dying daily, Asawa blamed himself for their sorry plight and went out into the raging storm to find the needed food or to die trying.

The outside world was swallowed up by the storm leaving Asawa surrounded on all sides by a sheet of driven snow. He pushed on blinded by the light, wandering aimlessly across the ice-covered plain. Within hours he was half-frozen and delirious, and he had long since given up hope of finding food or shelter from the storm. He would die soon, this was certain; there was no other way for a leader who had failed his tribe. However, he did not wish to die unprepared. If he fell to his death or was eaten by a wild animal, his spirit would wander forever between this world and the next. No man, no matter how ignoble deserved such a fate. Asawa sat down in the snow and performed the ritual deathwatch as prescribed by the elders.

And he waited for his spirit to depart. This lonely, solitary figure, buried under a mound of snow, had entered the belly of the storm. When the image first appeared, Asawa was sure he had passed into the great beyond and met the spirit of an ancestor. He could accept it being as white as snow there, but that it was as cold and that his body should accompany him on the journey dispelled the illusion. The image now spoke, but the words were in a strange language that sounded like wind blowing through trees, or water rushing down a canyon. The message was clear. There was food nearby, and It had come to show him the way. Asawa arose and followed the apparition into the storm and discovered all that his tribe would need in the weeks ahead. The way back was also shown, and when he arrived back at the cave, where all hope had been given up for his return, he spread before them the fruits of this new God. All bowed down in worship.

Under It's guidance the tribe prospered. Their every need was anticipated. Before the approach of bad weather, they were instructed to move on; if the game in one area was killed off, they were shown what seeds and nuts to gather. When a warring tribe planned an attack, they were warned ahead of time and escaped without harm. Although Asawa remained their leader, he had become but an instrument of divine will. In time all were able to look upon the face of their God and receive instruction. This contact allowed for a gradual but radical transformation of tribal beliefs and customs that would have met with much resistance if imposed on them by one of their own. This break with tradition uprooted them and made them even more dependent on their new God.

With the onset of more bad weather, lasting for nearly three years and further depleting an already limited food supply, the tribe was ready to follow their God across a thousand-mile expanse of frozen wasteland in search of a milder climate and new sources of food. Other tribes in the past had attempted such a crossing and failed. They were trying to duplicate the passage of their ancestors across the frozen land bridge between the old and new world. They remembered stories of them finding huge herds of mammoths, reindeer, oxen, and bison roaming a dry tundra. It was a hunter's dream and the tribes lived off these herds for many thousands of years. But theirs was a journey of only a few weeks and not the year-long trek that faced the current pioneers.

The great glacier had been receding for over a thousand years, leaving in its wake a patchwork of frozen and fertile lands. However, finding these small islands and their food supply, separated in any one direction by a hundred miles of ice, was the undoing of the others. Asawa's tribe, following directions, was able to pick their way across the wasteland, staying in one area only long enough to gather supplies for the next crossing, sometimes heading due north or south or even backtracking. Although the hardships of their journey were monumental, they lost only a half-dozen tribesmen from exhaustion but none from starvation. Every day saw a different miracle: new land beyond an ice-bound horizon, new ways of exploiting the area's unique plant and animal life. Their journey became a mythic record of week-long blizzards, of ice fields that stretched from horizon to horizon, of mountains that touched the sky. Their deliverance in one rescue after another bound them further to their God. After nearly a year, when they looked over the rim of this coastal range and saw the fertile valley below and the endless expanse of water beyond, the tribe gave homage to their God. And they were ready to give themselves over to him completely.

## 7.

On the drive in from the airport, Joyner had briefed Dr. Kellgren on his patients' condition. By now the new growths had begun to crowd out the body's own organs, and their diminished output had further lowered resistance to the takeover. Dr. Joyner's program was at a crisis point. His patients could no longer tolerate the treatment levels necessary to fight off the progress of the disease. The only therapeutic avenue open now was a better understanding of the process in hope of discovering some further means of combating it.

At the hospital, when Kellgren was shown photographs of the patients' chromosomes, he immediately asked Joyner if there was any incidence of polyploidy. There was some but not at a significant level. This surprised Dr. Kellgren. It was obvious from what he was seeing here, especially after hearing the background story, that the trail started in Roykenvik six months ago ended in San Martin six thousand miles away. If these "beings" were indeed responsible, their methods had changed and did not seem equal to the task. This kind of chromosomal rearrangement could only alter or change a function. It could not, or at least not in his experience, create totally new functions. For that you needed to expand the genome by polyploidy, like the plants in Roykenvik, and then the mutation of one of these duplicate genes could supply the new function. Of course that was how nature, given unlimited time, would proceed, but here the time schedule for this forced manipulation was somewhat abbreviated.

When Kellgren had thoroughly studied the row of photographs, he turned to Joyner. "And you've determined that a viral transposon is responsible for all the abnormalities?"

"We've discovered copies of them at nearly all the sites," Joyner said.

"But these elements jump around pretty spontaneously, too much so for anything this systematic," Kellgren said, watching Dr. Joyner's reaction closely. "Unless, of course, there's some kind of controlling element involved."

Joyner found this statement a little curious. Biological processes were not driven by intent but by instinct. Genes did not exercise choice; they were impelled by natural force. "Like what?" Joyner asked suspiciously.

Dr. Kellgren wagged a disapproving finger at his former student, asking for more patience. "I assume, given the radical genetic change here, you've considered the possibility this just might be some kind of speciation process?"

"Yes, I did," Joyner said, nodding his head.

"And I know you agree with the theory of punctuated equilibrium that a new species can arise suddenly, fully formed, and not by the steady gradual change of its ancestors."

"Well, I think the process could happen over a period of several generations to an isolated group cut off from the parental stock and subject to environmental stress requiring new adaptive changes. But, I don't buy the overnight, fully formed aspect of the theory."

"Even several generations is fast when you consider the immense biological undertaking inherent in such a process," said Dr. Kellgren, as he began pacing up and down. "Although I agree that rapid change is possible, I'm beginning to suspect that a mechanism more sophisticated than random mutation is involved."

"You mean the old Swiss watch theory?" Joyner asked with a broad knowing smile. He was referring to the idea that biological processes were too complicated to have arisen by accident, or that you could improve them by mutation alone. It used the metaphor of a Swiss watch to make the point, that merely changing one of its cogwheels would only make it inoperative. To make a better watch, you would have to adjust all of them at once.

"That says it well enough." Dr. Kellgren looked back at Joyner, not at all intimidated by his disapproval. "There is some kind of feedback system that takes input like environmental stress and makes all the genetic adjustments needed to adapt the body to changing conditions. I just know it."

"And that 'feedback system,' in your opinion, is what's directing the massive genetic change in my patients?"

"From what you've told me, there is hardly anything random about the spread of these growths."

Dr. Joyner had to admit that the chance mutation caused by

this viral transposon jumping around inside the cell's DNA could hardly account for the systematic takeover of the body by these foreign growths. But, in the absence of environmental stress, what were these patients adapting to, as Dr. Hunter had asked earlier?

"In fact, there is something unnervingly uniform about them," Joyner said, and motioned for Dr. Kellgren to follow him as he headed across the lab. It was night, and outside of a skeleton crew processing the latest round of blood tests, all was quiet. Kellgren stopped for a moment and watched one of the technicians at a computer console comparing one batch of these results against some standard measurement. He wanted to ask the operator some questions, but he could see his colleague waiting for him and hurried off.

"We did a gel electrophoresis comparing enzymes from several patients," Joyner said, and handed Kellgren a row of gel tubes. He now watched for a reaction. "And there was absolutely no variation between them."

This elicited a raised eyebrow as Dr. Kellgren studied the row of tubes. Now this was very interesting, he thought to himself, and he wondered what these "beings" had in mind. He had assumed they were engineering a precipitated evolutionary jump to the next subspecies of man. If that were true, then an increase in variability would be the hallmark, not complete uniformity. Unless, of course, it was not the next step in evolution but the last.

"I would say," Dr. Kellgren said, and he paused to build up Joyner's anticipation, "that this virus has triggered the same controlling element in all the patients."

"You mean the stress caused by their disease has the same adaptive force as a climate change, or decimation of a food source?"

"I'm beginning to think," Kellgren said with a sheepish grin, "what separates man from the rest of nature is his psychospiritual center, and because of that, his evolution may be subject to a different set of influences."

"Professor, this sounds like the transformational philosophies of the eighteenth century totally discredited by Darwin's variational theory."

"Not entirely. I don't believe we inherit acquired characteristics, but that man's psychological. . .environment can cause adaptive change."

"Well, when you can prove that something buried in our 'souls' has the power to transform matter, I'll consider your theory more carefully. But, until then, excuse me if I rely on a little twentieth-century medicine to save my patients."

Kellgren nodded his head in agreement, then handed back the gel tubes with the uniform staining band running across them. Joyner looked down at the tubes, and then up into his former teacher's smiling face and understood the implied message.

## 8.

Max Kellgren spent the next several days studying the test results, but it only reinforced his initial impression. Although the virus had triggered this speciation process, the uniformity of the new growths pointed to an extraneous element all the patients had in common. He interviewed them one by one, but he did not discover that missing ingredient. He had saved the Owens boy until last.

Kellgren watched him from behind a two-way mirror from the adjoining room. Carl was sitting in a heavy-duty chair bolted down to the floor, his wrists strapped to the arms of the chair. He had grown a full beard since his incarceration, and he was now glaring at them through the mirror.

"Has he been under sedation?" Kellgren asked Dr. Joyner.

"Don't I wish. He's a real pain-in-the-ass, but this local judge won't even let me administer the treatment without his consent."

Dr. Kellgren braced himself and opened the door to the interview room and stepped into the lion's den. When he approached the table, Carl turned and looked up at him with very intense eyes. He now pulled a chair out and sat down across from the young man.

"Carl, I'm Dr. Max Kellgren. And I'd like to ask you a few questions if I can."

"Yeah, well I'd like to ask you a few questions myself," Carl said belligerently. "Like when are they going to let me out of here?"

"I really wouldn't know. But, since your condition is still very unpredictable and you still refuse to cooperate with them, they'll probably keep you here until they get it under control."

Expecting more evasion, Carl was startled by this straightforward reply. He grunted a mild disapproval but was ready to continue with the interview. When Kellgren hesitated, studying him more closely, Carl gave him a bug-eyed stare in return.

Dr. Kellgren looked down and reread a few lines from Barry Hamilton's report, and then he began, "After this salesman dropped you off in town, did you feel any . . . different?"

"Well, about twelve hours later, I felt sick as shit."

"No, I mean nervous, on edge, or even elated. Any kind of intense feelings."

"Yeah, a feeling of doom swept over me," Carl spit out and then laughed. "What does this have to do with anything?"

"I'm trying to determine if this virus caused more than a biological reaction."

This took Carl totally by surprised. And he wondered how much the old man knew. "Yeah, I felt a little . . . odd right afterwards. Figured I was just tired from being on the road all week," Carl said in a more sober tone. "What about the others? Did they feel any different?"

Kellgren detected the change in Carl's attitude and found his interest in the others curious. "About what you described."

Carl nodded his head, as if he had expected as much. "Later that night, right before bed, and I'll admit I was feeling pretty drowsy by then, I had some kind of hallucination."

Kellgren tried to hide his excitement, flipping through his report as if looking for similar admissions. "What kind of hallucination?"

"Just a strange image that came and went, nothing much

else to it," Carl said and waited for Kellgren's response.

"A few of the others did mention seeing something strange, but theirs keep coming back," Kellgren said, trying to trap him.

After learning about the others, Carl shrugged his shoulders in a noncommittal reply. He decided not to reveal more about this image than was absolutely necessary. From the start he had recognized his deliverer in this image. Knowing the others were seeing it only confirmed the group nature of this extraordinary event. And, he thought, if that were the case, his personal salvation might be intimately tied in with them as well. He wondered what they thought of this image, if they treated it as friend or foe? But more importantly, given his present confinement, how was he going to communicate this understanding to them? It was while he was in deep contemplation that the visage arose from within to look back upon its sacred vessel. Its features were more fully defined, since its growth was unimpeded and found a willing acceptance in the host subject. Carl allowed it to sweep over him, to feed him with its tumultuous energies, to remake him in its own image. The last thing he remembered was hearing a sound like a giant waterfall crashing over him.

When Carl went into a trance without warning, Kellgren walked around the table to examine him. Watching from the viewing room, Joyner rushed in and came to his side.

"Has this ever happened before?" Dr. Kellgren asked him, taking Joyner's pocket flashlight and shining it into the boy's eyes.

"Not that I know of," Joyner said, as he took Carl's pulse. "But then we don't have him under visual surveillance."

Kellgren clicked off the light; the boy's retinas were fixed, and there was absolutely no reflex response at all. He now looked at him more closely; there was something strange about the angular structure of his face. He placed the palms of his hands over Carl's forehead and then slowly felt his way down the boy's face to his throat. He opened Carl's mouth, stuck his thumb inside and ran it across the palate and then down the arch on either side. Kellgren removed his thumb.

"Did he have this beard when you checked him in?"

"No. He's grown it since. In protest, I would imagine."

"Could we have it shaved off?"

"He's in the sheriff's custody. We'd have to ask him, but I don't see why he'd object."

"Okay, then let's get it. And while he's out, I'd like you to do a complete workup on him."

"X-rays?" Dr. Joyner asked increduously, and he now took a closer look at his patient's bearded face. "What are you looking for?"

Kellgren smiled. "I'll know that when I find it."

## 9.

When Carl had finished breakfast, he pushed the tray across the table and waited for the orderly to pick it up. He pulled out the morning paper and read it while he finished his cup of coffee. It had been an unusually hardy breakfast, and he could not help but wonder if they were preparing him for another series of intrusive tests. At least, with his full stomach, they would not schedule anything before noon. Carl expected a visit from Jennifer this morning, or at least he hoped for a reply to a message sent for her to visit him. Earlier he had rudely shunned all her attempts to see him, and he could only hope she would now forgive him. Carl was tempted to lure her with an obscure reference to this image, or even a sketch of those haunting eyes, but he decided against it. He knew they closely watched all contact with him, and he could only assume that they would check any written messages. The less the doctors knew of this image and its curative powers the safer they would all be.

Carl wanted to talk with her about the importance of this image, in trusting it fully. But he really wanted to see her again; he wanted to tell Jennifer how much he loved her and ask for her forgiveness. A cold dark part of himself was now slowly thawing out, and growing there was the seed of a new consciousness. As it pushed upward, breaking up the hardened residue, it had touched him with a love greater than he had ever known and moved him further beyond himself than he had ever ventured. In those moments, he sensed that it soon would push him clear out of himself, and that the person left in its wake would have little concern for mere personal love. Before that transpired, he wanted to look into Jennifer's eyes, while they were still full of recognition, and say his farewell.

At nine o'clock two orderlies came for him. Although it was before normal visiting hours, Carl still hoped, while walking down the hallway, that the men were taking him to the fourth floor interview room and that Jennifer was waiting there for him. However, the elevator went all the way to the first floor. They got out and walked past the admission's counter heading for the row of gift shops around the corner. When they walked into the barber shop, Carl was surprised to find the sheriff and two deputies waiting for him. He could not imagine what they wanted with him.

When Guy Joyner and Max Kellgren stepped in a few minutes later, they found Carl strapped to the barber's chair and held down on either side by two deputies, while Sheriff Howser shaved his beard off. Carl now spit into the Sheriff's face.

"Son-of-a-bitch," Howser said, and he wiped his face off with the sleeve of his shirt. He now turned to his towheaded young deputy. "Marty, take off one of your shoes and hand me the sock."

Without questioning the command, the young man sat down in a nearby chair, took off his left shoe and sock, and handed the sock to the Sheriff, who looked at Dr. Joyner and hesitated.

Barry Hamilton stepped forward. "Go on with it, Sheriff. I'm sure Dr. Joyner can appreciate the use of necessary force."

Howser rolled up the sock in a ball, and with his deputies holding Carl down, stuffed it in the young man's mouth. The Sheriff began shaving him again, but Carl kept whipping his head from side to side. Finally, one of them grabbed a hand full of hair and yanked his head back until he stopped. It only took a few more minutes to shave his right cheek clean. The Sheriff now wiped the boy's face clean with a hot towel.

Marty Keller, looking down at Carl's upturned face, was the first to see him. He immediately let go of his hair and jumped back in horror. Carl sat up in the barber's chair and looked around the room. Everybody was amazed by the sight of him. Finally, he swiveled the chair around to face the mirror. There staring back at him, if not yet totally realized, was the barest outline of the "image." Carl was delighted by what he saw. He now reached up with both hands and ran the tips of his fingers over these angular features. Dr. Kellgren stepped out of the group of paralyzed onlookers and approached him.

"Do you mind if I examine you?" he asked.

Carl looked around at him and with a new sense of his own personal power. "All right. But I'm not going to be anybody's guinea pig." Kellgren nodded his head in agreement. He lowered Carl's chair as the boy lay back for his examination, and he began to tap his finger along Carl's shortened jawbone.

The others had now shaken off their initial shock, and Barry Hamilton had a few questions for the eminent Dr. Joyner. "Do you want to tell me what the hell is going on here?" Hamilton asked, and for once, Joyner was without a ready reply.

"Frankly, this has caught me totally by surprise," Joyner admitted. "Dr. Kellgren suspected something, but I never thought the process would externalize itself."

"Oh, that's reassuring," Hamilton said, and he looked at Sheriff Howser for support.

"Damnedest thing I've ever seen," Howser said shaking his head in dismay. "Now, what I'd like to know, is what else can we expect?"

"I suspect that if left unopposed, and the process didn't break down on its own, the end result would leave the patients... unrecognizable."

"Are you telling me we could end up with a bunch of walking Picassos around here?"

This startling possibility, never contemplated until now,

burst upon Joyner with all the force of a terrible nightmare. He had always assumed that a speciation of *Homo sapiens* would result in an advanced race of humans you would want to invite home for dinner. But, faced with this harrowing alternative, Joyner shrank back from it in horror. Could it be confirmation of a highly contested theory stating that any daughter species would bud off from its parent stock in a drastically different configuration? Evolution by freak leaps, as one critic called it. And if so, did it also corroborate the second part of the theory: that the daughter species would spread out over the parent's entire range and displace it? Joyner turned and looked back at the Owens boy and wondered if he were looking into the face of a future subjugator.

"I'm really not sure what form it would take, but from what I see here, they could be 'drastically' different from us."

"Now that's just great," Hamilton said in exasperation. "It was bad enough when we thought we were dealing with a cancer epidemic, but this. . . ."

"This could cause a riot," Howser interjected. And the two officials now looked to Dr. Joyner for a solution to their problem.

"Well, from the beginning, I've suspected that this was not a benign process, and have tried to retard its growth by every means possible. The only option left would be full scale radiation treatment, but the dose needed could prove to be fatal."

That prospect, in light of what they had just seen, did not faze them in the least. "Maybe we should go back to the laboratory and discuss our alternatives," Hamilton said.

Dr. Joyner looked over at Max Kellgren, who was finishing up his examination. "We're leaving. Would you go along with the deputy and escort Carl back to his room?" Kellgren nodded his head in agreement.

When Linda went in for her next antibody treatment that morning, she had planned to confront Dr. Joyner and ask about the true nature of her affliction. There were numerous indications, besides the appearance of the image, that this was not a disease process but something far stranger. After years of yoga, of eating health food and taking care of herself, her body would know the difference. Although she experienced much discomfort and felt ill most of the time, it was the product of change, not dissolution. Also, increasingly, another part of herself, her psyche, was undergoing a quiet revolution. Her feelings for impressionist art, for cleaning up the environment, for Hitchcock movies had lost much of its affective value in these last few months. In its place arose strange, ineffable longings as yet only vaguely sensed. What was happening to her, she wondered?

Linda rounded the next corner and was hit by waves of intense energy before she recognized the source. She looked up to see Carl Owens walking down the hall toward her. When he got within fifteen feet, Linda saw in his angular features the image in her vision, and she was transfixed by it. They both stopped and stared at each other for a moment. Linda started to approach him, when Martin Keller stepped between them.

"Lady, step aside. This here is a dangerous psychotic."

Carl could only laugh at this description, and Linda was not deterred by it as she pushed the deputy aside. Dr. Kellgren reached over and grabbed the boy by the arm to hold him back. She now stepped up and placed the palms of her hands over Carl's face, and then starting with his forehead, she began to trace the outline of the image with her fingers. Linda filled in from memory the inroads yet to be made. This work put her in touch with the spirit behind the image. It was obvious that Carl was being consumed by it, that he had given himself over to it completely. And that prospect excited her.

The fact that Carl's progress exceeded hers and that of the others was due no doubt to his cooperation and to the lack of medical intervention. Was it too late for her to stop the treatment and make up the lost ground? Linda clasped hold of Carl's hands and turned to Kellgren. "Could you take me to Dr. Joyner?"

Dr. Kellgren nodded his head, and Linda gave Carl a hug before leaving. As they walked along, Linda finally turned to Kellgren. "Okay doctor, why don't you tell me how much you really know."

This question caught Kellgren by surprise, but after looking into Linda's determined eyes, he decided to comply with her request. "It started six months ago in Norway."

When Dr. Kellgren and Linda walked into the microbiology lab, Barry Hamilton, who was engaged in a heated discussion with Dr. Joyner, stopped short. Joyner turned around to see who was there. He now checked his watch. "Linda, why aren't you getting your shot with the others?"

"I ran into Carl Owens on the way there." Linda slowly looked around at the three men, making them all uncomfortable, and then finally said to Dr. Joyner, "I think you've been holding out on us."

"No, not really," Joyner insisted, "I'm just as taken aback by this development as everybody else."

"In other words, you suspected more than you were willing to admit to yourself or us until it stared you in the face," Linda said.

Joyner could only shrug his shoulders in beleaguered agreement. "You're right, but don't give up hope. As you can see, we've been able to retard its development in you and the others, and in time we might be able to stop it completely."

"On the contrary, doctor. Seeing him today has given me the only real hope I've had for some time." Linda looked around at the room full of startled faces. "Whether you know it or not, we've all been seeing the same image as Carl." Linda looked at Dr. Kellgren, then back at the group. "Until today I was unsure of its real nature, but now I'm convinced it is a deific being who's come to transform the human race. And I, for one, plan to cooperate."

Her statement totally confounded the others. Finally, Joyner turned to Dr. Kellgren for help. "Professor, will you please tell me what this is all about."

"It is my belief, based on the genetic analysis of the mutated plants in Roykenvik and the goat fetuses in Angora we've talked about, which bear similarities to the genetic anomalies seen here, that your patients are the subject of a planned genetic experiment by a scientifically advanced race of beings." Max paused to allow his audience time to absorb this disconcerting speculation. "Now, you can either ignore the facts of this case, fool yourself into believing it's a disease, or try to understand the real nature of this process and save your patients."

Dr. Joyner could only shake his head in total disbelief. "You can't be serious, professor?"

"Totally," Kellgren said, and then smiled winningly. "As a student you were always able to dispense with preconceived ideas and see what was actually happening in any given experiment. It was your true talent; don't let it desert you now."

Dr. Joyner was affected by his mentor's appeal, but with only the patients' test results as evidence, this was a purely speculative theory and a highly improbable one he was not inclined to believe. Barry Hamilton and the Sheriff, given Kellgren's international reputation, were more disturbed by his theory.

Hamilton turned to Dr. Joyner. "Is there any basis to this at all?"

Joyner gave his mentor a concerned look before telling Hamilton. "Admittedly, it is a baffling, unexplainable illness. And there's an outside chance this virus had triggered a speciation of the race, but there's no evidence that it's anything other than an aberrant natural process."

The two men were somewhat mollified by Joyner's insistence, but Linda was astonished by their ready acceptance of his empty rebuttal.

"You're going to buy that after what you've just seen?" Linda asked.

"We've seen a boy with a horribly disfiguring disease; if you can prove otherwise, I'm willing to listen," Hamilton said.

"A disease," Linda said in disgust. "That's all you people ever see. Well, you're wrong. And as of today, I'm off the treatment, and we'll see what develops." Linda turned around and walked out of the laboratory, leaving them stunned.

# PART II

# CHAPTER FOUR
# DYSGENESIS

*A syndrome including sterility,*
*mutation, chromosome breakage*
*in the hybrid progeny*
*of incompatible strains of Drosophila.*

## San Martin, California
## November 28

When there were no further outbreaks of the virus, the search for the salesman suspected of being the carrier had been called off. But, in light of recent developments, Barry Hamilton thought it wise to continue with that search. The first step was to follow up on the interviews conducted earlier by the investigators from CDC. After a week of tireless questioning, he made a major discovery. The photograph might have gone totally unnoticed had there not been something strange about the man's image. It was considerably brighter than his surroundings. The boy had shown it to his father, who remembered the photograph when Hamilton interviewed him some weeks later. What nobody else had noticed was that the salesman had turned his head halfway around to stare straight at the camera.

When Hamilton walked into the police department, Sheriff Howser was sitting at the dispatcher's desk. A big bear of a man, Howser looked fairly comical wearing an operator's headset.

"Listen Hot Dog," the Sheriff said into the headphone, "I warned you about. . . ." Static drowned out his message, and Howser reached over and tried to adjust the directional finder. "Keller, can you hear me?" The Sheriff received another earful of static, and he yanked off the headset and threw it down.

Howser then noticed Barry Hamilton standing at the counter, and he felt a bit foolish. "Ever since my day girl left, it's been a real nightmare around here." The teletype in the corner clicked on and started typing out a message. The Sheriff stood up, walked over and began to read it. Suddenly, the paper jammed on one side and fanned out on the other, and only the left side of each line of type was showing up. Howser tried to unjam the paper but only made it worse. Finally, the machine cut off itself. The Sheriff pulled out the sheet, took one look at the garbled message and threw it in the wastebasket.

"I'd better get a replacement real soon, or I'm going to lose my mind."

"Anybody else leaving?" Hamilton asked.

The Sheriff gave Hamilton a quick sideways glance before stepping over to his desk. He was being interrogated, and he did not like it. "Yeah, we've had one deputy who's left and one who's given notice, and this one dispatcher." The Sheriff gave Hamilton a long hard look. "And we've gotten off light."

"I thought your people were supposed to keep this to themselves."

"After the freak show in the hospital," Howser asked, shaking his head, "you expect my men to keep quiet?"

The front door now swung open, and Marty Keller came charging into the office. "Sheriff, what were you saying when we got cut off?"

Howser turned around, prepared to reprimand the young man in harsh tones, but he found that difficult looking into the boy's puppydog face. "I was saying that when you take your afternoon nap, leave your radio on for a wake-up call."

The boy started to protest, but Keller could never lie very well. "Sorry, Sheriff. Guess I ought to get to bed a little earlier."

"Well, you'll find you get more sleep that way," Howser said. "Now I know you young guys like to burn the candle at both ends, but just leave a little more wax for the job. How about it?"

Keller nodded his head, and the Sheriff then took his deputy by the arm and walked him over to the dispatcher's desk. He now handed him the headset. "See what you can do with this while I make my rounds."

The two men stepped outside and walked down the side walk. It was an overcast afternoon and unseasonably cool, and there were fewer shoppers out than usual. It appeared that the Sheriff knew all of them, and while he was talking with an elderly matron, Hamilton spotted Jennifer Barnak across the street. He watched her for a moment before he noticed that several people upon seeing her coming up the sidewalk were crossing over to the other side of the street. Hamilton nudged the Sheriff who looked up and immediately recognized the pattern.

"How long has this been going on?"

"Since we shaved the Owens boy last week, and the word got out."

"That's just swell," Hamilton said in disgust. "Have there been any violent incidents?"

"Not yet, but it's only a matter of time," Howser said. "I'm telling you, if you don't get these people off the street, it could get ugly fast."

They now came to the park bordering the north end of the town square and crossed the street to walk back up the other side. They walked on in silence for a moment. Hamilton now took the salesman's photograph out of his inside coat pocket and handed it to the Sheriff.

"Is this the man you remember?"

Howser studied the picture for a moment. "Yeah, that's him all right." He looked up at Hamilton. "He was a real regular guy. Hope he's not the carrier."

"Well, if we're ever going to get to the bottom of this thing, we're going to have to find him."

The Sheriff nodded his head in agreement, and he tried to hand the photograph back to Hamilton.

"Keep it. I want you to wire it across the state. Make it an all-points bulletin."

The Sheriff did not seem very receptive. "Let me assure you, Sheriff," Hamilton said with emphasis, "I have the authority to make this request."

"It's not that," Howser said, and walked on in a befuddled state for a moment. "It's just that, I really don't know how to send a photograph over the wire."

When Hamilton returned to his hotel, he called out for a sandwich and beer and turned on the network news. He watched it for fifteen minutes before he gave up; his mind was definitely elsewhere. He turned off the set and walked over to the card table that served as a desk. There was a stack of reports from the patients describing their contact with the salesman in question. There was something strange about these contacts, a pattern not yet evident but one he vaguely sensed. The eerie photograph only reinforced his suspicion. It was all very odd, and he was determined to solve this mystery.

His food came, and Hamilton spread out a couple paper napkins and ate at the table while he browsed through the reports. The spread of most infectious diseases by the primary carrier through casual contacts is usually haphazard. In this case there was something odd about the salesman's contacts. Several patients reported seeing him observing them before he came over and started up a conversation. Others said his appearance followed some kind of stressful incident, as if he were alert to it. All of them mentioned shaking hands with him and noticing that his hands were extremely hot. This indicated a feverish condition; the man must have known he was ill. Since he was not delirious but was clear-headed by all accounts, it certainly looked like he was selecting his victims and then infecting them.

Since all the patients spoke so highly of him, even after they learned he was the carrier, Hamilton could not believe the man that they described was such a monster. But he could be wrong. Another puzzle was why, since he was infected himself, he had not sought medical attention? Early on they had circulated his description to clinics and hospitals in the surrounding area, but the man never came in. Could he have been immune to the virus but still be able to infect others? Hamilton would have to ask

Joyner about that. Or maybe he did die but went unidentified and was buried as a John Doe. He made a note to have the Sheriff send the photo to city and county morgues as well.

There was one possibility that unfortunately fitted the case profile only too well. If the salesman were indeed an alien, as Dr. Kellgren had suggested, it would explain his apparent immunity to the virus as well as his mode of operation. Hamilton's offhand dismissal of this possibility earlier was more a professional than a personal stand. Although he had read books on the subject and found himself drawn to newspaper and magazine articles about UFOs, Hamilton had never decided whether he believed in their existence or not. If pressed hard, he would concede that, given the immensity of our universe and the wide dispersal of the necessary elements, life probably had arisen elsewhere. That other civilizations had developed a technology capable of crossing the vast distances of space and that they were presently visiting earth on a regular basis, as some would have you believe, was more difficult for him to accept. But, given the time span for such development and current speculation about travel at super light speeds, he could not dismiss it outright. And, if that were at all possible, would they not also have the technical expertise for the suggested experiment?

Hamilton now came to the last report with the photograph of the salesman clipped to it. He had had an expert examine the picture, and he had determined that the salesman's brightened image was not caused by either the processing or the printing. It was in the photograph itself. The expert thought the glow was light reflected from a nearby shiny object. Hamilton found this explanation a little lame, but then he could hardly use the photo as proof of the salesman's extraterrestrial origin either. In fact, he was more interested in why the salesman wished to be photographed. His turning around to face the camera made that assumption undeniable. The man was not startled; he had somehow anticipated the moment and taken full advantage of it. There was no doubt that he wanted to be identified. He would get his wish, Hamilton thought, and he could not help but wonder if that were not part of some master plan. And, if so, had his participation been as neatly arranged? He now took out a blowup of the man's face and stared into those remarkable eyes once again. After a while, and only with great effort, he pulled himself away.

## 2.

Since she had taken herself off Joyner's treatment in the past week, Linda could feel the process of her transformation accelerating. Already the first signs of Carl's angular features had appeared on her face. Also, her body felt different: lighter, less dense, thinner. And the musical notes replacing her thoughts were heard constantly now. Altogether the changes were still very minor, their effect was quite pronounced. People could sense her strangeness; it exuded from every pore of her body. An outsider unaware of its source might find it curious, but, for those who knew, it repelled them.

This was already evident at work. Linda found herself coming to school later and later each day. At first she chided herself for being tardy, especially since she was trying hard to keep a daily routine. But, halfway through the week, Linda saw that she was reacting to the other teachers' growing hostility by avoiding them. She imagined that word of Carl Owens's "change" had spread around town, and that this reaction would be a fairly typical response. Linda only knew a few of her new colleagues well, but was still hurt by their disaffection.

She was groggy that morning after only three hours of sleep, and decided to chance ducking into the teacher's lounge for a quick cup of coffee. The lounge was as steamed up by cigarette smoke as a sauna, and Linda hoped to slip in and out without detection. However, the drink machine kept eating her quarters, and she was forced to pound it several times before it spit out a half cup of black coffee. The others looked over and stared until Linda turned around. They went back to talking among themselves, but with hushed tones and with heads that kept nodding in her direction. At a few nearby tables, empty chairs were quickly filled with books and coats. Linda could only shake her head in dismay, and she walked out mumbling to herself.

In the hallway she passed several people, but she was too intimidated to offer her customary good morning greetings. One teacher even scooted over to the far side of the hall and walked past with her head down. When Linda turned the next corner, she saw Paul Jordan step out of his office only to duck back inside when he saw her coming. What was wrong with these people? Linda felt like walking past her homeroom and straight out the front door and never returning.

At lunch she found an empty table at the back of the room and ate with her head down to avoid the stares cast in her direction. When somebody stepped over to her table, Linda looked up with great trepidation. She was relieved to find Pam standing there.

"Mind if I join you?" Pam asked and then smiled contritely.

Linda was so glad to see a friendly smiling face that she completely forgot about Pam's recent desertion. "Are you sure you want to be seen with me?" she asked wryly.

Pam took her friend's ironic tone as a welcoming gesture, and she plopped down her overloaded tray and took a seat across from Linda. "Can you believe this? Even my helper called in sick all week." Pam took a bite out of her sandwich and continued while she chewed it. "You know what it is, don't you? Jeannie Faber dates someone on the police force, and they told her that something 'strange' is happening to Carl Owens." Pam put her sandwich down and looked over at her friend with concern. "Do you know what she's talking about?"

"They shaved his beard off and underneath found that his face had started to change."

"What do you mean by . . . change?"

"It appears he's slowly becoming the image in our visions," Linda said rather offhandedly. "I would assume that the face is only the beginning."

"Oh my God," Pam said, suddenly feeling very ill. "And we're going to be next?"

"Guess that really depends on the success of Dr. Joyner's program. Personally, I've never had much faith in it."

Pam found Linda's nonchalant attitude a little annoying. "You're certainly taking this well."

With a perfectly calm delivery, Linda told her old friend, "You're going to think I'm crazy, Pam. But I've decided to accept this 'process' for better or worse, and have taken myself off Joyner's treatment all together."

Pam stared at Linda in total disbelief. If this were merely a life-threatening illness, Linda would be committing suicide; but, given the new development, it was far worse. "You're right. I do."

"I know you don't see what I see, that your image fills you with fear. So did mine until I began to accept it. But that's our fear reflected back. It is love personified, and it is offering us a chance to share its life, to live that love, and I for one will accept."

"And I," Pam said, standing up and pushing her tray away, "would rather die first."

The following Sunday, Linda was invited to her parents' house for dinner. This was the first time she had seen them since stopping her treatment, although she had talked with her mother about it over the phone. As expected, her parents were appalled by her decision, which was why Linda had avoided seeing them until now. She wanted to give both of them, especially her father, time to calm down. Stanley Porter was accustomed to having his way. While growing up, Linda had fought with him over everything from her political views to the way she dressed. Looking back, she realized how much those views as well as her hippie lifestyle were a reaction to his values. Linda was clear about this decision, but she was afraid, given their past history, that her father would split her focus with another clash of wills.

Five years earlier her parents had moved out of their comfortable seaside home to a more palatial mansion in the foothills behind town. The dining room was as long as their old living room with a huge oak table and stiff highback chairs. They had also acquired more domestic help and now dined in a more formal atmosphere. It was enough to give a kitchen-eater like Linda a nervous stomach.

Maria, a young Mexican girl in her early twenties, was serving roast beef off a silver platter. The conversation was held up until she had left the room. Millie Porter now turned back to her daughter. "But Linda, dear. To stop the treatment now, especially after this...new development. Why it's tantamount to suicide."

"Well, I know it must look that way. But, believe me, if you could see what I've been seeing, you'd think differently."

Millie shuddered at that prospect. By now it was general knowledge that the patients were all seeing a disembodied image, and that Carl Owens and the others were slowly turning into it. It was clear that nobody envied them.

Stanley Porter watched the two women for a moment. Tall and dark, with a touch of grey at the temples, a frown spreading across finely etched features, Porter looked every inch the aristocratic scion of an old California family. "In other words," he said, pointing his fork for emphasis, "you know better than everyone else, and that includes two of the world's most renowned scientists."

"If this were merely a new type of cancer, strictly a medical problem, then I would agree with you. But it's not. It's something altogether different...something they'll never be able to 'cure' with their science."

"But you can?" Porter asked.

"Yes, by giving in to it, accepting it, and allowing it to unfold in its own wondrous way."

Looking at his once beautiful daughter, her face already stamped with the angular signature of this hideous disease, spout this mystical mumbo jumbo was enough to turn his stomach. Porter pushed his plate away. "It was one thing when you dropped out of college, only to go back years later; stopped going to church and followed every two-bit religious faker, only to come back here and take up your faith again. And every time, you knew. Boy did you know. Nobody, but nobody knew what you knew. There was no way to talk you out of any of it. So, we let you go, hoping that after each fall, after each setback, you'd learn. But you never did."

Maria came back into the dining room and, seeing all the half-finished plates pushed to the side and the frown on Mr. Porter's face, she assumed the worse and scurried around the table picking up the plates and hurriedly leaving.

While the girl worked her way around the table, Porter stood up and went over to the bar and poured himself a brandy. He now began to pace the floor. "But this is something entirely different. You are literally on your deathbed, faced with this horrible unknown affliction. And if you think I'm just going to pat you on the head, hope that this time you know more than the doctors, the scientists and everybody else, and allow you to just throw your life away, then you don't really know me very well at all."

Porter now stopped. "If you don't put yourself back under your doctor's care, then I will take you to court and have you declared incompetent, and force you back there. And I'm sure Tom will go along with me when I tell him what's going on down here." He turned to Millie. "Tell Maria, I'll take my coffee in the den." He walked out of the room leaving the women sitting there speechless.

Finally, Linda said, "I've never heard him talk like that before."

"Your father has always had strong feelings for you, that's why you've fought so much," Millie said, and she paused for a moment. "But, believe me, despite that or because of it, he'll go through with this. And don't expect me to take sides."

"So you think he'll call Tom?" Linda asked apprehensively.

"Well, it's about time somebody did," Millie said shaking her head.

"I didn't want him to get involved."

"The man's your husband, dear. He's already involved."

"Well, if the two of them think they can fight me on this, they're mistaken," Linda said resolutely.

## 3.

When Jennifer saw the restaurant's business slacking off, she went to Maggie and insisted on quitting. In the past few weeks, especially during her shifts, steady customers were avoiding the restaurant like the plague. And now that boycott threatened to drive them out of business entirely. At first Maggie refused to believe Jennifer's claim, until the other waitresses began leaving and telling her the same thing. It made her so mad she would have let the restaurant go bankrupt before firing her friend. Finally, Jennifer stopped going to work and would not return Maggie's phone calls. Her final paycheck arrived in the mail that afternoon, and she decided to spend it on groceries and hope for the best.

Pushing her cart up and down the aisles of the grocery store brought back fond memories when, as a little girl, Jennifer would sneak in with her friends to beat the summer's heat. They would hole up behind the water cooler, between the meat freezers, or under the produce bins. There they would while away the afternoon talking about boys, how they were horrible most of the time, wonderful some of the time, and impossible all of the time. Later, Mr. Clarke had mirrors installed making it more difficult to hide, but he never really chased them out, except when Ellie knocked over a whole bin of tomatoes. When his daughter was old enough to join them, their summer sanctuary was secured.

Jennifer still came here to shop, although she could get better prices at one of the national chains. Today the problem was what to get, not what it cost. Nothing appealed to her, or at least nothing that was good for her. Finally, she added to staples like brown rice, beans and vegetables, two bags of taco chips, and headed to the check-out counter. When Jennifer came around the row of freezer boxes, a little freckle-faced boy stepped out in front of her.

"Lady, you goin' to turn into an alligator, like they say?" He pointed to a group of older boys snickering from the next aisle.

Jennifer knelt down and motioned the boy over, but he

backed up a step instead. "Come here, I won't bite you." Finally, he was won over by the woman's gentle manner and her sweet voice. "To answer your question: no. But your friends, who make fun of what they don't understand, are going to turn into something far worse." The little boy absently listened to the words spoken, while he studied the angular contours of the woman's face. He now stepped over and ran his finger across the high arc of her deformed cheek bone. The skin was tender to his touch, the bone still fragile. It was so very strange, and yet so wondrous. The boy put his arms around the woman's neck, and she pressed him close. The feel of his loose body against her stiff muscles was comforting.

"Tommy, get away from her," a voice yelled out. The boy broke the embrace. His mother now walked up in a huff and grabbed his arm. She yanked the boy about ten feet with one vicious pull.

"Hey, that's not necessary," Jennifer said as she stood up.

"Don't tell me how to discipline my child," the woman said, walking back down the aisle. "And as for you, they ought to lock you up some place dark and throw the key away."

The woman turned around and dragged her son away. The other shoppers lingered a moment, expecting some kind of reaction from Jennifer, then walked off disappointed. Hugh Clarke, the owner, stepped out of his upstairs office to check on the disturbance, but when he saw that the Barnak girl was involved, he went back inside. Jennifer could not leave the store fast enough. When she overpaid her bill, and the cashier tried to call her back, she waved the girl off. At home Jennifer put away her groceries and then called the hospital to clear her long-delayed visit to Carl. She needed to talk with someone fast, or she would surely lose her mind.

At the hospital Jennifer was taken to the fourth floor's security ward which acted as the county's mental lockup. Here they had Carl in a closely monitored private room. The nurse unlocked the door and let her inside. Carl was sitting up in bed reading, and he looked up at her with surprise. The nurse pointed to the video camera on the ceiling. "This is not a conjugal visit. You have fifteen minutes." She turned and walked out of the room, locking the door behind her.

Jennifer stood back and looked at Carl in total astonishment. By now his face was clearly stamped with the mark of the "image." When she recovered from the shock of seeing him, Jennifer came over and sat down on the bed. Carl smiled at her, breaking up the angular features of his newly re-formed face and allowing a little of his old self to shine through.

"My God," Jennifer uttered, "I never realized it had gone this far."

"Before it's over it will go further," Carl said with a twinkle in his eye. He reached over and laid his hand over Jennifer's. "I wanted you to come," he continued, "to urge you to accept this 'change,' to trust it, give in to it, and allow it to work its miracle."

"I wish I could feel as good about it as you, but it all seems so. . .awful. I mean just look at us."

"We'll shed these cocoons soon enough," Carl said insistently.

"To become what? Alien creatures?" Jennifer asked, shivering at the prospect.

"I'm sure it will not be alien to our one true nature."

Jennifer begrudgingly nodded her head. "I know that you're right Carl, it's just hard to accept in the face of all this opposition."

"People will always resist change in others and especially in themselves until they come to see the greater life being offered. But, if we refuse to accept this burden, to fight this battle, for us as well as them, we all lose."

Jennifer thought this over. "Tell me, after this change-over, what kind of life can we expect?"

"Something far grander than we can ever imagine," Carl replied rather obliquely to Jennifer's further annoyance.

"Will we stay here, or go off...elsewhere?"

"I would assume. . .elsewhere."

"Well, are we talking Cleveland or what?" Jennifer asked testily.

"Jenny, you're asking me questions I have no answers for,"

Carl said in a raspy voice. "Don't worry about all of that, it'll take care of itself. Just trust the process and stick to it. That's all we can do right now, the rest is . . . out of our hands."

"That's asking an awful lot," Jennifer said resignedly.

"I know; it's asking everything in return for a promise," Carl said, and he put his arm around her shoulders. "It's your choice; I've made mine."

"And, since I plan to stop the treatment, I've made mine as well."

That night Jennifer had a dream. In it the archaic humans she dreamt of earlier were again roaming across an endless savannah in some prehistoric past. This dream was much more vivid; she could hear birds cawing, feel the hot sun on her skin and a light breeze blowing through the high grass, could smell the stink of the others as they moved across her path. She was there with them, stalking wild game, going in for the kill, eating the raw meat and enjoying it.

The scene shifted to another moonlit night where the tribe was gathered around a boulder engraved with the "image." But this primitive ceremony was much more than idol worshipping. They were in a group trance in communion with the spirit behind the image. Jennifer could feel its energy rushing through their bodies, greatly enhanced by the group as if each of them was a linked transformer stepping up the power of the source. In such ceremonies over countless generations, the species had been accelerated beyond its cousins along the path that ended, at this point, in the leap to modern *Homo sapiens*.

Soon, she sensed, they would be left on their own, the image itself deposited within the collective mind of the species for future recall. They would now have to find their own way through another two-hundred-thousand years of changing environments, past new predators, in search of new game until they would one day stand on a hillside overlooking a field of wheat and realize the secret of their survival lay in learning how to cultivate their own food. From there they would build a world civilization that would take them from the plains of Africa to the surface of the moon almost overnight in evolutionary time.

Yet she sensed, as their future passed before her, that this was only the first leg of their journey. That in time, after a greater unfoldment, their destiny lay beyond. Her dreaming self could not see that far ahead, and she woke up. Jennifer lay in bed for a brief moment and then stood up and walked over to the window. The moon had risen over the ocean, leaving a shimmering path of light that she followed up to its familiar surface. This was the same face she had looked upon as a child and had viewed with each full moon since. Jennifer now searched the immense star field behind it for some welcoming sign but found none. And she doubted if she was ready to take her place beside those who traveled these corridors so freely.

## 4.

Max Kellgren stood on the hospital's rooftop observation deck looking out over this small seaside community on a sunlit afternoon. He was convinced now that the "experimenters" were indeed extraterrestrials; he wondered what had brought them to their planet and what they hoped to accomplish in San Martin. It seemed unlikely they had come merely to test their experimental techniques on man. That they were experimental was obvious from their earlier failure with the Angora goats. Whether they would succeed this time was still unknown. If successful, did they plan to unleash a more virulent form of the virus and transform the entire species? This process seemed far too drastic for wholesale use. If they had that in mind, a more effective route would be to implant genetically altered zygotes in the population at large. But would mothers kill their alien offspring?

The door to the rooftop now opened. Andrea Hunter stuck her head out and spotted Kellgren. She now walked over, and he turned around to face her. "We couldn't find you, so Dr. Joyner went ahead with the PET scans."

Kellgren raised his eyebrows. "And was I right?"

Dr. Hunter begrudgingly nodded her head. "It does appear the GI tract is the next system to go 90 percent inoperative."

"Makes you wonder how the 'process' plans to nourish the body if it can't digest food."

"Of course," Hunter said defensively, "that's assuming 'it' plans to survive, or for that matter, that 'it' plans at all. That 'it' is not just an incredibly deadly disease, attacking the body system by system."

"Okay, then let's go down and have another look at this 'smart' disease," Kellgren said ironically.

In the treatment room, Carl Owens was lying on the table in the center of a donut-shaped structure, undergoing a series of PET scans of his internal organs. In the adjoining room, Guy Joyner watched a row of video monitors showing the computer-enhanced images. Nearby a technician was pinning up black-and-white reproductions of these images on the wall. When the last monitor went blank, Joyner looked up and watched the retractable table roll back in the next room. Carl sat up and then slid off the table into the waiting arms of two orderlies. They now led him from the room. As he passed the viewing window, he smiled at Joyner who was taken aback by the boy's friendliness.

Joyner stepped over and began to examine the new PET scans. It was now clearly evident that most of Carl's internal organs were slowly being phased out by the new growths. However, tests indicated that functions such as digesting food and eliminating waste matter were not being replaced. Though tissue-based, the organs were of an exceedingly strange composition. Seeing their growth from the last set of PET scans and again noting the absence of connective tissue, Joyner had to wonder how these organs planned to coordinate their activity. A greater mystery still was how it could support an organic system of any design.

It was now obvious to Joyner, despite the skepticism of many in his field, that this was indeed a speciation process of some unknown nature. The patients were rapidly evolving or being transformed into a new subspecies of *Homo sapiens*. All the hallmarks were there. It was surprising that it could happen this quickly, be triggered so easily, and that all the needed genes were already in place awaiting the right catalyst. The problem was whether his patients could survive this change-over, and if so, whether he should continue to fight its progress or allow this process to run its course. Most of his patients would rather die than go on it, but what about the needs of the race to express itself, to leap beyond itself, even if the results were not to his liking?

Max Kellgren and Dr. Hunter now stepped into the room. While Joyner finished marking up the PET scans, Kellgren started at the other end and worked his way down the row.

"What really puzzles me," Joyner said, as he stepped back to get an overview, "is how this process plans to support the body. I mean if it doesn't process food as an energy source, what keeps it going?"

Kellgren turned around. "There are other sources of energy like sunlight and charged particles in the air."

"And just how would it absorb and process it?" Joyner asked skeptically.

"Maybe it absorbs energy through the skin and processes it for use...like an electrical transformer," Dr. Kellgren said tentatively, testing the idea. He now nodded his head in confirmation.

Joyner gave this a moment's consideration before dismissing it as unlikely, then added, "Well, whatever it plans as a substitute, it had better kick in soon before the boy starves to death."

Kellgren turned around and looked at the row of PET scans. "I wonder if it isn't bringing all the body systems to a particular point, maybe Prigogine's 'Singular Moment,' before it, as you say, kicks in."

Andrea Hunter looked to Dr. Joyner for an explanation. "It's a point of maximum instability before an open or organic system either disintegrates or reorders itself at a higher level."

"If you mean 90 percent inoperative, it won't be too much longer by my calculations," she said.

Joyner stepped up to study the PET scans again. "If so, and

you may be right in this case, professor, the new system is nowhere near completion. I'd have to conclude the 'process' won't take."

"Since we don't know the basis of its operation, we can't really say that. It could be, for all we know, poised to take over right now," Kellgren added.

"Professor, I can't base my decisions on what may occur, but on what is mostly likely to occur," Joyner insisted. "What I see is this process robbing my patients of every bit of available energy for a switch-over to an incomplete body system."

"If you're right, given the pace of this change-over, we'll see signs of a breakdown in the Owens boy shortly. But, if you're wrong," Kellgren pleaded with him, "and you stunt its growth, you could leave your patients caught in the middle."

Joyner gave this some consideration. "I'm sorry, professor. But by the time the breakdown occurs, it will be too late for us to act." He turned to Andrea Hunter. "Let's increase the radiation dosage and see if we can't further retard the process."

Dr. Hunter nodded her head but was clearly saddened by this decision. Joyner looked at her questioningly. She said, with a tear rolling down her cheek, "I know you're right, but these poor people can't win either way."

Later that night, after the three of them had gone out to eat, Guy Joyner went back to his hotel room and called his girlfriend in San Diego. They talked for twenty minutes, which helped lift some of the gloom, but when he could not sleep, Joyner got dressed and drove out to the hospital. On the way to the lab, he picked up Carl Owens's PET scans in the X-ray department. He wanted to take one last look at them before ordering the next round of radiation treatments for his patients in the morning. He knew this might be a death sentence for them: there was little hope they could survive the new onslaught. What bothered him was the nagging feeling that he had not given Dr. Kellgren's theory enough consideration. He would now have to expand his thinking and explore new evolutionary pathways for such a developing body system.

In the past evolution was generally associated with a change in gene frequency, or the gradual replacement of genes within a given population by others bestowing more adaptability. However, this "sorting-out" definition had proven too broad for some experts. They would define evolution specifically in terms of an organism learning how best to extract energy from its environment. That definition was gaining popularity, because when you substituted information for energy in the equation, it could apply to all open systems in general. Joyner was not entirely comfortable with its goal orientation, but found the definition so useful he had since dropped his reservation.

The speciation process of his patients conformed to that definition: the body's energy-processing machinery was apparently evolving into a far more sophisticated system. However, it was doing that on its own without following a normal progression for evolutionary change. In general that started with changing environmental conditions (a dryer climate), requiring a behavioral shift (more grazing, less browsing), and resulting in a modified anatomy (more molars, less incisors). Even if Dr. Kellgren's mysterious "center" controlled the process, the body supposedly would continue to receive its energy from the environment. So, to better understand this process, Dr. Joyner would need to know what kind of energy source would feed a body system not designed for solid food consumption.

It was obvious after only a brief survey that Dr. Kellgren had discovered the most likely source: electricity, probably in the form of free-floating charged particles. And if that were the case, then this system would indeed be constituted differently. It would also explain why there was no connective tissue between the organs: the electricity would flow between adjoining electrodes. And could this be the first step in the evolution of what physicist Freeman Dyson called his "Plasma Beings?" He had speculated that as the sun dies out, *Homo sapiens* may evolve into a being composed of plasma—electrically charged atoms—that could live off the sun's diminished heat and eventually leave the frozen wasteland of our planet and live practically immortal lives in space, feeding off clouds of interstellar gas.

Could it be, Joyner wondered, and contrary to his past belief, that evolution was predisposed in a certain direction? And since this system was not an adaptation to current environmental conditions, was it a latent response to future conditions triggered a million years in advance? In time the sun would die out, and Tyson's "Plasma Beings" seemed like the logical next step. But could the seeds of that development have been planted several million years ago? If so, that would mean evolution was the unfoldment of some inherent quality rather than, or in addition to, the periodic adaptation to a changing environment. And that was contrary to most modern thought on the subject. Since, at this point, it was mere speculation, Joyner could dismiss it outright and continue with the planned course of treatment. But he was never one to bury his mistakes. If there were any chance this system could still save his patients, and that it might possibly be the next step in our evolution, Joyner decided to give it more time to activate itself.

**5.**

When Linda was called to Paul Jordan's office that afternoon and discovered Pam in his waiting room, she immediately knew the reason for the summons. In the past week Linda's situation had deteriorated to the point where none of the other teachers would talk with her, and parents were keeping her students home from school. When nasty notes began to appear in her teacher's box, Linda told Paul about it and he promised to investigate it. Although he had kept his distance recently, apparently he was not aware how hostile the others had become. Now, as Linda took a seat across from Pam, it was obvious from the way Jordan's secretary reacted to them that the situation had worsened.

Finally, after a tense silence, Pam looked over at her friend. "I would feel a lot better about this meeting if we weren't the only two asked in."

Linda shook her head in hopeless resignation. "Expect the worst."

Pam was about to give Linda another one of her pat speeches on positive thinking, but under these circumstances, she doubted it would sound very convincing and dropped the idea. The office door opened, and Paul Jordan stuck his head out. "Why don't you both come in now." He caught Linda's eye for a moment, but he could not hold her stare and backed into his office.

Inside Jordan took his seat behind a wide glass-top desk, and the two women sat across from him. There was a moment's silence as he nervously shuffled a few papers around. Finally, he looked up at them. "Imagine you know what this is all about?"

"The teachers have threatened a walkout unless we're fired," Linda said.

"That's the least of my problems," Jordan said, then wiped the perspiration off his brow with a handkerchief. "Lew Benjamin, the president of the school board, has been trying to get some straight answers about your condition from Dr. Joyner, but with little success."

"Well, you know it's not contagious. That should be enough," Linda said indignantly.

"Linda, we both know there's more to it than that, and it's got everybody up in arms."

"Oh, you think we're going to start sprouting horns any day now?"

"There have been some very strange rumors going around, and they just want Joyner's assurance that the students won't be exposed to something . . . upsetting."

"Don't you think we'd leave on our own before that?" Linda asked.

"Yes, I know that. But the board won't accept my word on it."

"It's just not fair," Pam said, with tears rolling down her cheeks. "I'm taking the treatment, doing everything expected of me." She now opened her purse rummaging through it for

Kleenex. "I just can't sit home, watching TV and waiting to die. Along with my husband, this school, these kids, are what's kept me going."

Jordan was affected by this outpouring of emotion and tried to think of a last-minute fix. "You could take this up with your union rep, have him file a protest."

"And get a hearing when...in six months?" Linda asked sarcastically.

Jordan wondered if she were telling him they only had that much longer to live, and if so he was greatly saddened by the news.

"Are you going to make us leave right now, without saying goodbye?" Pam asked.

"Of course not," Jordan said. And this time he was the indignant one. "Not until after the Christmas break, and maybe longer. It depends on how fast we can find replacements."

Linda stood up abruptly. Paul really had a lot of nerve, she thought, asking them to stay on while he looked for replacements. It was outrageous. "I'll stay until the break...for my students. But don't expect me to do you any favors." Linda looked over at Pam, who finally caught the drift of their conversation. When Linda turned to leave, Pam stood up and followed her out.

When she finally made it to her car, after arranging to take the rest of the afternoon off, Linda was so furious she had to sit for five minutes to calm down. This was almost too much for her to bear. It had been difficult enough facing this ordeal without the support of family and friends, but now they had taken away her students, her last source of comfort. Let them, Linda said to herself, try to take anything else from her.

While driving home, and still in a foul mood, Linda drove past a gasoline station and saw a man arguing with Jennifer. When she looked closer, Linda saw him pointing a gas nozzle at her while waving a lit cigar in the other hand. She made a quick U-turn to a cacophony of beeping horns, and she turned into the station almost running into the man's car. Linda jumped out of her car and rushed over.

"You and the others," the man said to Jennifer, while

vigorously twirling his cigar, "you're a menace to us all. I mean, Jesus lady, I've got kids in the backseat. Why don't you just go over and give them a big kiss, and I'll start takin' them to the vet."

Linda now stepped between them. "Okay mister, just put it down."

At first the man seemed puzzled by this request, but when he saw Linda looking back and forth between the gas nozzle and his cigar, he understood her alarm. He now put the nozzle into his gas tank and started to fill it. After grinding his cigar under the heel of his shoe, he turned to the two women. "What do you take me for? I'm Italian. I talk with my hands. No harm intended."

Linda was not completely convinced, and she took Jennifer by the arm and pulled her away from the disgruntled motorist. He put the nozzle on automatic, went over and picked up the squeegee and wiped his back window while mumbling to himself. Finally, as they watched from a distance, he came back and finished filling his tank. He now replaced the nozzle and walked up to the cashier's window to pay his bill.

Linda turned to Jennifer. "Maybe I did overreact just a little."

"Well, until you came, the guy had me scared half to death."

That surprised Linda. She would have thought Jenny could handle just that type of situation. But, looking through that face with its harsh angular lines to the soul inside this tortured body, Linda could sense a new vulnerability in the woman. "So, has it been that bad?" Linda asked.

"Yeah, and I don't know how much more of this I can take."

"I've got a great idea," Linda said, smiling mischievously. "Why don't we go over to Paco's and get bombed on margaritas."

"Now that's what the doctor should've ordered a long time ago," Jennifer said, pulling her wallet out to pay the attendant. "If you beat me there, order me a frozen margarita and tell Carlos to keep the blender running."

Linda could not believe what she was hearing. "Come on, Paco. How can you refuse to seat me? I was eating here when this place was a taco stand, and Rosita was causing three-alarm fires with her hot tamales."

Paco, a short wiry man given to speaking with elaborate hand gestures, paced up and down the stone veranda. "I am truly sorry, but what can I do?" he asked, shrugging his shoulders. "The man from the health department, Mr. Randall, is getting complaints from people who're afraid you'll contaminate the food if you eat here.

"Of course, I tell him this is ridiculous. Who prepares the food? Paco. Nobody else. So how could this be? But still, the man says if I serve you again, he will take away my permit." Paco stopped and looked up at the much taller woman. "You see how it is?"

Linda shook her head in disgust. Jennifer arrived at that moment, and Linda turned to her. "Can you believe this? He won't seat us."

"You mean we can't get a drink?"

The two women now turned and stared at the restaurant owner. Seeing a way to reclaim his honor, Paco called out to the bartender, "Carlos, two margaritas for the lovely ladies." However, when they started for the bar, he added, "To go, but on the house." They looked at each other, tempted to refuse the offer, but decided to take the drinks and run.

They sat in Linda's car in the parking lot and drank their frozen margaritas. The liquid ice felt good running down their parched throats. For a moment, as the liquor quickly went to their heads, they felt better. But, at least for Linda, it did not ease the pain of this latest rejection.

"It's one thing when people walk away from you on the streets, but quite another when restaurants refuse to seat you," Linda said, her anger building up. "I mean that's against the law. And no pencil-pushing bureaucrat is going to tell me I can't eat out anymore."

Partially drunk, Jennifer nodded her head in mock outrage. "Agreed," she said, but when she tried to slam her fist on the dashboard for emphasis, Jennifer missed by a long way and started giggling.

"I see you're in no condition to drive, so you'll just have to ride along with me," Linda said. She strapped her friend in and drove out of the parking lot.

When Linda charged into the Sheriff's office, Howser was watching television on a portable set. Seeing her combative expression, he reached across his desk and turned the television off and swiveled his chair around to face her.

"I want to file a complaint against the health department," Linda blurted out, as she walked up to his desk. "They don't have the authority to bar us from restaurants, do they?"

The Sheriff pulled a file out of his middle divider, opened it and handed Linda an official-looking paper. "They do when the courts have declared you and the others a public health hazard."

Linda read the decree in astonishment. Nobody had mentioned it to her. The legal response to the townspeople's growing opposition to their freedom had materialized all too quickly. She could only wonder if more forceful measures would follow.

"Linda, don't you think it's time you checked yourself back into the hospital where you can get the fulltime care you need?" Howser asked. "Anybody but Dr. Joyner would have insisted long ago. But, whatever his reasons, nobody is buying it. To them you've got the plague, and they're not going to feel safe until you're locked away."

"But I don't," Linda insisted, "and I'm not about to give in to their fear. I'm going to live the days remaining to me breathing in fresh air and soaking up the warm rays of the sun. And neither you, nor the rest of this town, are going to force me in a minute sooner." Linda turned and walked out the door.

The Sheriff shook his head in grudging admiration. The woman certainly had courage. When a squad car pulled up outside with its siren blaring, Howser stood up and followed Linda out the door. Barry Hamilton slid out of the backseat of the state police car followed by a scruffy-looking man in his late forties. He now pulled him up to the sidewalk and then turned to Linda.

"This the man you talked with the day you got ill?" Everybody took a step back, and Hamilton added, "He's been checked out, and he's no longer carrying it."

Linda had immediately recognized him despite his shabby, unshaven appearance. "It's him all right. What happened to him?"

"They found him at a detox center in Eureka," Hamilton said. "Said he's been in and out of the place five times in the last three months."

The Sheriff stepped up and got a good look at him. "I'd say he'll need about a gallon of coffee before he's ready to talk." He motioned for his two deputies to take him inside.

"Sorry Sheriff, but Dr. Joyner has the first shot at him."

"Says who?" Howser asked petulantly.

"Henry Bilford, head of health services for the state," Hamilton replied.

The Sheriff turned around and walked back into his office mumbling something about bureaucratic assholes under his breath. Barry Hamilton now turned to the deputies. "Are you going to take him over, or do I ask the state patrol?"

While the deputies considered Hamilton's request, Jennifer came stumbling out of a bar up the block and waved to Linda. "Hey Linda, come on down. Ed says he'll serve us. Says nothing we have could harm his clientele."

Linda headed up the sidewalk to rescue her friend. The salesman turned to Hamilton. "If it's all the same to you, I'd rather go with her."

He grabbed the drunk by the arm and shoved him back into the state patrol car. "Boys, how about a ride to the hospital?"

"Sure, we wouldn't want to burden the local police with such a dangerous criminal." The two state patrolmen had a good laugh, got into their patrol car and drove away.

## 6.

When Linda returned home from her last day of school, she plopped her things on the kitchen table and went back to her bedroom for a nap. Trying to act cheerful at the Christmas party, while feeling so terrible about leaving, had given her a colossal headache. She never did tell her students she would not be coming back after their vacation. No doubt Paul Jordan would explain her departure without upsetting the poor darlings. Linda was never one to keep the truth from her students whatever their age. It was her job to instill in them a hunger for the truth, and to distort it or otherwise tamper with it was a great disservice. Others of her profession were somewhat less disinclined.

When she woke up, Linda fixed herself a sandwich and ate it while she put her books away. She did not know what to do with her presents, many of them still left unopened. Linda had planned to write each of the givers a thank-you note, but she could not bring herself to pen them. Finally, she just shoved the lot of them in the bottom drawer of a kitchen cabinet. With a cup of hot tea in hand, Linda went out and sat on her screened-in front porch. Somewhat later, as the twilight faded into night, Reverend Taylor drove up and parked out front.

As he walked up the sidewalk, Linda went over and opened the screen door for him. "Reverend Taylor, what a surprise," she said sardonically, suspecting that he had come to persuade her to reenter the hospital.

He stood in the doorway for a moment shuffling his feet. "Hope this isn't a bad time for you?"

"It's not the best of times," Linda said, "but do come in." Reverend Taylor was not dissuaded by her lukewarm reception and walked through the opened screen door onto the front porch. "It's getting a little chilly out here, would you like to go inside?"

"If you don't mind, and I'll only stay a moment," Reverend Taylor added.

When they were seated in the living room, and after he had declined a cup a coffee, Linda asked him rather rudely, "Let me guess. We're holding church services two days early?"

The minister cracked a smile. "I'll have to admit Sheriff Howser suggested as much. But I had to remind him that the church has always been the last refuge for those broken in body and spirit, and that mine would continue to be such a sanctuary."

Linda was taken aback by this show of intestinal fortitude, and she now regretted having received him so poorly. "Well, Reverend, that was certainly kind of you," she said, still wondering why he had come.

Taylor shifted in his seat nervously, while turning the ring on his little finger around. He now looked up. "Linda, I'm somewhat at a loss to explain to myself why you have chosen to discontinue your treatment in the face of almost certain death." He paused for a moment searching the woman's now disfigured face for signs of this mysterious image. "It makes me very curious about this vision you've been seeing, and your absolute faith in it. And I just wanted to know if we could talk about it?"

"And what would you like to know, Reverend?" Linda asked, somewhat taken aback by the minister's inquiry.

"Is it true all of you are seeing the same image?" he asked.

"Yes, if at various stages of its development."

So it had an objective reality, Taylor thought, outside their own minds. "Does it talk to you or otherwise instruct you?"

"Not in words," Linda said, "but one gets the distinct impression it's communicating with us at a deeper level."

"And what is it . . . communicating?"

"It appears that its language is that of feelings. And it has filled us all with the most ineffable longings," Linda said, her eyes tearing up. "It's as if we're only half-complete, and that in its boundless reaches we'll find our completion and know a love unimaginable to us now."

Linda was able to communicate to Reverend Taylor what she was feeling, and it moved him greatly. And yet he still clung to his suspicion. "And yet it's killing you?"

"One part of me is falling aside to give way to another. What I truly am can never die," Linda insisted.

The woman sounded as if she had just stepped out of the pages of the Bible. Taylor looked deeply into eyes that had unmistakably looked into the face of some deific being, and through an inexplicable process she was becoming what she had seen. That it was the God he prayed to, he did not know. Would he know Him, the minister wondered, if he looked upon His face like this woman had? Or would he feel compelled by his training to deny the reality of what he had so often talked about from the safe distance of his pulpit?

"I feel the truth in what you say," Reverend Taylor finally conceded. "And it disturbs me."

"Well, maybe you should see it and form your own impression," Linda said.

Taylor sat back in his seat. For a moment he wondered if she were going to call up a visitation here and now for his review. "How would that be possible?"

"In one of the caves excavated during last summer's big archeological dig in the mountains, they found a series of hidden chambers with this image engraved on its walls." Linda paused for a long moment. "And, if you like, I could show it to you."

Reverend Taylor was momentarily stunned by this revelation, and before he could stop he heard himself say, as if from a distance, "When?"

As he stood there, covered from head to toe with dust, Reverend Taylor looked up into the face of this unknown God and shuddered. It was not what he had expected. Conditioned by biblical paintings from the Middle Ages, his own personal God-Image was somewhat more beatific. Although these eyes contained a knowingness beyond man's, there was a terrible harshness about them. He felt more acrimony than love staring out at him. Since this was a drawing, that could be merely the artist's perception, but he doubted it. Yet it did make him curious about these archaic humans. Were they easily frightened primitives and was this vision merely a bad dream? The elaborate nature of their religious rituals as depicted here spoke otherwise. And one had to wonder how much insulation such trappings provided when you were face to face with your maker. From what he had heard, the image invoked in the other patients a similiar emotion. Taylor was sure he would find such a vision equally as terrifying. Yet Linda saw it in a different light.

"I'll have to say that I don't find this image very comforting," Reverend Taylor said.

Linda stood beside him transfixed by the sight of it. Finally, she turned to her minister. "I know what you're feeling. At first it scared me to death, but I've since come to accept it, and see love and not terror reflected back."

"So that's the price of admission."

Linda smiled. "Well, Reverend, hasn't it always been that way?"

He looked askance at the impertinent young woman, and then he walked around the inside of the pyramid-shaped temple. "Now what did you say they used this for?"

"The shape itself was used to focus energy," Linda said, "for various kinds of initiations. The drawings suggest that the whole tribe walled itself up in here alive as a test. Since the only way out this side of death was straight up through two thousand feet of solid granite, they either transformed themselves or died."

Reverend Taylor turned around, not sure he heard her correctly. "Into what?"

"Beings capable of transmuting themselves into pure energy."

"And how on earth would they do that?" Taylor asked.

"I believe the process is called ascension. And it's done by raising the vibratory rate of the body."

"You mean like...," Reverend Taylor started to say but could not bring himself to complete it.

"Yes, in some traditions," Linda said, "Jesus was one in a line of ascended masters."

Reverend Taylor did not agree with her; Jesus was the only son of God come to free man. But, since the minister had come in hope of understanding this mystery, he would allow more of its story to unfold before he disputed its claims. "And how does this image fit in?"

"Be it alien, ascended master, or God himself, I believe it is the image of our future selves. And as we let go of our fears and accept its love we'll be transformed by it."

"Are you telling me this disease is the first stage of this 'process,' and that you and the others are following such a path?" Taylor asked incredulously.

Linda walked closer to him, and when he turned back to her, both their flashlights were enough to illuminate the spot.

"Reverend, we are all on that path, but some of us have just been speeded up a million years or so."

He now swept his arm around to encompass the walls of the temple with their numerous tribal paintings. "But surely these ancient people didn't suffer from the same disease?"

"I believe they were more in touch with the world of spirit, while we need a jolt to break down our defenses and open us to the influx of new energies."

When Reverend Taylor turned and again shined his light on the temple wall, looking up into the face of this ancient God, Linda walked away leaving the small pool of light behind until the darkness of the cave had totally engulfed her. Out of its bottomless depth arose more images of this lost tribe. Here she saw them living in the valley, saw them evolve over time from a band of half-starved hunters into a sacred society. And from this base, Linda caught glimpses of a future glory that thrilled and excited her. But one she could not yet claim for herself.

In the years since the tribe had settled in the coastal valley, the great abundance of food coupled with their isolation from other warring tribes had loosened the bond of tribal cohesion. Also, when Asawa, their only true leader, had retired to his mountain cave to live out his life in communion with their God, he had freed them from the last vestige of tribal custom to follow the law of their own inner being. Here, in increasingly vivid dreams, they received personal instruction from their "Great Man" on everything from good hunting areas, to the approach of inclement weather, to herbal remedies for illness and potions for increased sexual potency.

To the degree they followed such guidance the more helpful were their future dreams. Those tribesmen who chose not to listen, or broke the inner code of moral conduct by cheating or stealing, drove the "Great Man" away and were forced to rely on their own resources. There were several migrations of the fallen ones to other fertile lands, where new tribes were formed and old customs and rituals reinstated. After the last of them had left, the remaining tribesmen found a new harmony amongst themselves, as they were better able to identify in each other that greater part. In time all disputes were settled and all major decisions made by calling on their collective "Great Man."

This ability to see in others what they saw in themselves further blurred the demarcation between the inner and outer world. As a dream could foretell the approach of a storm, finding an odd-shaped stone of rare composition could trigger a complementary dream of its symbolic import. For them everything was infused with spirit, alive with its possibilities. Before picking fruit one would ask permission from the tree's spirit, when killing a deer one would offer homage to its counterpart. And death was merely the transition from body to spirit, followed by the return through birth into another embodiment.

The more they identified with this greater part of themselves, the more gifts of the spirit were manifested. The tribesmen had entered a dream state halfway between this world and the next, and they were ready for the next stage of their planned development. Asawa was given the necessary instructions, and he came down from the mountain to live among his people and pass on the new teachings.

The main precept was the total love and acceptance of self. The people were told that in their striving to transcend themselves they had become overidentified with their higher selves, and until they could love what they resisted in themselves and others, parts they had tried to push aside, they would remain incomplete. With such acceptance they would come to realize the totality of themselves. They were immortal beings capable of spanning time and space, but had become trapped in physical embodiment returning time after time until they were able to transform matter into spirit and reclaim their heritage. The people heard what the prophet had spoken, and they took it to heart and made it their own.

Sometime later there was a drastic change of climate when the southern part of the great glacier shifted and began to recede in their direction. Average temperatures dropped steeply, killing off most of the local game and vegetation. The tribes in the inland valleys, descendants of the fallen ones, were hit the hardest. When starvation decimated whole tribes, those remaining gathered together and summoned the courage to cross the coastal mountains to enter the forbidden valley of the Ancient Ones. They had hoped that this valley was spared, and that they would find fields of fresh vegetables and forests stocked with game. When they found neither and saw that the inhabitants were immune to their common tragedy, they sought to kill them and feed off their flesh. The Ancient Ones removed themselves lest they cause the others harm and sought refuge in the mountain caves. Here, under Asawa's guidance, they prepared themselves for the final transition from men to Gods.

## 7.

It was clear to Guy Joyner after several more weeks of development that the process, as Dr. Kellgren had predicted, was converting the body from a chemical to an electrical-based system. In itself, given the speed of the change-over, this was amazing. What was even more astounding and what seemed to settle the current debate on the subject was that the speciation of the race proceeded without a great influx of new genetic material. The viral transposon that had triggered the process did contain an extraordinary if small complex of genes, but one would assume such a drastic process would be fed by considerably more.

The problem, as Joyner reviewed the matter, was that science still did not know at the genetic level what made species different, or the difference between a parent species and its offspring. As an example one could identify in a comparison between humans and chimpanzees every bone belonging to either species. But, at the genetic level, there is almost a perfect match between the amino acid sequence in similar proteins like the beta chain in hemoglobin, whereas many species that look alike are genetically quite different. Apparently species are characterized by more than their genetic makeup.

This has led to much speculation about the genetic steps in man's evolution. Was the progression of early man that saw great changes in height, cranial capacity and jaw size the result of natural selection working over a long span of time and due to a change in many genes; or were the genes already in place awaiting the right combination to trigger a quantum leap instead? The evolutionary theory of "punctuated equilibrium" postulates such a change. It states that most species are intractable units that require an unusual "genetic jolt" to break out of their adaptive mold. New species appear when small segments of the parent stock are subject to great stress, when they are pushed to the limits of their tolerance. The result is rapid change at all levels.

From the beginning Joyner had deduced that this was a speciation process. But, since the "genetic jolt" in this case appeared to be a packet of "foreign" genes, it made him wonder if, to take Dr. Kellgren's speculation one step further, this were not a crossbreeding experiment instead. In the past there had been much speculation about what would result when you transferred genes from one species to another. Would they begin to resemble each other progressively with each new allotment of genes, or was the order less important than the sheer amount of genes? Another possibility was that only with the transfer of a particular group would you see any resemblance, and nothing sooner. In this case, the viral transposon with its fifteen-odd genes was enough to precipitate the current development.

Ken Olson stuck his head into Dr. Joyner's makeshift office. "Deborah's ready whenever you are." Joyner nodded his head in acknowledgment while he gathered his papers together and placed them back in their folder. He stood up and followed Olson out to the lab's computer center.

Here he found Dr. Kellgren talking with the young lady. Seeing him arrive, Deborah Bronsky sat back down at her console and began to type in the instructions. "Dr. Hunter, using the latest test results, and keying in on Carl Owens's data, has projected the future development of the 'process' by comparing it to known patterns of evolutionary growth."

Bronsky looked around to see if the others were ready, and then she started the program. On the terminal screen an animated drawing of a male *Homo sapiens* appeared. It now slowly progressed through various stages of development: its body becoming thinner, its head expanding greatly, arms and legs shrinking proportionately until the final result was a creature that looked like an organic spark plug.

"Like I thought," Dr. Kellgren said, "the body is being transformed into some kind of organic electrical generator. No doubt the honey-combed cranium is a receptor for drawing energy out of the air, from sunlight, maybe even from the stars."

Joyner studied the animated figure for a moment. Whether it was a speciation of man or an alien crossbreed, the result was a creature halfway between organic matter and something more transcendent. If it were an adaptation to life a million years into the future or to an entirely different ecosphere, it was singularly unsuited to life here and now.

"Well, even if it were to succeed, I wouldn't hold out much hope for their survival," Joyner said. "Sunlight alone would burn out something that sensitive pretty quickly."

"That's assuming this is the end result," Kellgren added. "Maybe it has a dual purpose: to survive at low energy levels, or use an overload to propel itself forward?"

This possibility suggested to Joyner a two-tiered model of evolution that seem to fit in with his earlier speculation that it might be as much the unfoldment of an inherent quality as periodic adaptations to changing conditions. Was it in fact a matrix in which the long-term process of evolution could be speeded up under the right circumstances and run to completion?

If so, was Dr. Kellgren's "center" the determining factor?

Andrea Hunter now came walking up to them, carrying a large computer printout and looking very concerned. She stopped and stared at the figure on the terminal screen.

"And what do you make of this?" Joyner asked her.

"It might be the next stage in our evolution, but it won't be reached at this frantic pace." She now set down her bundle, took a computer disk from the top of the stack and handed it to Bronsky. While the disks were being switched, Hunter turned back to the others. "As Dr. Joyner has suspected, with the body's food processing system nearly turned off and the new system still incomplete, the process would burn out any energy reserves long before a change-over could occur."

The new program now came up on the terminal screen and began to run. It showed the same male *Homo sapiens* as earlier, but concentrated on the early development of the process up to a point just past where Carl Owens was now. On either side was a series of numbers rapidly clicking off. When it came to that point, the numbers froze and began flashing in red. "So I ran a program on the body's consumption of such reserves, and it showed that at this point," Hunter said and nodded at the screen, "about ten days away for Carl, two weeks for the holdouts, a month for the others, the process burns up those reserves, leading to an irreversible collapse."

This assessment left them stunned. Andrea Hunter now turned to Dr. Joyner. "And by my calculations an increase in radiation treatment two weeks ago or now wouldn't make any difference."

Joyner nodded his head in agreement, but he still could not help but feel guilty about his earlier decision to forestall additional treatment. What bothered him now, as much as anything, was the fact he had considered such a drastic process as being anything but destructive. In the body, disease was always more rapid than healthy growth. Part of the problem was that this process contained a little of both elements: while it destroyed parts of the body, it also built healthy new tissue, if of an unknown nature, to replace them. It was a "constructive disease," as one of his colleagues had dubbed it. That term also described much of modern research: inducing destructive processes for constructive purposes. It made him wonder once again about this being somebody else's failed experiment.

Dr. Joyner now turned to Dr. Kellgren who continued to study the animated figure of the re-formed man. "Well, professor, this looks like the end of it."

"It may be the end of their physical reserves, but is that all they have to call on?"

Joyner looked questioningly at his old mentor. "But this system is still incapable of processing other forms of energy."

"Since it's only a matter of time, maybe we can somehow bridge the gap until total change-over."

"What do you suggest, plug them into an electrical outlet?" Joyner asked in frustration.

"Now that's an interesting idea," Kellgren said, looking off into space and thinking about it.

It was early evening before Linda could get away and run off to the beach. Dr. Joyner had called earlier to tell her his latest prognosis, and ask if she would come for additional blood work. After that the phone never stopped ringing with calls from family and friends checking up on her. She appreciated their concern, but since she felt he was mistaken, their condolences were mostly annoying. Since when had Joyner understood the nature and the course of this process? She would like to have heard the opposite: that her faith was backed up by hard evidence, but she was not about to accept less.

There were several people taking a stroll on the beach. The breeze blowing in off the ocean was cool, and everybody was wearing either jackets or sweaters. As Linda walked past one couple, they stopped and rudely stared at her. She quickly moved on. Her transformation was going through its ugly stage, and by now her face was badly deformed. Most people who did not know her would assume it was a birth defect. This aspect of the process was for Linda, who had always been very pretty, a real trial. Looking in her vanity mirror every morning, charting the progress of the change, she had to force herself to love this face, accept it as part of herself. What was even more difficult was to allow people their reaction without judging them.

To love herself that completely, in spite of the world and its sometimes harsh opinion, had always been a key issue with Linda. She had always sought the world's approval and the fulfillment of herself in its embrace. In the 1960s it was through political activism, in the 1970s it was spiritual groups, and more recently she had sought to find herself in a material lifestyle and the love of another. But she found she could only lose herself in them, not fulfill herself. Returning home to San Martin was the beginning of her journey back to herself. This process was its culmination. And the image, the primordial self she had come to reclaim. From the beginning she had known to trust it, to allow it to work its wonders, but now that trust in the face of so much overwhelming opposition would be severely tested.

After her walk Linda climbed the wooden stairs that zigzagged their way up the side of the seaside cliff to the park that ran along the palisade for several miles. At the top she found Max Kellgren waiting for her.

"Thought I might find you here," Max said, extending his hand and helping her up the last giant step.

Linda took a moment to catch her breath. "It was a lot easier going down them."

Max nodded his head toward a bench under a nearby pine tree. "Would you like to sit down?"

"No, I'm all right," Linda said, then added mischievously, "contrary to popular belief." She now offered her arm to him. "What I would like is a stroll through the park."

Max took her arm, and the two of them walked down the winding sidewalk that ran along the cliff's edge. The sun was setting over the Pacific, and they watched it in silence as they went. It was a clear evening, and they could see the golden disk slowly sink beneath the horizon leaving a trail of clouds lit in a reddish hue. The sight left them momentarily speechless.

They walked on, and after a while Max spoke up, "I assume Dr. Joyner called about this latest development?"

"Yeah, says I'm going to die next month instead of the month after," Linda said, shaking her head. "But then I've never been very impressed with his past diagnoses either."

"Unless something remarkable develops, I'm afraid I'll have to go along with this one."

Linda could see the distress in her newfound friend and patted the good doctor on the arm to reassure him. "Well, what's one more miracle anyway?"

He nodded his head in amused agreement. "Yes, why not?"

The path now hooked around a fenced-off precipice, and they walked around it peering over the edge of the cliff and down its rock-strewn side. Linda looked back at Max. "The problem with Dr. Joyner is that he deduces meaning from facts: the process is going to collapse because its running out of energy; whereas I have faith in the process, my meaning, that it will create the factual basis for my survival."

"You mean mind creates whatever it believes in?" Max asked.

"That's one way of saying it, but I would prefer to say that since mind is everything, it becomes whatever you believe in."

Max found this distinction rather academic faced with the evidence at hand. "Frankly, Linda, it's not something I'd stake my life on."

"In a way you have," Linda said insistently, "because you believe you're going to die and your essence will die with you." Max stopped and turned to Linda, annoyed by this effrontery. "It's a belief; change it and you change your possibilities," she said looking back at Max with such a well-intentioned smile that it mollified his anger. "Fortunately, your disbelief doesn't alter the nature of the soul's immortality. But it can change the outcome of things more mutable, including this process."

"In other words, if I believe there's a solution to this problem, you're saying that belief helps create one." Linda nodded her head in agreement. "I only hope you're right," Max said.

"I know that I am."

## 8.

At Christmas Linda Boyer's estranged husband Tom came down for the holidays, staying at her parents' house outside town. He arrived late in the day, and her parents insisted on taking the two of them out to dinner at their favorite restaurant that evening. Linda told her father to check first, that they might refuse to seat them. Stanley Porter said the owner, a longtime friend, had called to invite them. Linda was relieved to hear that. When Tom called, inviting her over early so they could talk, she insisted on meeting him at the restaurant. Linda preferred seeing Tom in a social setting first so the shock of her appearance and the fact she had kept so much from him would not lead to a nasty scene.

Fisherman's Catch was located on a bluff overlooking the Pacific. For the last several years, they had a Christmas buffet dinner now famous all along the coast south of San Francisco. The crowd this year was larger than ever, and even with reservations it took them fifteen minutes to be seated. While waiting in the lobby, Linda's presence had sent two couples storming out the door. The others kept their distance and did not say anything. Now, as the busboy filled their water glasses and laid down pats of butter, he kept looking over at Linda in astonishment. Porter was about to say something to him, when Millie stood up and pulled her husband to his feet.

"Why don't we go through the buffet line now, and give Linda and Tom some time alone."

Porter looked over at his daughter; her clothes were hanging loose on an emaciated frame, her face badly deformed. She looked so vulnerable, in need of his protection. He turned to Tom who understood his role in this situation.

"I'll attack the first person who says anything," Tom said rather flippantly. Millie could not help but laugh, much to Porter's annoyance. Somebody from a nearby table now walked past with a steaming plate of food. This was enough inducement to get him moving toward the buffet line. After they left, Tom turned to Linda. "I was waiting for your father to punch out the busboy."

"Do I look that bad?" Linda asked self-consciously.

"No way. You look just fine," Tom said, and then added when she questioned his reply, "okay, if somebody didn't know you, they'd think you had a birth defect. For those who do, you look. . . different. But so what; it's still you."

Linda looked back at him in astonishment. Since when had he become so sensitive? She suspected her mother had talked with him. "That's nice of you to say, Tom, but I look in the mirror every morning and I know better."

He started to protest but could see it would be in vain. Now, in a tone more like his old self, Tom said, "Let me tell you one thing, when your father broke the news to me, I was absolutely furious with you." He stopped for a moment trying to keep his anger from flaring up. "How could you keep something like this from me?"

"Well, at first, nobody knew anything and I didn't want to worry you about it. But, when they discovered the scope of this thing, all you could do was insist on more medical care," Linda said, rubbing her temples with the onset of yet another headache. "And frankly, I didn't need to fight off another concerned but misinformed. . . friend."

"Yeah, well I'm a little more than a friend, and I should've been told," Tom insisted, but less stridently.

The busboy now came up to the table with two plates stacked high with roast turkey, cranberries, and sweet potatoes. "The man sitting here said to bring these to you."

Tom took the plates from him and set one down in front of each of them. He now took a dollar out of his pocket and handed it to the boy. When he turned back, he saw Linda staring at her plate. "Did they forget something?"

"On the contrary, I can hardly eat any of it," Linda said, wondering why she had let them bring her here.

"Why, do they have you on a special diet?"

Linda pushed the sweet potatoes onto a side plate and began smashing them down with her fork. "Yeah, potatoes mashed to a pulp."

Tom shook his head in disbelief. "You're kidding, aren't you?"

Linda had finished mashing the potatoes and was now looking down at the mess. "Well, eventually I won't need food, but until then, this is about all I can handle."

Since he had heard her disease was fatal, Tom almost asked if there had been a change in her condition, when he remembered being told of Linda's delusion. Seeing his once beautiful wife in this condition, her body wasted to nothing and her mind unraveling before his eyes, was too upsetting for him to eat his dinner. The two of them pushed their plates away at the same time.

The band now played a familiar old waltz, and they listened to the melody for a moment. "But I can still dance, if anybody's interested," Linda said. Tom stood up and escorted his wife to the dance floor.

It had been ages since they had gone dancing, not since the first year of their marriage. At first, given Linda's current lack of coordination, they ended up stepping on each other's feet with every other dance step. But Tom held her close to him and swept her along as they twirled around the dance floor. The others hardly noticed her, and those who did were too busy having fun to let it bother them. Halfway through the next number, an arm-flailing, hip-gyrating fast dance, Linda lost her breath and had to be taken off the floor.

They went out onto the restaurant's deck for some fresh air. Leaning over the railing, Linda began breathing in the cool ocean air until her lungs started to burn. Tom took his sports coat off and draped it over her frail shoulders. They both stood there and looked out at the ocean for a long moment.

He now turned to her. "Linda, you don't know how badly I feel about all of this." Tears welled in eyes long dry to them, and his voice became choked up with emotion. "To think how stupid and pig-headed I've been. If only. . . ."

Linda placed a finger over his lips to quiet him. "Please Tom, no regrets. Just kiss me."

They kissed with all the longing of two people who had allowed love to slip through their fingers until now it was out of their grasp. It was a wild, desperate embrace, and finally Tom had to pry himself loose from her.

"The lady is a tiger," he said, aroused by his wife's passion. "Could we. . ." he started to say before catching himself.

"I would love to," Linda said forlornly, "if the equipment still worked."

Tom was shaken by this revelation, and was becoming increasingly overwhelmed by the mounting toll of his wife's tragic illness. He grabbed hold of the railing for fear his knees might buckle under him.

"Tom, please do me a big favor and go back to San Francisco in the morning," Linda said. Before he could protest, she went on. "I don't want you to stay here and watch me change into something you could never relate to. It's best to think of me as dying, because the part of me that you know, truly is. Leave now and remember me as I was when we first met." Linda stepped over and took hold of Tom's hands. "Can you do that for me?"

At this point Tom was too devastated to offer any resistance, and he nodded his head in reluctant compliance with her wish. He put his arms around his stricken wife and held her close to him, and they stood there in gentle embrace while the moon rose behind them over the distant horizon.

In time the chilly night air made Linda cough; she pulled away, taking a handkerchief from her pocket and placing it over her mouth. When it had passed, Linda took off her husband's coat and handed it back to him. "Tom, it's getting cold out here and I'm tiring fast. Time for me to go while I can still drive."

"Let me take you home, and I'll pick your car up in the morning."

"No, but thank you anyway," Linda said, resisting an impulse to place herself under his care. "I need to keep doing things for myself." Tom could understand that but still worried about her getting home safely. They lingered for a moment, realizing this might be the last time they would see each other. Finally, Linda began backing up. "Tell mom and dad I'll call in the morning." Tom nodded his head, watching her slowly fade into the darkness. Linda now called out to him, "Tom, I love you. And goodbye."

The Monday after Christmas, Jennifer finally sent the last of her presents. There were only six left, and everybody would certainly understand if she was not able to make the effort, but it was important for her to complete this project. Or, at least it seemed so when she left the house that morning. Jennifer was not feeling well and now wondered if it had been such a good idea. There were only a few people in line at the post office, and only one of them had a package to send. Finally, shaking very badly, Jennifer stepped up to the counter and laid her packages down.

The old postal clerk, Mr. Samuels, hidden behind this stack, said to his customer, "Looks like somebody's a little late for Christmas." When he took the top two packages off to weigh them, he saw that his customer was Jennifer and was sorry he had spoken up.

"Please, can you hurry. I'm not feeling very well at all."

"Sure thing, Jenny. Just take a minute," Samuels said as he hurriedly weighed, stamped and placed the packages in the outgoing bins. As Jennifer paid him, her rickety hands struggling with her wallet, the old man waited patiently remembering her as a young girl. She would come in on the first Friday of every month to buy the new block stamps for her collection. With pigtails and a red ribbon in her hair, she was always a welcome sight. Seeing her eaten up with this illness was unbearably sad. He now handed Jennifer her change and clasped her hand between both of his. "I hope you're feeling better, Jenny."

She smiled back, as much as it hurt, and tried to reassure him of it. Outside, she sat down on a bench to gather strength for her walk home. She had been feeling worse the last few days, ever since Dr. Joyner called with his "wonderful" prognosis. As much as she wanted to maintain a positive attitude, Jennifer was finding it increasingly difficult, faced with both the medical findings and her own rapidly deteriorating condition. She knew in her heart that Linda was right, that their only hope for survival was an absolute faith in this vision, but she was new to this way of thinking and was riddled with doubt.

Jennifer struggled to her feet and walked down the sidewalk. After a few steps she began swaying from side to side and had to grab a parking meter to keep her balance. She now used a row of them as support and proceeded from one to the other. Seeing her struggle, someone asked if they could call her a cab but she refused their help. Jennifer was still smarting from earlier rejections by the townspeople and wanted to make it home on her own.

At the corner she waited for two lights to change before attempting to cross the wide boulevard. She was now in a daze and wandered along carried by the flow of the noonday crowd. Halfway across Jennifer was jostled by an oncoming pedestrian and knocked to the pavement. Momentarily stunned, she lay there as a circle of onlookers gathered around her. The faces gawking at her were partially hidden in their own shadows giving them a sinister look. For a moment, while staring up at them, Jennifer was seized with terror: would they finally gang up and kill her? And then in the opening at the top of the circle a shaft of light shown through. In it she saw her image, now fully formed, its eyes beaming with love, and her fear abated.

And then, as the others looked on, Jennifer underwent a spontaneous transformation of her face, its angular contours collapsing further inward. There was a collective gasp from the crowd as everybody stepped back. The process drained every last ounce of energy from her already depleted body, leaving her helplessly floundering on the ground. Finally, she struggled to one knee, her hand extended as she reached out for help.

Marty Keller, the tow-headed young deputy, was passing by the town square on his day off when he saw the crowd gathering. He now pushed his way through to the center where he found the Barnak woman struggling to get up. She looked like a wounded animal to him, like the baby deer he had freed from a trap as a young boy. Keller stepped forward, knelt over and scooped the woman up in his arms. "I'm going to take you to the hospital." Jennifer nodded her head in beleaguered agreement.

CHAPTER FIVE

# CONJUGATION

*The union of two cells,*
*during which chromosomal material*
*is transferred from the donor*
*to the recipient cell.*

## San Martin, California
## January 2

When they finally allowed Linda to see her, Jennifer's condition had greatly worsened. Dr. Joyner kept his patients segregated, but since Linda was in better condition than the others and he wanted more blood work from her, he decided to give her access in exchange for it. The first thing she noticed when entering the room was the coldness. She walked over to check the thermostat and discovered that it was set on sixty-four. There was an index card stuck underneath the metal backing that warned against adjusting the temperature. Shaking her head, Linda stepped over to the bed and stood next to Jennifer. She was asleep but it was a disturbed sleep. Tossing and turning, she never settled in one spot for very long. Although she lay on a waterbed, the angular contours of her body could find no solace. Linda pulled a chair over to the bed and sat down. She was quietly watching her friend, when Jennifer suddenly rolled over on her side and opened her eyes.

Jennifer looked at her for a moment, her eyes still unfocused. "Linda, is that you?"

"Yes, it's me."

"I was dreaming just now, and you were in it," Jennifer said, then questioned herself, "or at least someone who . . . felt like you."

Linda reached over and took Jennifer's badly deformed hand out from under the covers and held it. She started to pull it away, then stopped herself. "Sorry, I'm being silly, but they discovered that heat feeds the process."

"Is that why it's so cold in here?"

Jennifer nodded her head. "As if that would make a difference." She now rolled her eyes. "They're even giving some of us ice baths."

Linda gritted her teeth in exasperation at Joyner's continued wrongheadedness. "Since they think we're dying anyway, why don't they just push in the other direction and see what happens?"

"I think they'd rather see us all dead than transformed into something beyond them."

"You know you're right, but fortunately this process is bigger than all of us combined," Linda said with deep conviction.

Jennifer squeezed Linda's hand hoping her faith was contagious. "I wish I could feel as confident about it."

"Well don't deny how you feel. That's how it communicates with us. And if it's dread you feel, then feel it deeply, intensely," Linda said with great conviction. "That's the energy that feeds the process from within us. Absorb it and your feelings will change."

Linda stood up. "I know you're tired, so I'll let you get back to sleep." She placed Jennifer's hand back under the covers and then pulled them up to her chin. "I'll stop in to see you tomorrow."

"Come earlier, I'm better in the morning."

"You're getting better now," Linda said, as she backed up to the door, opened it and left.

Jennifer watched her friend leave and then rolled over on her back. Of any position this was the most comfortable, if still very painful. By now the physical pain had become excruciating. It did sensitize her, however, to her feelings. They now arose in wave after tormenting wave from the deeper recesses of her shattered psyche. Although the images summoned up from the past were familiar to her, they now spoke with a strange new intensity. She saw herself as a child being punished unfairly, as a schoolgirl afraid to tell on a teacher who had taken liberties with her, as a junior in high school unjustly accused of cheating. Finally, she relived her last meeting with Carl before he left town leaving her with a broken heart. It was her history, the material of her psyche, but the anger she now felt, the outrage was heightened beyond her past feelings about these incidents. It was as if a message was being delivered to her. Confront your feelings of powerlessness, of being a victim; own them, and they will empower you. Jennifer opened herself to this outpouring, allowed the anger to spread through her, felt it deeply, intensely. Surges of energy ran up her spine; her body twitched like a live wire, and then it exploded in her brain. Lying back, sunk deeply in the waterbed, Jennifer now lifted her hands into the light and saw them spontaneously re-form themselves.

When Linda stepped into the therapy room, she looked around for Pam but did not see her. She was about to leave when an ice-encrusted head popped up out of a high steel tub. As Linda walked up to her, Pam wiped the slivers of ice out of her eyes.

"Are you joining the Polar Bear club?" Linda asked.

Pam tried to smile in response but the effort was too painful. "I think we're both overqualified."

Linda came over and put her hand in the tub of ice. "Been sitting in here long?"

"A couple hours." When Linda failed to remove her hand, Pam said, "Feels good, doesn't it?"

Linda had to admit that the cold soothed her dried-out skin, seeped down and numbed the awful pain in her joints. But she now pulled her hand out of the ice bath and wiped it off on a towel hung over the side. "Yes, but the price is too high."

Pam narrowed her eyes and seemed to purse her lips. "You mean living longer?"

"Come on, Pam. These are only half-measures. Why prolong such a miserable existence when a new life, a greater life awaits us?"

Linda's past pronouncements on the subject were aggravating enough, but given their present condition, her present remark made Pam furious. Tiny beads of ice melted on her forehead and streamed down her face in little zigzag patterns. "You know I'm getting awfully tired of hearing about this new life of ours," Pam said and pulled her badly deformed hand out of the ice bath and draped it over the side, "when the old one is turning into a Saturday morning creep show."

"But don't you see," Linda said, lifting Pam's hand, "this is just a transitional state."

"You keep saying that, and we keep getting worse."

"I think we have to bottom out before we can turn it around."

"Well, we're right on schedule then," Pam said sarcastically.

"No, we all have a few things to let go of first."

"Yeah, well I've got about two quarts of good blood left, if that's what you mean."

Linda faced the onslaught of this anger with a gentleness that absorbed it like a sponge. "It seems the process is intent on stripping us of all our 'knowns,' from our physical identity to our mental framework until we are left naked and alone facing the great unknown before us." Linda picked up her friend's robe and now held it open for her. "Clinging to the past, to our old selves, to our outmoded ways of thinking and feeling, is what's killing us, not the process."

As Linda spoke, Pam found herself slowly sinking deeper into the tub of ice until only her head showed. Yet the truth of these words were able to penetrate that icy barrier. She had been clinging, Pam had to admit, and quite desperately, to what she had always considered an ironclad identity. Yet it was one this process could so easily undermine. Since she still felt a sense of self, it made her wonder where her true identity lay. If this identity were not composed of all the givens in her life, from social position and religious beliefs to political ideology, could it somehow be connected to this "image?" Pam had to wonder if giving herself over to it was a form of surrender or reacquisition?

Either way it meant trusting a process she could never control. And that was the big issue here. Could she just let go and allow herself to be swept away? Pam arose from her icy bath and climbed out of the tub. She stood naked on the tile floor as the water streamed off her now shortened body and ran down a nearby drain. Linda stepped over and helped her friend on with her robe, and the two of them walked out of the therapy room together.

**2.**

The three men were sitting next to the two-way mirror looking into the interview room where a hypnotist, Dr. Aaron Grossman, had put the salesman into a trance and had just completed his preliminary questioning. Joyner now turned to Barry Hamilton. "And what exactly is this supposed to prove?"

"Well, just wait until you hear this, and you tell me," Hamilton said somewhat dubiously, and then glanced at Dr. Kellgren hunched over in his seat, looking like a wizened old gremlin.

Dr. Grossman now cleared his throat, took a drink of water, and proceeded. "Charlie, that morning, Friday, September 6, you are driving up Pacific Coast Highway. It is five o'clock. Please tell us what happened next."

Charlie Bonner, the salesman, stretched out on the reclining chair, now drew his arms in closer to his body. "Well, the fog has been rising now for the last couple hours, and the visibility is next to nothing. I'm looking for a roadside diner to pull over and catch a few hours of sleep until the road clears.

"That's when I see this one headlight parked on the other side of the road. I figure the guy's having car trouble, so I pull off and stop flush with what should be his bumper. But there isn't one. And now I see the light is too high for a headlight."

Bonner's voice began to quiver with strain. "This is where it gets strange. I start to hear this voice in my head, like somebody turned on a radio in there. The voice says that by stopping to help what I assumed was a stranded motorist, I have shown the compassion necessary to carry through an important mission. They would like me to work with them on an experiment that could have a great beneficial effect on my race." Charlie's breathing had become labored and his fear more evident. "I start to ask who 'them' is, and what this experiment is about, but I don't really want to know. I just want to get out of there."

"But you feel," Grossman interjected, "that you are communicating with an alien intelligence?"

"It sure the hell isn't a Xerox salesman," Charlie said, trying to laugh but coming out with highpitched squeals instead. "The voice says it's my choice, but if I refuse to help them, no further contact would be made and all possible benefit to mankind lost. Now that puts me on the spot. I mean, what if they have the cure for cancer or something, but we lose it if I don't play along with them?"

There was a long pause, and after a moment, Dr. Grossman said, "What's going on now, Charlie?"

"I'm thinking about it," the salesman said curtly, and then after a long pause, "I ask them what would I have to do anyway, and they say nothing at all. But, if I'm right in the middle of what's going on, I'll have to do something. The voice says I'll be unconscious the whole time and won't remember a thing. One of them will inhabit my body for several days and do what's needed, while I'm asleep. I ask if it's safe. And they say they do it all the time." There was another long pause. "When you think about it, that's probably the best way. What I don't know can't scare me shitless. So I say, what the hell, do it."

"And the next thing you remember it's two days later, and you're sitting in your car in Sausalito?" Dr. Grossman asked.

"Yeah, and hung over to boot."

"That's very good, Charlie. Now I want you to lie back in your chair and relax." Grossman turned to the two-way mirror. "Essentially that's the same story I've been getting from the start."

Dr. Joyner's voice now came over the speaker box. "Could he

have made it all up, doctor?"

"I seriously doubt that," Dr. Grossman said, somewhat irritated by the question. "I've been working with him for a week now, ran him through a dozen tests, and he checks out perfectly. He's not lying; he's telling us exactly what he experienced, and I'll stake my professional reputation on it."

There was a long pause on the other end, and the sarcasm now evident in Joyner's voice indicated what he thought of the man's professional opinion. "Isn't it true, doctor," he said with particular emphasis, "that a drug-induced hallucination, when recalled under hypnosis, can sometimes be mistaken by the patient for a real experience?"

Dr. Grossman put his fingers to his temples and started to massage them. "There have been some studies that suggested as much," he said with a voice quivering with emotion, "but nothing really conclusive. And besides, there's no indication of drug use, only alcohol, and that's even less likely to cause such a misreading of events."

In the other room Joyner put his hand over the microphone. "I take it the good doctor has never seen an alky on rampage." Hamilton nodded his head but with less conviction. Joyner now turned back and addressed the hypnotist. "Dr. Grossman, I want to thank you for all your time and effort. Please send us a bill for your services, and it'll be promptly paid."

Hamilton now reached over and took the microphone. "And doctor, don't forget you've signed a nondisclosure agreement, which we take very seriously." Dr. Grossman shook his head in mild amusement, when Hamilton added, "Before you leave, the deputy standing outside has been instructed to search your briefcase." Grossman looked back at them. "As if anybody would believe this story to begin with."

Dr. Grossman now proceeded to bring him out of his trance. The three men pushed their chairs back from the mirror and stood up. Hamilton looked around at the two doctors. "So what do you think?"

Joyner stood there for a moment, his arms folded across his

chest, his chin resting in the upturned palm of his hand, as he thought about it. "We know so little about the mind, especially one under the influence of drugs or alcohol, to take such a recital at face value. I mean, besides being a hallucination, it could be a memory, maybe a scene from an old movie, played back before his eyes as if it were actually happening."

His audience of two was not impressed with this explanation. "Since I've used hypnosis before in my line of work, and generally with good results, it's my feeling that Dr. Grossman could tell the difference," Hamilton said.

"So you want me to believe this story. That our friend here," Joyner nodded at the salesman being escorted out of the next room, "ran into a spacecraft on the way to San Martin one morning. He allowed one of the aliens to inhabit his body, and, in this disguise, then entered the town and passed along a genetically altered virus capable of transforming those infected?"

Dr. Kellgren stared back at Joyner for the longest time, and he finally said, "And it was that simple."

Joyner did not expect a levelheaded assessment from his addlebrained old professor, but to see the hardnosed Barry Hamilton seriously considering it made him think twice. If this were a planned experiment which, given the artificial nature of this "disease," he could not entirely dismiss, why was this scenario any more outlandish?

Seeing Joyner's hesitation, Hamilton added, "Since we've yet to discover the source of the infection, this would tell us where and how the virus was contracted. But, more importantly, that it is a live source capable of another outbreak."

"If one were to believe the salesman's story," Joyner added.

"You have to realize I deal in worst-case scenarios. And if there's any validity to his story, and a threat to the community still exists, then I have to check it out."

"You're not going to pass this along to your people in Sacramento, are you?"

"I'm not sure yet, but what if this is true and these aliens are just fine-tuning their methods?" Hamilton now turned to Dr.

Kellgren. "Or what if these patients somehow pull through and turn into. . . ?"

"Homo electrus," Kellgren said, smiling back mischievously.

"Right," Hamilton said, shaking his head. "Either way, somebody is going to want to know why they heard it first on the six o'clock news."

"And what do you think they'll do about it?" Kellgren asked with concern.

"Well, the higher it goes, the worse it's going to get."

And the more control, Joyner thought to himself, that he would lose. He stepped over to the mirror and looked into the now deserted interview room. Also, the less likely that his patients would receive the needed care and attention. In fact, there were people in Washington capable of just locking them away in a dark hole someplace until they were all dead. He was horrified at that prospect. If he could not cure them, Joyner decided, he would rather see this supposed experiment succeed and have his patients transformed into a life form "alien" to him and his race.

Dr. Joyner turned back to Barry Hamilton. "Frankly, Hamilton, with only the salesman's story to go on, I think they would laugh you out of the department at this point. In time, with further research, my team might be able to corroborate this claim with some hard evidence."

Hamilton thought about this for a moment while Kellgren looked on in surprise. He knew his former pupil too well to accept this explanation. It made him wonder about Joyner's real motives.

"Believe me," Hamilton finally conceded, "I'm in no hurry to air this story."

"Well, if this helps," Dr. Kellgren added rather slyly. "As long as we keep this experiment going, our 'friends' won't need to try it elsewhere, giving you more time to build your case."

Joyner had to turn back to the two-way mirror to hide his smirking grin. So Max figured it out, he thought. He will definitely need his help trying to understand the nature of this experiment, if indeed there were one, and how to push to its completion. With his back still turned, Dr. Joyner said, "Why don't we look in on the Owens boy?"

## 3.

After seeing Jennifer's rapidly deteriorating condition, Linda decided to visit Carl before his condition worsened. She had never actually met him, seeing him for the first time in her doctor's office months earlier, but she had heard from Jennifer that he was the first among them to recognize the true import of the "image" and accept the process. Linda was hoping to find in him the kind of ministering angel she had become to the others. She did not have doubts that needed a hearing but sought the reassurance of one equally committed to the same course of action.

Carl was now in the intensive care unit, and when Linda walked into the nurse's station, an orderly sitting behind a corner desk looked up from his paperback novel. Before he could stop her, Linda went over to the window and looked into the dimly lit room next door. There she saw a figure lying on a bed huddled under the covers. She turned back to the orderly. "Is that Carl Owens in there?

"Lady, you supposed to be in here?" he asked as he searched through the top drawer of the desk for his clearance sheet.

"Dr. Joyner said I could see the others when I wanted."

"You got that in writing, because he told the head nurse otherwise."

"You could page him if you like," Linda said staring down the befuddled little man.

That would take more responsibility than he was willing to assume. If he were lucky, he could stall her until the head nurse came back from her break.

Linda now started out the door. "I'm going to go in and talk with him for five mintues."

The orderly stood up to stop her but then decided against it. He did not want to physically restrain her. Although the official word was the freaks were safe to handle, he was not taking any chances. The man sat back down at the desk, picked up his novel, and began to read it.

When Linda stepped into the hospital room, she stood at the door for a moment while her eyes adjusted to the dim light. She wondered if Carl's advanced condition required the low levels. If so, would the onset of such a sensitivity signal her own decline? Linda now walked up to Carl's bed and stood over his covered body for a long moment. There were a number of wires running out from under the covers connected to monitoring devices at the head of the bed. When Carl rolled over on his side, the covers fell away to reveal a body harness that restrained his movements and kept him from pulling the plugs out of the equipment. Linda shuddered at the added pain this must be causing him, and she decided to tell Dr. Joyner her feelings about it.

She reached over and took Carl's outstretched hand as it hung over the side of the bed. And the moment their hands touched, she felt a surge of energy race up her arm and spread throughout her body. It was like sticking her hand in a toaster oven. Carl opened his eyes and looked up at her with total recognition.

"Florence Nightingale, I presume," Carl said in a scratchy voice, then tried to swallow but could not do it. He now pointed to a water pitcher just out of reach on a nearby table. "Could you pour me a glass of water?"

Linda let go of his hand, stepped over and filled the glass. When Carl reached behind himself for his pillow and got tangled up in the wires, Linda came back and propped the pillow up for him. He now scooted up the bed to a sitting position, and she held the glass to his mouth while he sipped from it.

When he finished, Linda placed the half-empty glass on his nightstand and turned back to him. Carl now reached out and took her hand. "After three months in here, I know a nurse when I see one."

"Well, I don't do bedpans," Linda said with mock sternness.

"That's all right. I can't piss worth a damn anyway."

Looking at Carl from close range, Linda could now see how far along his collapse had progressed. By now his face was a mass of jagged edges: his nose a single narrow slit, his mouth a gaping hole, his ears mere flaps of flesh. Only his magnificent eyes seemed to have grown with added intensity while the rest of him withered away. In them, reflected back in pools dark and deep, were the eyes of their "image."

"So, looks pretty hopeless, huh?"

Transfixed by those eyes, Linda absently shook her head. "No, not at all." Slowly she tightened her grip on Carl's hand.

"Oh yeah?" he asked curiously and then searched the face that now bore down on him so intently. In her eyes Carl soon found himself looking back at the all too familiar "image." Now separated, the two halves of this primordial whole sought unity. The energy began to build in slow pulsating surges that rocked their bodies back and forth in its rhythmic embrace. Coursing through them, it absorbed pocket after pocket of blocked energy, adding to its already tumultuous flow. Locked in and interfaced, they had soon become a single integrated circuit of energy. The last thing either one of them remembered was hearing the monitoring alarms go off in the nurse's station before they both lost consciousness.

When Max Kellgren and Guy Joyner, followed closely by Barry Hamilton, walked into the nurse's station, Mrs. Barrows was seated behind her desk. Dr. Kellgren went over to the window to look in on Carl and saw Linda standing beside his bed. He turned back to the nurse. "How long has she been in there?"

Joyner had been checking the monitoring devices against the far wall, but he now stepped over to look for himself. Mrs. Barrows nervously cleared her throat. "She told the orderly you gave her permission."

He shook his head in annoyance. Linda's visiting privileges certainly did not include access to intensive care, and he thought that he had made that clear to her. Mrs. Barrows stood up from her desk. "If you like, I can ask her to leave."

Joyner was about to nod his head, when Kellgren tugged at his shirt sleeve. He turned around and watched the scene developing in the next room. Linda was holding Carl's hand, and the two of them were silently staring into each other's eyes. And then they began to rock back and forth, and even in the dim light, you could see their bodies twitching. "What are they doing?" Joyner asked.

"I believe it's called channeling energy," Kellgren said.

Joyner looked down at the climate control board for the unit and slowly turned up the light level. And the men looked on in utter fascination as their patients danced to the beat of this unheard music. They could almost feel each new surge of energy as it twisted them about. Soon they found themselves as caught up in viewing this spectacle as the patients were in experiencing it. When the first alarm sounded, neither of the scientists could pull himself away. Mrs. Barrows went over and checked the electroencephalograph; it was recording short intense spurts of alpha rhythms that grew shorter with each passing moment.

"Dr. Joyner, I think you'd better see this!" she called out to him. He finally pulled himself away and came over. The alpha state had long been known to induce deep relaxation, welcomed in their condition, but now as their brain rhythms dipped down into theta, and grew more intense, he became worried. If the rhythms went any lower, the two of them might slip into a coma. But, before he could act, alarms started sounding off on the other equipment.

Joyner raced back to the window. "What the hell is going on?"

The two men were staring into Carl's room gaping at the sight before them. As Joyner looked on he saw what appeared to be a spontaneous re-formation of Carl's face to a stage prior to the breakdown of the process. Linda's face was in profile, and despite the light levels, it was hard to tell if she had been as affected by the exchange.

"Dr. Joyner," the nurse called out, "the boy's heartbeat is down to twenty-five, and losing ground fast!"

Joyner turned to Dr. Kellgren. "If we don't stop this soon, it could kill both of them."

Kellgren nodded his head in agreement, and the two men raced out of the nurse's station and into Carl's room. They went up to their patients and could now see that Linda had experienced some re-formation herself, if not to the extent of Carl's. And as they looked on, little aftershocks of change were rippling across their faces.

"We better do something before they get hit with another surge," Joyner said, looking to Dr. Kellgren for a suggestion.

"We've got to break the circuit," Kellgren said, and indicated that Joyner should grab hold of Carl's wrist and he would do the same with Linda's, and for both of them to try pulling their hands apart.

Joyner hesitated for a moment, but with the alarms continuing to ring, he overcame his fear. He grabbed hold as instructed and pulled. Both men were hit by a jolt of electricity that knocked them three feet back. But they had pulled the two patients apart, quieting the alarms. Carl slumped down into his waterbed; Linda fell backwards into Kellgren's arms. He sat her in a nearby chair, and she slowly revived. The two men now took a closer look at their patients, and they were astounded by the extent of this re-formation. It went far beyond their science's ability to remedy. Dr. Kellgren looked at Joyner, their eyes met, as they silently asked each other if further "channelings" might bring more progress. From the other room, Barry Hamilton continued to view the patients as he considered the same possibility.

## Sacramento, California
## January 9

### 4.

Henry Bilford, secretary of health services for the state of California, sat behind an imposing oak desk with Barry Hamilton seated across from him. In his early fifties, he was a big man who dressed casually, spoke plainly, and felt more comfortable in party caucuses than in roaming the halls of the state capitol. He was a career politician as interested in the welfare of his sponsor, the governor, as in that of the good citizens of California. To assure the proper execution of his duties, Bilford was backed up by a superb team of administrators and technical experts. While he waited for his chief analyst to join them, Bilford nervously drummed his fingers on his desk. The intercom now buzzed, and he reached over and pressed the call button.

"Jerome's here," his secretary said.

"Go ahead and send him in." Bilford looked over at Hamilton, trying to gauge his reaction. He could see his top field agent was less than enthusiastic. "I'm letting Jerome sit in on this," he finally said with a conciliatory smile.

Hamilton nodded his head, as the door to the office opened. Jerome Hall, preppie to the hilt, now stepped in and came over to them. Hamilton stood up, and the two men shook hands.

Hall held up his rival's report. "Good work, Hamilton," he said, as he took his seat and turned to Bilford. "But, if we don't watch it, things could get out of hand quickly."

"How so?" Bilford asked, sitting back in his chair and folding his hands under his chin.

"Until now, Dr. Joyner has certainly lived up to his reputation. In record time he determined this was not a viral cancer epidemic, and that the resulting disease posed no threat to the general population. This early assessment quashed plans for a premature quarantine of the area that would have most certainly become an embarrassment to this office."

"Maybe we could cool his heels with a citation from the governor," Bilford said to the polite but condescending smile of his assistant.

"We all agree that he's done an admirable job, but it's over. The disease will die out with the last patient, and any remaining threat will be removed." Hall now looked over at Hamilton. "To switch his efforts at this point from the containment to the enhancement of this 'process,' as you call it, is not only ill-advised, it's damned irresponsible."

"That's a little strong, isn't it? I mean he's just trying to save lives, and he is the expert . . . remember," Hamilton said pointedly.

"'Herr Doctor,'" Hall said with a German accent, "I believe they call him in certain scientific circles." Hall now took out his notorious fingernail file and started filing his nails. "He may indeed be the expert, but he's working for us and our top priority is the public's welfare, which is not being served here."

Bilford nodded his head in complete agreement, then turned to his agent. "Jerome's right. Tell Joyner to wrap it up, or we'll bring someone in to do it for him."

"And if he refuses?"

"I'll have the National Guard deliver my next request," Bilford said and looked over at Jerome, who seemed impressed with his boss's tough stand.

"Henry, we're dealing with someone with a lot of clout. He's not going to be so easily intimidated. And what if he decides to go public with an appeal to save the 'freaks'?"

Before Bilford could respond or ask Hall's opinion, his assistant spoke up. "Look Barry, nobody wants to deny these patients the best possible medical care. I mean, didn't we bring Joyner in?" He now tossed his report onto his boss's desk. "And besides, I seriously doubt this approach would work anyway. It sounds like a bunch of mysterical crap to me, and I'm sure Joyner's colleagues would think much the same," Hall said. "No, the last thing our friend wants at this point is to go public." He reached over and picked up the before-and-after photographs of Carl Owens. "But, if this cockeyed approach held out any real hope, it would be all the more reason to shut him down now."

Hamilton looked back and forth from Jerome Hall to Bilford and got the implied message in this last statement. They wanted these freaks dead and buried to prevent any possible future outbreak of this hideous disease. At least he knew where they stood.

Hall now picked up the pack of polaroid snapshots and thumbed through them. "I still find it hard to believe that a viral package of only a dozen genes could trigger such a drastic process," Hall said shaking his head. "I know something about genetics, and that's an absolutely astounding feat." Hall now stared intently at Barry Hamilton, wondering if he was withholding any information from them. "And to think this virus just, to quote Joyner, 'picked these genes up along the way.'"

Hamilton did not know enough about the subject to argue with this technocrat, but he had to admit that the man's instincts were uncanny. Using his foot, he now pushed the briefcase containing the salesman's tape further under Bilford's desk.

When Barry Hamilton walked into his office, his secretary, wearing headphones, was typing out one of a slew of dictated letters he had brought back with him from the field. He went over to her desk and opened the left top drawer where she kept the manila envelopes.

"What're you looking for?" Rhonda asked, pulling her headphones down around her neck.

"Got it," he said, as he yanked a 9 X 12 envelope free. Before Rhonda could volunteer her services, he turned around and walked back to his office closing the door behind him.

Inside Hamilton took a red felt pen out of his pencil holder and wrote across the front of the envelope: FOR HENRY BILFORD: Personal and Confidential. He now took the salesman's tape recording out of his briefcase and placed it in the envelope. He licked and sealed the flap and then taped over it. Hamilton walked around, opened the top drawer of his desk and laid the manila envelope inside. He next closed and locked it.

Hamilton sat on the edge of his desk flipping the key up and down in his right hand. He knew that withholding this information was a serious breach of policy that, and even if he disclosed it later, would no doubt lead to his dismissal. Hall would insist on it and then hire one of his cronies to replace him. And it would be impossible for him to find similar work elsewhere. This was a fateful decision, and Hamilton knew it. Yet, as he had asked himself repeatedly in the last few days, he still did not know why he was sacrificing his career to help them. Joyner's ploy to hold out for more evidence was exactly that: an excuse. It was only after seeing the partial re-formation of the two patients that he realized there might still be some hope for them. But that was not his real reason.

Slowly, almost imperceptibly, Hamilton was beginning to realize that, despite himself, he believed the salesman's story. Admitting that and acknowledging it as the reason for his present action brought a welcome relief. Charlie Bonner's recollection under hypnosis was believable, and he had seen enough hypnosis sessions to know when someone was faking it. But it was the great difference between the man photographed earlier and his double that really convinced him. He now opened his briefcase, took out the salesman's photograph and studied it for the hundredth time in the last two days.

It was obvious that outside of their physical resemblance

these were two totally different people. From the cast of his body to the tilt of his head, the man in the photograph exuded a tremendous sense of power, even when he underplayed it. Whereas the salesman, despite a certain down-at-the-heels charm, was a walking wreck. But the telltale difference was in their eyes. One pair were so hypnotic you had to fight them off, while the other looked like those of a tired bloodhound. And this was no mere change of personality, but the replacement of one with another. Were they different facets of the same person? He doubted it. Only the salesman's bizarre story could explain everything else that had happened convincingly.

With this acceptance also came a belief that ultimately the purpose of their coming here and the true nature of the experiment were benign. The patients' present condition seemed to belie that optimism, but as Max Kellgren had pointed out, that could merely be a stage. But they would never find out if he did not choose to cooperate with them. And that was what struck him the most about the salesman's story: this enormous venture hinged on one man's faith. Could each step along the way require the repeated acceptance of others? Maybe everybody from the doctors to the patients to the townspeople were part of some grand design. Well, either way, he would pay the price for his cooperation, and he wondered if the others when called upon would do the same.

Hamilton walked out of his office, closing the door behind him. He went over to his secretary, who had spun around in her chair at his approach. "Rhonda, I've left a manila envelope in my top desk drawer, addressed to one of your favorite people." He waited to see if she understood whom he was talking about. He then handed her the key to his desk. "I might ask you to deliver it for me at some point, and I just wanted you to know where it is."

With Barry's sad expression, Rhonda assumed the worst. "Am I going to see you again?" she asked, visibly upset.

"You'll see me again," Hamilton said reassuringly, then leaned over and kissed his longtime secretary on the forehead. "It just might not be in these hallowed halls." He walked out leaving

Rhonda dabbing her wet cheeks with a handkerchief.

## 5.

After the "exchange" between Linda and Carl resulting in their partial recovery, Dr. Joyner had extensive blood work done on both of them. It showed high blood levels of an unusual sugar, seen in small amounts in all the patients. And as expected there were also elevated levels of the new enzymes associated with the process. Wondering if there was any connection between the two, they ran tests on the production of one of the new enzymes in the presence of the blood sugar and another in its absence, and they discovered a key mechanism in the transformative process. It helped to explain why the system seemed to be failing and offered hope for a remedy.

The blood sugar was an inducer, a substance that could accelerate as much as one thousand times the production level of certain enzymes. In this case it seemed to trigger all the new enzymes produced by the physical transformation. It accomplished this amazing feat by binding to the repressor molecules that normally blocked their synthesis. So, in the absence of the blood sugar, key biological processes under the negative control of these repressors were inactive. The problem, as they now saw it, was that as the process drained the body of its energy reserves and phased out its food processing plant, production of the needed inducer fell to a level that eventually closed down the process itself.

One obvious solution was synthesizing large amounts of the inducer and injecting them into the patient's blood. However, at this point, with such low blood levels and with the other body systems nearly inoperative, there would not be enough backup support to prime the process. Also, since the enzymes would be largely unused, their buildup would soon trigger the process of feedback inhibition resulting in the shutdown of further production. What was needed was large amounts of readily available energy to activate the entire system. The channeling of energy by his two patients seemed to have done just that. It appeared, as far as they could tell, that the unfinished electrical-based system was able to process and convert enough of this energy to produce the desired results.

Unfortunately, the effects of this one-shot charge of energy were beginning to wear off. Every day Joyner could see his two patients losing ground: a prominent cheek bone falling down, a little finger hanging loose, a chin receding. The scientists calculated that the "channeling" had pushed back a still inevitable collapse by two weeks or so. Yet there was hope of future gains if they could better understand this phenomenon. They needed to know the power of this channeled energy: would a longer session have a proportionate effect or even greater, or were there limits; how much energy could the patients take at one time; would smaller multiple exposures have the same effect as a massive dose? To answer these questions, Joyner had set up a controlled link-up experiment between Linda and Carl that afternoon.

In the laboratory the two scientists now watched as Andrea Hunter ran a new program on her terminal screen. Here they saw an outline of two human bodies. At points corresponding to organs and major body systems, numerical counters were running off numbers at an amazing speed. These organs now began to change, evolve into the new electrical-based system. It progressed at a different rate for each body as the counters stopped on the left one first. They waited in silence until the other system completed itself.

Dr. Hunter swiveled around on her chair and looked up at the two scientists. "This is my estimate on how much energy would be needed to prime these body systems to the point where production levels of the needed inducer can push the process to its completion."

"But I wouldn't be a bit surprised, if we see some kind of leveling effect as distribution of the generated energy gets allocated by demand," Kellgren said.

Hunter looked to him for an explanation. "By linking them

up via a blood line," he insisted, "we create one single dissipative structure, more complex and interactive than either by itself. And one that would require less energy to perturb it."

She now turned to Dr. Joyner. "Do you agree with him?"

"Well, according to Prigogine's theory, if I remember correctly, the more complex the structure, the more energy it needs to maintain its connections."

"Yes, but we don't want to maintain them," Dr. Kellgren said, "we want to rearrange them, shake the system up, allow it to reorder itself. Which is what the process has been doing from the start."

"Either way, it all depends on the amount of energy this channeling can generate," Joyner said. "Andrea, were you able to figure out how much it took to reform them last time?"

"A rough estimate that, if applied here, wouldn't hold out much hope for completing it," she said. "But that was only a brief exposure, not a true test. For all we know, the charge could increase a hundredfold once it passed a certain point."

The console phone rang, and Hunter answered it. She listened to the caller for a moment before she put her hand over the receiver. "It's Dr. Whitehouse. He wants to know where you're at. Sounds like he's getting cold feet."

Dr. Joyner turned to Kellgren. "We better get down there, and get started." He nodded his head, and the two men turned and walked out of the laboratory. They headed down the hallway for the operating room at the far end.

Finally, after further thought, Joyner said, "What I can't understand, is if you're going to engineer a process that transforms a body system, why would you build in such an interactive dependency?"

"Maybe we've been so caught up in our little discovery, charting its genetic wonders, that we've failed to see the real implications here," Kellgren said, coming to a stop, as Joyner walked past him and had to turn around. "What if this experiment wasn't set up to test whether they could transform single biological units, but if we would, as a race, cooperate in the transformation of the species as a whole?"

"You mean our participation could be as vital as the patients'?" Joyner asked.

"Maybe they can only take it as far as we are willing to go ourselves." Dr. Kellgren started walking again, anxious to get on with it. "What an elegant experiment," he said in astonishment. He now turned to Joyner. "I would definitely like to talk with these beings."

Joyner could only shake his head at such an outrageous prospect, and he was relieved to have finally arrived at the operating room. He pushed the doors open and went inside as Kellgren followed after him.

Dr. Whitehouse, the head of surgery at the hospital, a tall thin, high-strung man always perturbed about something, was adjusting the valves on the blood circulating machine to be used in the experiment. When Max Kellgren and Dr. Joyner walked in and came over to him, he gave them a highly skeptical look. "And I suppose you're going to tell me the computer program checks out?"

"Well, it shows good prospects for more gains," Joyner said, alarmed by the man's great agitation, "but just how much we can't tell."

Whitehouse could only shake his head in disgust. "Nobody has ever done anything remotely like it before, not to mention the splendid condition of our two patients." He now turned back to work on the machine. "But the figures add up."

Dr. Joyner waited for a lull in this sea of agitation, then asked, "Are the two patients ready?"

"They're bringing them down now," Whitehouse said curtly.

Joyner looked back at Kellgren, and the two men exchanged worried looks of concern. The surgeon's cooperation was essential if they hoped to proceed with this line of therapy against mounting opposition.

While Carl waited to be taken away, his parents, who had come to witness the experiment, stopped in to wish him well.

This was only the third time in the course of his long hospital stay that they had visited. He knew how hard his illness was on them, and so he had encouraged them to stay away. They had lost him to the road for five years, only to have him return and die a horrible death before their eyes. It seemed to suck the very life out of them; both had aged ten years in the last three months.

Matt Owens stood at the foot of his son's bed nervously twirling his key ring. His eyes were cast down, studying the dot pattern in the linoleum floor. When he looked up, he could only glance briefly at Carl before turning away. The sight of him was too harrowing to endure much longer. Just being in the same room with him made the palms of his hands sweat. He hated reacting this way; the boy was his own flesh and blood, but there was also a part of him, growing stronger each day, that was a stranger to him.

Wilma Owens was sitting at her son's side holding his hand. Looking at him was as hard for her as for her husband, but she saw through the horrible mask to the beautiful little boy he once was. "Dr. Joyner told me what they planned, but I couldn't make any sense out of it." Wilma now turned around to her husband. "Did you understand him?"

"Nope," he said with his eyes still cast down.

Carl explained, "This genetic change has closed down our food processing plant, so we're slowly starving to death. But they've discovered the new system can use the kind of etheric energy generated by prayer or meditation to feed itself, and that's what we're trying to create."

Wilma thought this over. "Well, if that's what it lives on, you're becoming angels not monsters."

Carl broke into a craggy smile, delighted with his mother's description. Matt looked up and stared at his son hoping to see some sign of it. The boy looked more devilish than angelic at this point, but then his appearance could change. He now decided that he had been unfair, out of fear and prejudice, and he would give this process more time to show its true face.

Matt Owens was standing there looking down at his son

when the orderlies came in. They quickly unplugged Carl from the monitoring equipment, and moved him to a wheelchair for the ride down to the first floor operating room. Wilma now leaned over and kissed him on the forehead, and Matt surprised himself by reaching out at the last moment and grasping hold of Carl's hand. "Hang in there, son." Carl looked up at his father, and one last solitary tear from dried-out ducts edged its way down the jagged edges of his face. They now took him away, and a woman in a candy-striped dress offered to escort Matt and Wilma to OR1's viewing gallery.

When they wheeled Carl into the operating room, he saw Linda sitting in a wheelchair being hooked up to a machine. The orderly steered him over and stopped right in front of her. A nurse stuck an IV into his arm and plugged it into the circulating machine. Dr. Whitehouse now ran a couple of tests to see if the system was working correctly.

While they waited, the two patients looked across at each other. "Do you have this straight?" Carl asked.

"We sit here holding hands and meditate," Linda said nonchalantly. "I do it all the time."

"Must save on electricity," Carl said.

Whitehouse finished up just as Barry Hamilton walked into the room. He set the machine on ready, then went over to the man. "So what's the official word?"

Hamilton looked around at the three men. "That you haven't shown enough justification for such an unorthodox experiment, and to cease and desist."

Dr. Whitehouse was greatly relieved by this pronouncement, but when Hamilton failed to follow through on his orders, he asked, "And so?"

"And so what in the hell do they know anyway," Hamilton said, and he made a gesture with his hand for them to proceed. Dr. Whitehouse was furious with him, but looking around the room and seeing little support for his position, he turned and walked out of the operating room in a huff.

Joyner looked over at his two patients, who now joined

hands, then he stepped over and flipped the switch on the circulating machine. The pump whirled into action with the clicky-click of its rotating disk drawing blood from the patients into the lines. He waited until he was assured of the machine's smooth operation before joining the others in the monitoring booth. There were a half-dozen specialists from as many fields viewing the experiment. All were close personal friends of Joyner, who were willing to risk censure from the scientific community to participate in what promised to be an historic experiment. Joyner now signaled for the cameraman to start filming the scene.

Five minutes into the experiment they witnessed the first spontaneous re-formations. The sunken left side of Carl's face pushed outward into a more defined angularity developed just prior to the breakdown of the process. In Linda the back of her head expanded into a larger cranial cavity. And they were both experiencing ripples of small changes, such as the color of their eyes. The scientists looking on were astounded by physiological changes taking place at rates a thousand times faster than even fetal development. In fact they were so captivated nobody had even bothered to check their instruments. They realized that the data recorded there would not convince anybody who had not seen it themselves.

In the operating room the exchange of energy between Linda and Carl was now rocking them back and forth in their wheelchairs. Each new surge was experienced in the body as a series of felt shifts slowly building in intensity until they exploded in the brain, firing off synapse after synapse. You could see the patients' eyes blinking, even when closed, their heads bobbing up and down to the beat of this orgasmic dance. And with each surge the image seen in their minds' eyes grew, re-forming them in its likeness once again. By now the rocking had stopped. They were one with the energy and offered no resistance to its flow.

In the viewing gallery the patients, their friends and their relatives watched in hopeful anticipation. As the process pushed past its previous limits, Linda and Carl began to shed their ugly malformed appearance. In its place a glimpse, more image than an actual embodiment, of the beings struggling to emerge could be seen. There was a collective gasp from the audience. Sitting there in the place of these two cretins were what could only be described as angelic beings. Several people broke down crying; the others were equally affected. And then, in a moment, the image evaporated into the mist as the process reached its peak and then reversed itself.

The monitoring devices in the booth began sounding off, and the scientists were forced to turn away from the spectacle to view the data in hope of halting this collapse. They quickly determined that production of the needed blood sugar, the inducer that propelled the process, had stopped. This was due to the diminished influx of energy after it had reached its peak level. What they could not determine was why the energy stopped flowing. After conferring with the others, Dr. Joyner turned to Kellgren. "Max, do you have any idea what happened?"

Kellgren stood in silence for a moment watching the two patients slowly being re-formed. It was now apparent that the collapse did not follow the previous line of development; it also looked as if the patients had leveled out at the same stage. "The integrated structure worked well enough; they were able to absorb more energy together than separately, but still not enough to complete the process."

"Well, if that's the case, then there's nothing we can do right now."

"It doesn't look that way," Kellgren said with disappointment. "But I wouldn't pull the plug yet; I think they'll level out further along than before."

Joyner nodded his head in agreement. The two of them now walked out to the operating room to check on their patients. Linda and Carl opened their eyes at the same time and looked at the scientists. He could see that they were both in a great deal of pain, but there was nothing he could give them to ease their discomfort. It was one of the risks of the experiment.

"If it's any consolation, I think this helped show us what's really needed to push the process to completion," Kellgren said.

Carl smiled. "Well, that's fine. But, we had better do it next time, because this body can't take much more."

"Did we go as far as I think we did?" Linda asked.

Kellgren nodded his head. "Just wait until you see the video."

## 6.

In the street across from the hospital, the Red Cross's bloodmobile had been parked since early morning. There was also one at the main fire station on Butt and at Earl Warren high school, but this particular converted RV unit, because of its location, had attracted the largest crowd. A sign posted on the side of the vehicle declared that large amounts of blood were needed for an operation that would hopefully save the lives of the local residents afflicted with the strange genetic malady. Some townspeople, upon reading the announcement, just walked away shaking their heads in disgust. However, the great majority of them stepped into the long line to give blood.

Paul Jordan, the school principal, was told of the blood drive halfway through the week, and he now pulled up to the hospital in a mini-bus filled with his neighbors. It had not been hard convincing his friends to donate the much-needed blood. Since the first experiment a week earlier, word had spread through town about the spectacle witnessed by those in the viewing gallery and the promise it held out to the patients. For Jordan it was also an opportunity to redeem himself. Earlier, acting out of fear, he had shunned Linda and acceded to her unjust dismissal from school. It had weighed heavily on him. She was not only an old, dear friend of his, a former pupil and a respected colleague, but she was deathly ill. The disease that afflicted her and frightened him and the others must have been a thousand times more terrifying to her. Yet all he considered was his own miserable skin. Jordan hoped there was still time to save his friend and reclaim his self-respect.

He led his neighbors to the back of the line, and then Jordan headed for the crowd gathered around the notice to talk more of them into donating blood. Walking along he caught the eye of old-time friends like the grocer Hugh Clarke and his wife Naomi, Mike the Butcher, Paco and his son Jose, who looked away feeling guilty about their past treatment of the patients. A yellow school bus now pulled up, and Reverend Taylor stepped off followed by members of his church choir. When he passed Jordan heading the other way, the minister stopped to talk.

"Looks like a good turnout, Paul."

"Certainly does, Reverend. And I've heard the other two are doing nearly as well."

Taylor raised his eyebrows, truly impressed with the townspeople's response. These were good decent people, understandably scared by the specter of this dread disease, but also capable as they had now shown of rising to the occasion. "Well, don't let them leave until after Joyner's conference, cause you've got a lot of people in there who'll want to give." Jordan made a mental note of it, as Reverend Taylor crossed the street and headed up the stairs into the hospital.

In the main auditorium, the patients and about a hundred concerned relatives and close friends had gathered to hear the results of the first link-up experiment. Many of them had been there and recognized, despite its apparent failure, the real possibility of this unorthodox approach. On the stage, Dr. Joyner now stepped up to the podium. "If everybody will take a seat, we'll get on with this." Kellgren was talking with Dr. Hunter at the side entrance and now hurried back to his seat.

"I think we have some very good news for everybody. The link-up experiment between Linda and Carl, while it didn't push them into full transformation, did show great potential for doing just that. The problem as we see it has more to do with creating a structure, in this case a greater link-up of patients, capable of absorbing enough energy to propel the process further along. But that is, if the other two important elements not under our control: the source of energy, which appears unlimited, and the new system's ability to process this energy, perform to our expectations."

Joyner now turned around and motioned for Kellgren to step forward. "Since it was Dr. Kellgren who first recognized the importance of this link-up structure, I'm going to let him explain what we have in mind. But, let me add, that in my judgement, it represents your best and possibly only hope for survival."

Kellgren took the microphone from Joyner, who went back to his seat behind the podium and sat down. "I know how much all of you have been through, and I would hate to create false hopes, but I'm convinced that such a link-up will succeed. Computer analysis tells us that the earlier attempt pushed Linda and Carl right up to the brink before their circuits were overloaded. What is needed is an even more complex integrated structure formed by no less than twenty-five of the thirty patients. Such a dissipative structure would be able to absorb the needed energy, but by being more complex, it would also be more unstable and easier to shake up and send into full transformation."

Kellgren waited a moment to allow his audience to absorb this complex explanation. "But, I must add, it will take a link-up of at least that many of you to have any hope of succeeding. It appears that nobody can make it unless most of you try."

The implication of this statement was not lost on his audience. The patients looked around at each other; those for the experiment watched those against it for any change of heart. Dr. Kellgren sensed the nature of their conflict and sought to allay the fears of those afraid of what they might become.

"A question I'm sure everybody is asking themselves is what form would the transformation take? We assume you'd become the image in your so-called visions. Although the genes precipitating the change are unknown to us, basically they are rearranging what is already there, if latent, in our genetic structure. Therefore the result is most certainly of human origin, although you would be as dissimilar to us as we are to the chimpanzee, whose genetic makeup is quite similar to our own."

Kellgren paused before delivering his summation. "No

doubt this represents an extraordinary evolutionary leap. In the past, subspecies developed in response to environmental shifts, requiring new adaptive modes of behavior eventually resulting in physiological change. In your case, the shift is more of a psychospiritual nature, and as this experiment proved, so is your adaptation. I believe you are the first to respond to a shift in the collective consciousness of the race, one that will soon affect all humanity, and by accepting this change you may make the transition to this new subspecies possible for the rest of us."

The next afternoon Reverend Taylor led a procession of townspeople to the sacred caves in the mountains behind the city. He had told them the history of the caves and described the tribe who had once inhabited them. Also, he explained that the patients had been seeing an image which was discovered on the walls of these caves, engraved there some ten thousand years ago. However, they were still unprepared for the eerie strangeness of the caves, the drawings on the walls and the culture they depicted, and the haunting image now staring down at them from the slanted walls of the inner temple. The people of San Martin had gathered to pray to this unknown God, to beseech him to spare their brethren from this awful affliction, and, if not to restore them to their former lives, to guide them through this passage to the new ones that awaited them.

Although few of the townspeople would at first acknowledge the existence of any but their own God, they could not deny this miraculous visitation here in their town. To accept it, whatever it may be, and to allow those who followed it their truth, had affected them in a strange, wonderful way. It seemed to open closed-off parts of themselves, to call forth their greater half. As a consequence they were willing to accept more of the world's great multiplicity. This included the God of this ancient people, and it allowed them now to pray to it for the deliverance of their family and friends.

Reverend Taylor now began his invocation. "We humbly beseech thee, O Great Spirit, God of this lost race of men, who hath appeared again for reasons only known to thee, whose image now burns bright in the minds of the afflicted among us, to have mercy on them. We know not what designs thou hast for them, but they have suffered much and now cling to life by the thinnest margin. If it is within your power, as we do believe, to release them from this great travail, we implore you to return them to their former health and well-being or to speed the transition to the greater lives that await them. For this we now pray."

The minister knelt down on the hard clay floor of the cave and looked up into the harsh eyes staring down at him and offered a silent prayer. The others followed after him, and each searched their hearts for the words that best expressed their own personal supplication. Some wished to have their loved ones returned as they once were, others would have them transformed into the beatific beings seen earlier, but all prayed for a quick resolution that would alleviate their present torment. In time the outpouring of these feelings, directed upward at the image, focused and intensified by the pyramid-shaped room, began to have an effect. Reverend Taylor was the first to notice it, and then a rush of excitement spread through the gathering. Those huge cold eyes began to soften, other features slowly took form, until they now looked up into an angelic face. Tears welled up in those sorrowful eyes and began to flow down the side of the wall forming a pool at its base.

For Reverend Taylor the only way to explain this phenomenon was to call it a miracle. What else could account for this drawing coming to life and crying real tears? In itself it shattered a worldview in which such things just were not possible. And if drawings could cry, he now thought, why could not humans be transformed into angels? Taylor stood up, walked over to the wall, bent over and dipped his finger into the pool of tears. It had an unexpected sweet taste that spread through his body and seemed to envelope him. And it left him with a wonderful feeling of total well-being. He now dipped his hands into the pool, drew the waters up and poured them over his head.

## 7.

With the full link-up experiment set for the next day, Guy Joyner had been busy overseeing the final preparations. One last minute problem was how to feed the extra blood supply to the patients without interrupting the flow by replacing bottles every few minutes. The blood was needed for the greatly accelerated biological response to the transformational process. This would include increased production of the inducer and the new enzymes, and it would create an added load of byproducts the patients' impaired kidneys and livers could never filter out without it. Working with an engineer, they designed a makeshift system using a water pump to draw blood from a central supply and still feed it to each patient individually. Dr. Joyner had already determined that, due to the patients' altered body chemistries, their differing blood types were now fully interchangeable.

After a successful test of the system, and when all the new monitoring equipment checked out, Joyner left Ken Olson to finish the preparations and headed back to the laboratory. It was early evening, and the halls of the hospital were fairly deserted. And he was able to walk along lost in thought without interruption. Dr. Joyner had been so caught up in the events of the last few weeks that he had little time to consider the implications of this breakthrough for his work and for genetics in general. It had always been his dream that one day, if not in his lifetime then in the near future, the tools of this powerful science could be used to "remodel" the human species. He would like to see more altruistic, cooperative, less competitive traits enhanced at the expense of those aggressive tendencies that had wreaked so much havoc on society in the past.

Joyner was among those modern scientists who felt that changing the behavioral foundation developed over our long evolution was critical enough for our survival to justify such a drastic intervention. And although their science was still decades away from the needed technology, recent research indicated that behavioral patterns did indeed have a genetic basis and thus could be open to modification. Geneticists working with the sea slug Aplysia had discovered that its stereotyped ritual for laying eggs, made up of seven separate behaviors, is orchestrated by a single gene producing a string of peptides that coordinate this fixed-action pattern. In this way complicated behavioral repertoires in animals as well as in humans could be built up. If so, replacing the gene could eliminate or greatly modify the unwanted behavior.

Joyner had to admit to himself that, given the events of the past few months, the attitude that man was little more than a combination of genes or the instructions contained therein, mere programs to be manipulated, changed or largely rewritten, was hopelessly inadequate. Among his colleagues he followed the most humanistic approach to his work; his desire to improve the species was a sincere response to the pain and suffering he saw around him. But Joyner now realized that he saw that goal in terms of building bigger and better machines. He thought that if you could only replace the biological basis for such unsavory traits as greed and warring aggression, you could build a more peaceful world. What he was seeing in San Martin, not only in the patients but in the townspeople, himself and the others involved, was the kind of self-transcendence that truly characterized the species and was its best hope not only for survival but for its greater evolvement.

As Joyner was walking through the main lobby, someone leaving the building called out to him. He stopped and stared through the revolving glass doors but could not see who it was. When he turned back, Joyner found himself standing in front of the elevators. The feeling that he would like to talk with Linda suddenly swept over him. The elevator door now opened, and he stepped in and pressed the button for the fourth floor.

When Guy Joyner walked into her room, Linda was sitting up in bed with her eyes closed. At first he thought she might be sleeping, but when he came over to her bed, Linda opened her eyes and looked up at him.

"Are you nervous about tomorrow?" Linda asked.

"Shouldn't I be asking you that?"

"Either way it'll be over for us, but you have to stay behind and dish out the explanations."

"If what I think will happen does," Guy said, "then nothing I say will explain it."

Linda nodded her head in agreement, then stopped and listened as if to a faintly spoken voice. She now turned back to Guy. "They won't believe it unless they see it themselves."

"Well, I saw it and I can hardly believe it."

"But you've conditioned yourself not to see what you don't believe," Linda said half-jokingly.

"Oh yeah," Guy said, almost taking offense before he conceded. "Good old scientific objectivity."

Linda was impressed with Dr. Joyner's new attitude. "And you're that sure about the experiment?"

"If the energy holds out, and we assume it will, then Max Kellgren's system should work just fine."

"You mean we finally agree on something?"

He nodded his head. "Ain't that amazing."

The two of them looked at each other like two barroom fighters who have slugged it out so long neither could remember why they were fighting. Finally, Guy broke the silent contemplation. "I know we haven't been on the best of terms, but I just want to say how much I've come to admire your courage in the face of overwhelming opposition for your stance and against insurmountable odds for your survival. It has helped me to understand that the spirit of man," he said, and then added with a smile, "and woman, is the missing element in the evolution equation."

Linda reached over and took Joyner's hand. "And yet," she said, "it's always been there, working in the background. But as a scientist, representing our objective awareness, your recognition of it will do as much to activate its potential as our acceptance of its influence."

"Oh, it's nice to know we can take part of the credit after all," Guy said facetiously.

"Well, after a slow start, you did finish strong," Linda

countered, then added in a more serious tone, "It seems that our culture, now largely characterized by its scientific approach, has swung so far out of balance it has awakened its counterpart."

"Which is?" Guy asked.

"Those feeling, intuitive qualities that are the truly transformative force at work within ourselves and our society."

Guy thought about that for a long moment. "If so," he said rather sadly, "I'm afraid I've got a long way to go yet."

"You're making progress," Linda said, then smiled mischievously. "But, if you'll give me your other hand, I'll see if I can't jump-start the process."

Guy instinctively stepped back from Linda, but he remained tethered to her by a firmly held hand. Already the energy was moving through this lifeline, breaking down his resistance. He looked back into eyes, dark and deep, from which the image now rose. He stared at it for a moment feeling its irresistible pull, and then he stepped over and extended his other hand to her. When she clasped both of them between hers, it felt like he had placed his hands into a hot oven.

Charlie Bonner, the salesman, had been walking past the unattended nurse's station when he heard the monitoring alarms go off. He stepped inside and walked over to the viewing window. Here he saw Dr. Joyner holding hands with the Boyer woman, rocking back and forth on the heels of his shoes. He assumed she was, in the parlance of the day, channeling energy to him. Charlie smiled. The scientist could definitely use a jolt to loosen him up, he thought.

As he watched, he again heard that faintly spoken voice inside his head. For the last three days, it had been asking permission to once again inhabit his body for a brief period. This time, however, it wanted him to remain conscious in case "they" needed to consult with him. Since the hypnosis sessions with Dr. Grossman, Charlie had gradually begun to recall the strange events of his roadside encounter back in September. But, since that incident had left him with a bad case of the nerves, driving him to drink heavier than ever, he was not too receptive to their latest request.

Another monitoring alarm went off, but since the scientist had his back to him, blocking Charlie's view of Linda, he could not see what was happening to either of them. But it was obvious she was trying to help the one person who had held up this change-over, as some were now calling it, from the start. If his own cooperation, as was indicated, would help her and the others, the least he could do was go along with them one more time.

Bonner walked out of the nurse's station, closing the door behind him. He hoped it would give the two of them more time together. He walked back down the hallway heading for his room at the far end. Everybody was now coming back from their dinner break, but few of the nurses and orderlies paid any attention to the broken-down old drunk. When Bonner reached his room, he stepped inside but stayed there for no more than thirty seconds. The man who now stepped out into the hallway, although he wore the same terrycloth robe and looked exactly the same, carried himself differently. As he walked back down the hall, more people took notice of him. He now opened the door to the stairwell and hurried down two flights of stairs to the second floor. He was heading for the auditorium which had been set up for tomorrow's link-up operation. He needed to look over their equipment and possibly make some fine-tuned adjustments.

# CHAPTER SIX
# TRANSFORMATIONS

*The act or operation*
*of changing the form or external appearance;*
*in genetics, the direct modification of a genome*
*by the external application of DNA*
*from a cell of a different genome.*

## Sacramento, California
## January 23

Jerome Hall was standing at the window in Secretary Bilford's health services office looking down at the mall five stories below. It was lunch time, and the secretaries were taking advantage of the unseasonably warm weather by eating on the park benches surrounding the fountain. Hall absently watched as he nervously pulled at and released his lower lip. Something was bothering him, a nagging suspicion that he could not quite shake. He now looked down at the telegram in his hand and read it for the tenth time:

> JOYNER REFUSES TO QUIT. GOING
> AHEAD WITH EXPERIMENT TOMORROW.
> THREATENS TO GO TO THE PRESS
> IF WE INTERFERE. WAITING
> INSTRUCTIONS.
>
> B.H.

Henry Bilford came into his office wearing casual clothes and gave Hall a very angry look. He had taken the afternoon off to play nine holes of golf while the good weather held, and he was on the verge of beating the state's attorney general, Bill Jeffries, when they flagged him down. Without saying a word, Hall now stepped over and handed his boss the telegram. Bilford read it through twice before looking up.

"A little late to be calling for the cavalry isn't it," Bilford said.

"He's been down there for two weeks without a word, and now this." Hall started pacing the office. "He's been holding out on us, I know it. But I can't figure out what it could be."

"Well, if anybody would know, it's his secretary...what's her name?"

Hall stopped and nodded his head. "Rhonda."

When Hall walked into Hamilton's office, Rhonda was talking on the phone. Seeing him enter, she immediately cut the call short and hung up. Rhonda did not like this pushy, bureaucratic hatchet man, and she was just a little afraid of him.

"Rhonda, when Barry was here last, did he say anything about his assignment in San Martin that might lead you to believe he was holding back something?" Hall watched her carefully, and he was certain from the way she lowered her eyes that Rhonda knew something. "Henry thinks as much, and if it should come out later that you knew, and didn't tell...."

Rhonda shook her head in disgust. If she was not a single mother with two kids to support, she would love to tell Hall where he could shove the key she now took out of her drawer. Rhonda tossed it across the desk at him; it hit once and popped into the air, where he grabbed it.

Hall looked at it for a moment. "And what does this go to?"

Rhonda grabbed her purse and stood up to leave. She now walked around the desk and stopped in front of him. "I'm sure you've got plenty of locked cabinets; you figure it out." She went out the door, leaving him there staring at the key.

Hall took out his key ring and compared keys until he found a match. He walked back to Hamilton's office, entered it and went around to unlock his desk drawer. He retrieved the manila envelope addressed to Henry and opened it. He took out the reel of tape and looked for a letter of explanation but found none. Hall guessed, however, that whatever was on this tape would eliminate one more rival. And he could not wait to hear it.

When he returned to Bilford's office, he played the tape as the two of them listened in stunned silence. Afterwards they looked at each other in partial shock, like two survivors of a plane crash unable to comprehend it all. Finally, the only response either of them could muster was a request by Bilford to play it again.

Hall rewound the tape and played it from the beginning. When it came to the part where the salesman was asked who had stopped him, the two of them leaned over the desk and listened carefully.

> "This is where it gets strange. I start to hear this voice in my head, like somebody turned on a radio in there. The voice says that by stopping to help what I assumed was a stranded motorist, I have shown the compassion necessary to carry through an important mission. They would like me to work with them on an experiment that could have a great beneficial effect on my race. (Long pause) I start to ask who 'them' is, and what this experiment is about, but I don't really want to know. I just want to get out of here."
>
> "But you feel that you are communicating with an alien intelligence?"
>
> "It sure the hell isn't a Xerox salesman."

"I don't believe it," Bilford said, reaching over and flipping off the tape recorder. Hall nodded his head in agreement before Henry clarified his statement. "I mean, how could Barry keep something like this from us?"

Hall smiled. "But you accept what he said about the 'aliens.'"

"Don't quote me," Bilford said, sitting back in his chair, "but I once talked with a brigadier general in the Air Force, who claims we have a hundred-foot-long freezer full of UFO crash victims at a base in New Mexico."

A glazed look passed over Hall's face as he sought to distance himself, as he always did, from a serious consideration of such subjects. They made him uneasy, and yet he could never pinpoint the source of the discomfort and deal with it. So he avoided them or made fun of them and never questioned why.

"Well, I don't believe a word of it, but if Joyner pulls off a miracle and this gets out, it could create one hell of a panic."

"Agreed," Bilford said rather wearily. "You better go down and try to stop him, and I'll get the governor to call out the National Guard and close the whole place off." And then as an afterthought, he said, "And if you see Barry, tell him he's fired."

The decision was made for Hall to wait until morning before flying down to San Martin. That night the governor called out the National Guard, but it would take twelve hours for them to mobilize and head for the city. Since the situation there was still unclear, and they did not know whether the local sheriff could contain it, they decided not to alert the renegade doctor until the Guard was within striking distance.

As Hall flew over San Martin the following morning, it looked peaceful from the air. It was now ten o'clock in the morning, and everything appeared perfectly normal.

Chris Gates, the helicopter pilot, leaned over so his passenger could hear him over the noise. "Where do you want me to set down?"

"On the street in front of the Sheriff's office."

The pilot did a double take, but Hall pointed his finger at the spot two blocks over. Since this was a military operation and Hall was acting on behalf of the governor, Gates followed the orders against his better judgement. He waited until the traffic cleared below him, and then he slowly set his helicopter down on the street to the sound of honking horns.

The Sheriff had stepped out onto the sidewalk when the helicopter first approached and tried in vain to wave them off. Now, as Hall opened the plastic canopy door and stepped out of the passenger's side, Sheriff Howser walked over to the pilot. "Get this thing out of here!" Gates shrugged his shoulders and offered a sheepish smile in apology, and then he slowly lifted his copter until it had cleared the telephone lines, and he could speed away.

Hall stepped up to the Sheriff and extended his hand, but the man declined to shake it. "Sheriff Howser, I'm Jerome Hall from Secretary Bilford's office, and I have a message for you from. . . ."

"Look Hall, I don't care whose messenger boy you are, don't you ever pull another stunt like that in my town again."

The Sheriff turned around and walked up the steps to the police station, as Hall followed after him. Inside he reluctantly took the envelope, opened it and read the letter from the governor. Despite himself, he was impressed by the man's calling card if not the message itself. He read it again, stalling for time to think.

"Do you understand what it says?" Hall asked.

"I can read all right," Howser replied angrily, then took his hat off and ran his hand through his hair.

"Good. So get your men together and let's get over there," Hall insisted.

Sheriff Howser could not refuse a direct order from the governor, as much as he hated complying with this police action. But he could insist on conditions that would ensure the safety of the patients. "Okay, but if we're going into the hospital, no guns, and just the two of us and my deputy." The Sheriff studied Hall's reaction, and he concluded that the bureaucrat would accept his demands, if under protest. "Otherwise, you can wait for the National Guard to take you in."

Time was more important at this point, Hall decided, than police force, and he reluctantly nodded his head. "Then let's go, Sheriff."

**2.**

In the second floor auditorium, which had been converted into a makeshift operating arena for the link-up experiment, the patients in wheelchairs were sitting in a circle holding hands fed by blood lines running between them. After more than an hour, the link-up had pushed several of the patients, Carl and Linda in particular, up to the brink of total transformation only to have them regress back to a leveled-off position where all the patients now hovered. Although there were fluctuations causing some movement up and down the scale, it was minimal at this point.

Inside the observation booth, there was a row of monitors displaying the readings for each of the patients. Andrea Hunter now typed instructions into her terminal that resulted in a series of comparative figures appearing on her screen. Joyner and Kellgren were leaning over her shoulder viewing the figures.

"It's the patients on the low end of the scale, the marginally committed ones, who are somehow holding it up, but it's still pretty close," Kellgren said.

"Maybe we should've screened everybody first," Dr. Hunter said.

"And how do you test for this kind of faith?" Joyner asked, and everybody shrugged their shoulders.

That response surprised Dr. Kellgren, and he studied his former pupil for a moment. There was something different about Joyner today. It intrigued him, but he certainly had no time to figure it out.

One of the other scientists, Dr. Kanter, a molecular biologist from Stanford, had overheard this conversation and stepped over. "I guess we just couldn't weed out the patients with the low figures, and regroup around the others?"

"Taking anybody out of the loop now would probably kill them and send the others into a downward spiral," Dr. Kellgren said, questioning the man's compassion.

Joyner nodded his head in agreement and then turned back to the terminal screen. He studied it for a moment. "Andrea, give me a reading on the average level of the blood sugar inducer." A figure now flashed on the screen. "And how does that compare with our estimate?" he asked.

Another figure, lower than the previous one, now came up on the screen. "It's above what we thought would be necessary to push the process to its completion."

Joyner shook his head in frustration. "Then what is holding

it up?"

Dr. Kellgren walked over to the window and looked out at the patients. He went from one to the other searching for an answer. They were poised in the middle between two worlds, as this energy poured into them from above precipitating the biological reaction within. And yet they held the key. Suddenly, it dawned on him. He remembered his talk with Linda on the beach, how she insisted that belief created reality. At this point it was strictly a matter of faith. Kellgren turned back to his colleagues. "Enough of them don't believe it's possible, despite what they've seen and what we've told them, and that's doing it. Belief is the catalyst that triggers this process."

"And like I said, how do you instill that kind of faith?" Joyner said in agreement.

"I think a demonstration would help," Kellgren said rather mysteriously.

Joyner passed this off as another one of his mentor's quirky statements, and he turned back to Hunter's terminal screen where the latest patient readings were now appearing. When he saw a new pattern emerging, Joyner looked up to call Dr. Kellgren over, but he apparently had left the room. Joyner looked out into the operating arena, but he was not there either. Since the new development required immediate action, he consulted with the other scientists, but he remained mildly annoyed with Dr. Kellgren for stepping out at such a crucial point.

An advance unit of the National Guard had arrived at the outskirts of town and was setting up a barricade across the coastal highway, stopping all traffic into San Martin. For the moment they were leaving the outgoing lane open. Sergeant Elmore Miers, a six-foot-five-inch black warehouse foreman from Fresno, and his unit had beat the other units heading south from the Bay Area and north along the coastal highway from San Luis Obispo. Coming in from the west, he had cut through the Los Padres National Park on a little-used fire road, hitting the coast just south of Big Sur. He had been in touch with the other two units all morning. The agreement had been that whichever arrived first would set up a roadblock at their end of town and then go in to barricade the hospital, while the other two units stayed back and manned the roadblocks, prepared to move in if needed.

With the roadblock in place, Sergeant Miers was now ready to move the rest of his unit into town for the more difficult part of this operation. He had finished lining up the caravan of troop carriers, tanks, and jeeps, when he heard a commotion at the roadblock. Until now traffic had been turned back with hardly a grumble from the sidetracked motorists and truckdrivers, but from the shouting he assumed somebody was refusing to cooperate.

Miers walked up to the row of sawhorses stretched across the road. A well-heeled executive type was arguing with one of his men.

"What's the problem here, Parker?" Miers asked.

"Been telling this...gentleman that the town's under quarantine, but he won't listen."

"If it's under quarantine," the irate motorist interjected, pointing to the outgoing traffic, "why are there cars leaving town?" When the Sergeant hesitated, the man continued, "I talked with my father last night, but he didn't say anything about this supposed epidemic."

Miers told himself he needed to come up with a story that would settle this dispute quickly, while showing his men how to handle future complaints. "Well, it's not exactly a quarantine, or at least not yet," he said, and then in a confidential tone, "and between you and me this story about an epidemic we're telling people is just a cover."

This made the motorist even angrier. "Well, there had better be a good explanation for this!"

Sergeant Miers nodded his head, his face a mask of seriousness. He now began to step closer to the motorist with each new revelation forcing a retreat. "Did your father happen to tell you about the strange disease going around town causing... genetic disorders?"

"Yeah, but I thought they'd contained it."

"Well, they did and they didn't," Miers said obliquely, taking another step and lowering his voice further. "It seems that all the patients became pregnant, even the men, and they're starting to give birth to. . . ." The Sergeant ran his hand over his face. "I've seen the pictures and, all I can say, is that they're not human."

The man was now backed up against his car. The story was getting a little far-fetched; no doubt the Sergeant was joking with him. He decided, however, that a town overrun by these gun-toting kids, was far more dangerous than what the Sergeant described.

The man got back into his Mercedes station wagon, and by making a sharp turn, he was able to spray the Sergeant and his men with a line of loose gravel from the side of the road. Miers wiped the sand off his face, and he then let out an uproarious laugh that was answered by hoots and howls from his men. When they had settled down, the Sergeant turned to them. "Okay ladies, let's move out."

When the gap between those patients at the bottom and at the top of the scale again began to diverge, Joyner's immediate reaction was to bring the patients back to a common level by adjusting the flow of blood and the circulation of the inducer to each patient. But, remembering Dr. Kellgren's insistence that this link-up was designed to create a more complex integrated system vulnerable to such fluctuations, which hopefully would reorder and transform it, he decided, against the advice of the other scientists, not to interfere with the process.

When Joyner heard his name called out and looked up from the terminal screen, he could hardly believe what he saw: Dr. Kellgren was standing in the doorway dressed in a hospital robe. Joyner walked over to him. "Max, you picked one hell of a time for a nap."

Kellgren threw his head back and laughed. "I had something just a little more strenuous in mind." He grabbed Joyner by the arm and pulled him out into the operating arena. There an orderly waited for him with a wheelchair.

Joyner took one look at the wheelchair and understood what Max had in mind. "Professor, I can't let you do it; it's suicide."

"For someone with six months to live, it's a calculated risk."

Joyner knew his old mentor was ill, but he did not realize it was that serious. "I'm sorry to hear that, Max. But isn't that all the more reason for you to live out the rest of your life instead of throwing it away on a wild gamble?" Joyner began pacing back and forth. "I mean, even if you helped them, it could kill you."

Dr. Kellgren took a seat in the wheelchair and nodded for the orderly to push him over to the circle of patients. Joyner followed closely behind. "Well, Guy, I've been a scientist all my life; I've believed what I've seen with my eyes and could prove with my mind. Faith for me was a fool's crutch. But, in these last few months, I've seen too much not to believe in other possibilities."

"I can go along with that," Joyner said with sincerity. "But nobody's asking you to stake your life on it."

"Well, that's the thing about faith: it requires that you believe totally and completely. If you don't, it's not faith you have but mere conviction," Kellgren said, and looked up at his young colleague. "I have complete faith in this process and total trust in the beings who are directing this transformation, and because of that, I am willing to stake my life on it."

Joyner could hardly contest such a pronouncement, and he could only hope the man's current faith was as well-founded as his previous science. "And you think the others will rally around you, and together you can push the process to its completion?"

"I believe it," Dr. Kellgren said with a twinkle in his eye. When they pulled up to the circle of wheelchairs, a place was opened for him and the orderly pushed him into his slot. A nurse now stuck the IV needle in his arm, hooked him up to the blood line, and turned the circulating pump back on. Max Kellgren looked around the circle of stunned patients. "You didn't think I was going to let you go without me, now, did you?"

## 3.

The Sheriff pulled up in front of the hospital and parked his patrol car on the street. Jerome Hall jumped out of the car and raced up the hospital steps, while the Sheriff and his deputy followed at a more leisurely pace. When the two of them walked up to the front desk, Hall was arguing with one of the nurses. In frustration he turned to Howser. "Sheriff, would you please tell this old witch who I am?"

"Mable, this gentlemen is Jerome Hall from the Department of Health Services in Sacramento," Howser said, then added disdainfully, "and a close personal friend of the governor himself."

"Well, I don't care if he's married to the old fart, he won't get anything out of me until he learns some manners." The elderly nurse went back to her register and made a notation.

Sheriff Howser could not help but smile at the woman's orneriness, and then he took his time before asking, "Mable, would you tell me where I could find Dr. Joyner?"

The nurse looked up, and in her most flirtatious voice, she said, "Why sure Sheriff, anything for you; he and the others are in the second floor auditorium. Just take the elevator and. . . ."

Hall rushed off before hearing her directions. At the elevator he waited for ten seconds, tapping his foot impatiently, and finally took the stairs up to the second floor. He looked around for a sign, but, not finding one, he chose a direction and raced off. Hall peeked in every doorway and opened every closed door until he came to the end of the hall. He cursed to himself, then turned around and walked back. He finally decided to ask for directions and stopped a woman passing by in a candy-striped dress.

"Hey lady, where in the hell is the auditorium?" he asked.

The woman looked at him and shook her head in disgust. She now pointed back down the hall. "First left, second right."

When Hall finally found the auditorium and walked inside, the light was so bright that he had to put his hand up in front of his eyes to block it out. Turning aside he saw Barry Hamilton a few feet away, and he walked over to him. "Henry said to tell you

you're fired."

Hamilton did not appear to have heard a single word spoken to him, as he continued to stare into the light, transfixed by a vision seen. By now Hall had adjusted his eyes to the light and looked off in the same direction. He could hardly believe what he saw. Some of them were still sitting in wheelchairs, others were getting up and shedding their oversized hospital robes, while a few of them walked around the room in an apparent daze. They were about four feet tall with incredibly thin bodies, and at first glance they could pass as emaciated twelve-year-olds if it were not for their enormous heads. They were dome-shaped and appeared almost porous, and it was hard to believe these childlike bodies could hold the weight of such heads. But, by far their most distinctive feature was light blue eyes set back under a bulging forehead, as if they had been tunneled out of the surrounding flesh. The central body cavity was too thin for ribs or a spine, and Hall wondered what it used for support. The arms and legs were thinner still, and these naked bodies had no hair or genitalia.

Everybody in the room was crying softly, and you could hear a chorus of gasping breaths. Hall thought that if he stared at this incongruous sight much longer he would surely lose his mind. He turned away and, spotting the Sheriff and his young deputy, stepped over to them. "Sheriff, aren't you going to do something?"

Howser, his eyes brimming with tears, found this call to hostile action ridiculous. He looked back at Hall and shook his head. When the others moved in for a closer look, the Sheriff and his deputy joined them, leaving Hall standing alone. Seeing their reception by the townspeople, he realized that he would have to wait until later to take action against these alien beings. With the National Guard set up around the hospital, he would have plenty of firepower to handle these little monsters when the time came.

Hall turned and started for the door. That was when he spotted the salesman. The man was leaning up against the wall watching him. He found the intensity of the man's stare annoying, and when he passed by him on the way out, he asked, "And so who the hell are you?"

The man stepped over flashing his dazzling smile and extended his hand. "Charlie Bonner, salesman extraordinaire."

Hall was almost fooled by the man's sudden friendliness, but then he remembered this name from an earlier report and recognized the voice from the tape recording. He took one look into those hypnotic eyes, pulled his hand back before making contact, and practically ran out of the building.

In the operating arena, family members watching from the gallery had now joined the others and looked on in amazement at these magnificent beings. Although they had seen the transformation of their loved ones take place, it was still hard to believe. The patients, or "transees," as one onlooker had dubbed them, were now drifting about in a daze. Since they looked exactly alike, an impression that was modified upon closer inspection, nobody could easily spot their transformed relatives, adding to the confusion.

Millie and Stanley Porter were circulating around the room looking for Linda. Although they were reassured in the presence of these beings about their daughter's transformation, they still wanted to gaze into her eyes and see some sign of recognition. When one of the transees stopped and stared at them from across the room, Stanley grabbed his wife's arm and nodded at the one who was now walking over. It stopped ten feet away and looked at them. The glow surrounding its body began to grow with each passing moment until it reached out and enveloped them. They were now suffused with a love that set their bodies on fire. It stepped over and put its long willowy arms around Millie's waist and pressed its enormous head to her stomach. When it extended a hand to him, Stanley took it and then read its plastic identification bracelet: Linda Boyer. "It's her, Millie," Stanley said with tears streaming down his face, as he reached over and put his arms around the two of them.

Guy Joyner had been watching this scene from the control booth where everybody was in a jubilant mood. Ken Olson had even gone for a bottle of champagne and was now passing out Styrofoam cups of it. Although he was delighted with the success of the experiment, despite the uncertainty of the transees' future welfare, he was not certain how to proceed from here. Olson had spotted a military unit setting up outside the hospital, and although Joyner had alerted the press and hoped their presence would prevent any hostile action, there was no guarantee of that. It appeared that a public appeal for the transees' safety was the best course of action at present.

The door to the control booth now opened, and one of the transees stepped inside. For the scientists, watching these developments from their glass booth was like viewing a science fiction movie. But now the little alien had jumped off the screen and hopped into their laps. Everybody stopped in mid-motion and quietly watched the creature move down the aisle, the electronic equipment on either side greeting its passage with some quirky behavior. It stopped in front of Guy Joyner. He lowered himself to a squatting position eye level with the transee. Guy read its bracelet: it was Max Kellgren. He put his arms around his old friend and cried the first tears of his adult life.

Max pulled back to arm's length and looked at Guy intently. You could see the folds of brain matter moving across his still soft forehead; Guy watched and waited but nothing happened. Max now touched his head and then reached over and tapped Joyner's. He was definitely trying to communicate something.

"Dr. Joyner, I think he's trying to talk with you telepathically," Olson suggested.

Guy pointed at his assistant asking if Max understood him, but he shrugged his shoulders in a decidedly human gesture. Max now went over to Dr. Hunter's computer terminal, and she scooted her chair out of the way. Everybody gathered around. He passed his hand over the keyboard, and it turned itself on and began to type out a message on the screen: FOR UNEVOLVED TYPES YOU GUYS ARE ALL RIGHT. Everybody in the control booth broke out laughing. Max took Guy's hand, and then made another pass over the keyboard: THERE'S SOMEONE YOU NEED TO MEET. He now pulled his friend away and led him out the door.

In the auditorium, more families had found their loved ones and were having a tearful reunion. Max brought him over to the salesman, who was watching the scene. He turned to them. "Oh Max, there you are. You'd better go over and round up the others. We'll be leaving shortly." Max put his arms around Guy's waist and gave him one last hug, then turned and walked back.

"He understood you," Guy said.

"The verbalization was for your benefit, doctor."

Guy looked at the man skeptically, but he could not deny that Max had understood him and followed his instructions. Upon closer inspection, he could see this was definitely not the salesman they had interrogated earlier.

"So Dr. Joyner, we finally meet," the salesman said mischievously. "You know I've been following your career for some time now."

"Have you?" Guy asked dubiously.

"Do you remember that chemistry set your parents got you for your tenth birthday?" the salesman asked, and Guy nodded his head in astonishment. "Well, we kind of 'persuaded' them to buy the deluxe model. I think you'll agree it was a good investment." He gave Guy a moment to recover from the shock. "We don't have much time. So, if you'll follow me, we'll go somewhere for a quiet chat." He took the dazed scientist by the arm and led him away.

**4.**

When Jerome Hall stepped out onto the front porch of the hospital, he was reassured by the sight before him. The National Guard had set up a barricade across the front lawn using two tanks and 150 infantrymen. With two more Guard units waiting to join them, and an army battalion heading their way, Hall felt confident he had enough firepower to manage the situation. However, while walking down the steps, he could see that this National Guard unit lacked a strong military posture. The men were loosely strung out along the line joking and horsing around with each other. Since they were also brought in to control the local citizens, who were now gathering at the barricade, he found their behavior unprofessional.

Hall walked up to the black noncom in charge. He read the man's name tag. "Sergeant Miers, I'm Jerome Hall from the governor's office." The man nodded his head but did not react otherwise. Hall turned and looked down the line of soldiers. "Sergeant, your men don't seem to be taking this deployment very seriously."

"Is that a fact," Miers said, as he turned and watched the line of soldiers for a moment. "Yeah, well, we're not regular army: we don't get paid to stand at attention until we drop."

"Then maybe we should wait until a regular unit arrives," Hall said, as he carefully watched the Sergeant's reaction.

"If you can get your 'friends' in there to wait for another six hours, I'll be happy to pull my men back to the nearest bar," Miers said. When Hall gave him a skeptical look, the Sergeant walked over to a nearby jeep and picked up the radio phone.

Hall glared at the man for a long moment before turning away. The Sergeant put the phone back. "You don't have to worry about these men; they'll snap to it when the time comes."

"Well, I hope so," Hall said, resigned to the situation for now.

Hall watched the crowd forming around the outside of the barricade for a moment. He was not sure how much force would be needed to place the "patients" under protective custody, which was the standing order in the event Joyner did succeed with the experiment. He wondered how much force these townspeople would tolerate. Hall kept reminding himself that, despite their otherworldly appearance, these "beings" were the friends and relatives of the people gathered here. If the reception afforded them inside was any indication, they might have to clear the square before proceeding.

"Sergeant, if we need to call in the other two units, how long would it take?"

"Have them here and set up within fifteen minutes."

"Okay, then radio and tell them to stand by," Hall said.

Miers was walking over to the jeep when a helicopter swooped in at treetop level and buzzed them. A moment later another one flew over from the other direction with a cameraman hanging out of the side filming them. When the first helicopter circled around and then hovered over the town square, Miers stepped clear of the others and tried to wave them off. When the pilot ignored him, the Sergeant called out to a soldier who had just popped his head out of the tank's hatch. "Castleman, send this turkey a message for me."

Shading his eyes with his hand, he looked up into the sun and read the CBS call letters on the side of the helicopter. "I hope Dan Rather is up there." He slid back down inside, and a moment later the tank's turret swiveled around and its gun rose and pointed directly at the helicopter. It quickly lifted up and sped away; the other one followed after it, and the two of them landed in the park at the far end of town.

Hall raced after them on foot and caught up with the two film crews halfway between the hospital and the park. The news teams were from the CBS and NBC affiliates in San Francisco that Dr. Joyner had called that morning. Hall now stepped out to block their way. "This city is under military quarantine, and I'm going to have to ask you to leave immediately."

The director of the CBS crew, Bart Travis, answered his request by turning to his cameraman. "Go ahead and roll it, Hank." His commentator, Leslie Howell, now stepped in front of the camera and read the teleprompter. "We are in San Martin, California, where a strange viral agent has triggered a genetic process resulting in the transformation of several local residents into a new species of humans." Howell now put her hand up in front of the camera. "Is this for real or what, Bart?"

"That's what we've got so go with it," he said shaking his head in dismay.

Howell now turned to Jerome Hall and stuck out her microphone. "I am now speaking with. . . ." Hall ran his hand through his hair. "Jerome Hall from the Department of Health

Services. And that is a totally unfounded rumor. I have personally met with these patients, who are suffering from a terrible disfiguring disease, and nothing more."

A commotion coming from the town square disrupted the interview. The director of the NBC crew, Mark Paxton, who was waiting to interview Joyner, turned to his CBS counterpart. "We're going up ahead and catch what's happening, and then we'll trade." Travis nodded his head in agreement, and the other crew started off.

"Hey, come back here," Hall yelled out, but the interview resumed before he could rush after them.

"We were alerted to this situation by Dr. Guy Joyner, the renowned geneticist, heading the medical team treating these patients," Howell said.

Hall could feel himself losing control of the situation, and he lashed out in anger. "Well, Dr. Joyner has been under a great deal of stress, and however qualified, his is only one opinion. Other team members of equal scientific stature do not concur with this conclusion." He could see his statement had the desired effect. "I want to emphasize that their extraordinary condition is not the result of genetic experiments by scientists, human or otherwise, but strictly the result of an unknown disease process. And that this virus is not, and I repeat...not contagious. There is absolutely no threat to the general population."

The director was frantically scribbling a message on a cue card, which he now held up. Howell read it and turned back to Hall. "Excuse me, but Dr. Joyner never said anything about genetic experiments."

Jerome hmm'd to himself before replying. "There was a rumor going around, again totally unfounded, that the virus precipitating this change had been genetically altered."

Cued by her director, Howell asked, "And when you said 'not by scientists, human or otherwise,' what exactly did you mean by 'otherwise'?"

Hall could not believe he had been so careless, and he tried to gloss over his mistake. "Another crazy rumor unworthy of your attention," Jerome said offhandedly, but from the woman's suspicious look, he knew she would not let it drop at that.

Howell was about to grill him further, when the director stepped between them waving his arms. Travis was receiving a message through his earphone, and when it concluded, he told them, "Okay everybody, we're heading over to the hospital and catch the action there firsthand."

Travis and Howell walked off at a brisk pace, while the technical crew packed up their gear. Hall followed after them, and the three of them arrived at the hospital together. Mark Paxton fought his way over to them through the now massive crowd. "Somebody made an announcement that Dr. Joyner would be coming out shortly with the patients, and asked that the news teams be set up to film it."

"Sorry, but I can't allow that," Hall insisted. He was about to raise a further objection when a crowd surge swept him off to the side.

"What do you think?" Paxton asked. "Can this guy close us down?"

"Not on your life," Travis spit out vehemently. His crew had arrived on the scene, and together they pushed their way through the crowd to the barricade and started setting up their equipment.

Guy Joyner had been sitting in the small office across the hall from the auditorium listening to the salesman's story. He now sat back in his chair and closed his eyes. After the events of the last six months, coupled with the incredible transformation of his patients only moments ago, it would have been easy to accept even the most outlandish scenario without critical evaluation. But he resisted that temptation.

"Let me understand this," Joyner said, leaning forward again. "You say you've been here setting up this experiment for a hundred years?"

"This phase of it, but actually it goes back much, much further."

"Well, if it's an object lesson about the right use of genetic engineering in man, you're still a hundred years early."

"I'd say fifty. In a hundred, you'd have so altered the true course of your evolution that it'd be sidetracked forever."

"And our friends out there," Joyner nodded in the direction of the auditorium, "represent, I take it, the preferred end result?"

"Preference has nothing to do with it," he said emphatically. "It's an evolutionary unfoldment that not only includes your species but all species on the planet, all planets within your solar system, and all star systems within the galaxy as a whole."

"And yet, from what you've told me of the science involved and from what I've seen of my patients' development, it was genetically engineered," Joyner replied.

"Oh, was it indeed?" the salesman said, and gave Dr. Joyner time to question that opinion. "Or, was that planned to activate the only transformative force capable of such an evolutionary leap?"

Dr. Joyner had assumed that the experimental channeling of energy was a desperate attempt to salvage a doomed process. He had never suspected that in itself it represented, in whatever form, another evolutionary force besides the two accepted by Darwinian thinking: gene frequency and the phenotypic characters of the organism (those behavioral traits that affect reproduction). "And what exactly would that be?"

The salesman paused a moment for hightened dramatic effect. "What you would call the spirit or soul of the individual."

"And it is that development, I take it, that accounts for your advancement?"

"You could say that."

"And this technology?" Joyner asked.

"Borrowed from other 'races' and adapted to your species' unique requirements."

"These others races, did they make good use of their science?"

"In time all saw its inherent limitations," the salesman said. He paused, as Dr. Joyner looked at him with heightened curiosity, and then he continued. "Among other things, what we wanted to demonstrate was that life, all life, is created and sustained by the interface between spirit and matter. Each is a perfect reflection of the other. To change, by altering or merging, the inherent pattern in any life form will cut off that pathway until it withers and dies away."

Joyner now thought about the pain his patients had suffered, and he wondered. "But surely there must've been an easier way to deliver your message?"

"If it were merely that, we would've sent a telegram," the salesman said. "And if a demonstration was all that was required, then we would've sent a troupe of actors."

"But instead you set up this elaborate experiment to do what: activate this 'force' in a few people?"

"And for the effect that would have on the race itself," the salesman conceded.

"Which is what, if I may ask?"

"To be determined in the next stage of our little experiment," he said, then added rather obliquely, "which will require your cooperation and that of a 'few' more people."

## 5.

The two news teams had set up their cameras and were waiting for Dr. Joyner's entrance. Bart Travis was talking to Leslie Howell, who was doing a quick make-up job on her face, when the front doors of the hospital swung open and the salesman stepped out onto the porch accompanied by the transees.

"Jesus Christ," Hank said, and yelled to his director. "Bart, take a look at this." The cameraman practically poked his eye out jamming it into the eyepiece of his portable video unit. He brought the picture into sharp focus and flipped it on.

Travis and Howell turned around; they were both dumbstruck by the sight before them. She dropped her compact on the pavement, but did not even hear the mirror shatter. Mark

Paxton stepped over to them. "I can see why they wanted to keep a lid on this."

"Well, they didn't," Travis said ecstatically, "and we just stumbled on to the story of the century."

The salesman was now joined by Dr. Joyner, and the two of them followed by a small contingent of the transees began to walk down the steps.

Sergeant Miers turned to his men. "Don't anybody do anything."

When they reached the bottom of the steps, the salesman looked around for moment and then walked straight up to the CBS director. "I would like to make a statement to the world community, can you arrange that?"

Travis thought about it for moment, when Paxton spoke up, "Our local affiliate has a portable satellite unit we could send it out on."

"That's great, Mark. Let's do it." Paxton hurried off to arrange for the satellite feed. Travis turned back to the two men. "Now which of you is Dr. Joyner?"

Guy stepped up. "I'm Joyner."

"If you're Joyner, then who's he and what's he going say?" Travis asked, confused by this mixup in identities.

Joyner looked at the salesman, who gestured for him to explain. "He's one of them," he said, and pointed to the group of transees, "and what he's going to say could very well change the course of human history."

"Okay," Travis said, somewhat taken aback. "Coupled with a shot of your little friends here, and with your introduction, I think you've got your audience." He now looked over at the salesman. "For how long depends on you."

"Don't worry," the salesman said, "I'm going to knock them dead in Des Moines."

Looking into the salesman's eyes, Bart did not find that as reassuring as it was meant to sound. However, his news sense told him that whatever transpired, he would be known for the rest of his career as the man who got this story out. He now motioned for Leslie Howell to come over, and he introduced her to the two men. "While we're setting this up, we need to get a little background story for Leslie's lead-in." They nodded their heads in agreement and followed the woman off to the side.

Along the barricade the transees were now approaching the soldiers. You could almost feel the tension rippling through the line, hear a collective dry gulp from the men. Sergeant Miers was watching this development with concern. "Okay boys, everybody keep cool," he said, and as they came closer, the Sergeant added, "Why, they look about as harmless as a bunch of fawns." A transee now stepped up and put its arms around one of the soldiers. Terrified at first the man slowly warmed up to the creature and returned the hug.

Another transee walking down the line stopped and stared off into the crowd in what appeared to be puzzled recognition. The bystanders pushed forward, and someone reached through the line, took its hand, and read the hospital bracelet. He turned back to the others with tears streaming down his face. "It's Betty. . . Betty Carr." Everyone looked on in astonishment at this creature who had been their neighbor, a Girl Scout leader, and a civic organizer before her devastating illness. To see her transfigured overnight into this celestial being swelled their hearts with great joy. They all pushed forward, breaking through the barricade and sweeping her up in a collective embrace. This scene was repeated up and down the line until the crowd had absorbed the soldiers and the transees into its body.

The two camera crews were now ready to record the salesman's statement. Dr. Joyner was standing with the woman reporter on the hospital steps surrounded by a small group of transees. Bart Travis was standing off to the side talking into his headset with the technicians in the remote unit on the street. He now stepped forward and turned to the cameramen. "Okay, we're ready. I want you to open with a fifteen-second shot of the. . . transees, then pan up to a two-shot of Leslie and Dr. Joyner ending up with full shot of everybody. Okay?" The two men nodded their heads in agreement, and Travis stepped back and gave Howell her cue.

"This is Leslie Howell of CBS News coming to you from San Martin, California. You are looking at former patients here who were infected with what at first appeared to be a strange new virus, but which in fact had been genetically altered to precipitate the evolution of what one expert has called a new subspecies of *Homo sapiens.*" Howell now turned to Joyner. "I have Dr. Guy Joyner with me, the world-renowned geneticist called in to deal with this crisis. Tell us, Dr. Joyner. How did this startling development occur and who is responsible for it?"

"At first we thought this was a viral agent that could trigger cellular transformation, or cancer, in many different organs. But it soon became apparent that these were healthy tissue growths of an unknown nature. Closer study of these new cell types revealed the kind of wholesale reshuffling of genetic material one would expect to see with the emergence of a new species."

Joyner paused and looked over at the director, who nodded his head for him to continue. "However, it became evident after awhile that the genes precipitating this evolutionary advance were genetically engineered by a science far in advance of our own. That our patients were in fact subjects of a genetic experiment conducted by . . . 'offplanet' beings . . . ."

At the state capitol, Secretary Bilford was in the governor's office watching the broadcast from San Martin. Sitting at his desk, Governor Walker tried to follow it, while talking with the President on the phone. "Yes, Mr. President," he said, wiping beads of sweat off his forehead with the sleeve of his shirt. "But, we just found out about it yesterday." While he listened to another tirade about bureaucratic snafus, Walker put his hand over the phone receiver and turned to Bilford. "Dammit Henry, I thought you said your man could handle this."

"I can't imagine what happened," he said sheepishly. "Jerome should've known better than to let them broadcast this circus live." The Governor gave his longtime crony a chilling look before answering the President's next question.

Bilford turned back to the television, where Dr. Joyner was seen standing on the hospital steps surrounded by the transees. "...that our patients were in fact subjects of a genetic experiment conducted by...'offplanet beings,' as they prefer to be called."

Governor Walker put his hand back over the phone receiver and turned back to Bilford. "Who did he say was responsible, Henry?"

"Off-planet...beings, whatever that means," he said in exasperation.

"It means Joyner has either lost his mind or we're about to lose ours."

At the Pentagon in Washington, the Army Chief of Staff was sitting in the War Room watching the broadcast from San Martin with heightened concern. His counterpart from the Air Force came into the room and pulled up a chair. "Is this some kind of joke?"

"Let's hope so, General."

The two grim-faced men along with the military personnel on duty looked up at the television monitor on the wall. Dr. Joyner stepped aside after introducing the salesman, and the camera now focused on him as he began to talk.

"Let me begin by saying that the gentleman through whose body I now speak has willingly volunteered his services so that this message can be delivered to you at this time. In my true state I am pure spirit, but once I was like you, trapped in embodiment here on this planet until that glorious day some ten thousand years ago when, as the Indian chief Asawa, I ascended from this plane. I have returned at this critical time in your history to initiate a course correction that will assure an evolutionary ascent that will one day, sooner for some than for others, return you to your rightful place among the stars."

"Can't we get this off the air?" General Hahn of the Air Force asked.

The Army Chief nodded his head and picked up the phone. "Ted, get me the President on the line."

In San Martin, Jerome Hall had finally fought his way through the crowd, and he now stepped up to the CBS director. "I insist that you stop this interview right now."

"Talk to my news chief," Travis said and turned his back on him.

Next Hall walked over to Sergeant Miers. "Sergeant, since this town is under military quarantine and since I'm acting on the Governor's behalf, I command you to stop this interview."

Miers looked around at the town square filled with civilians, at his soldiers intermingled with them, and finally at these vulnerable little creatures. He turned to Hall. "I only take orders from my superiors."

Hall walked over to the jeep and picked up the radio phone. "Well, then let's call them and get this settled." The Sergeant motioned for him to go ahead and make his call.

On the steps the salesman continued. "For all of you are descendents of the same great race of beings as myself. Our story on this planet began some five million years ago, when we happened upon this blue oasis in an endless sea of black space. Here we encountered something not found elsewhere, and we have traveled 'widely,' a physical form offering an array of new sensations that proved irresistible to us. So we chose a promising race of primates and embodied into their life cycle."

On the streets of Manhattan, as in cities across the country and around the world, people had dropped whatever they were doing and found the nearest television to watch the broadcast from California. There shoppers bundled up on a cold midwinter day were crowded around the main display window at Macy's.

The salesman was saying, "Thus began an evolutionary ascent accelerated by the light burning in each of you that precipitated the development of this humanoid form into one capable of greater physical and mental expression, culminating in modern *Homo sapiens*. But, in time, after countless incarnations, we began to lose awareness of our original state of being and became identified with this form. Until now, for most of you, it is all you consciously know. But, buried deep within, patiently awaiting its time, your greater self sleeps. That is, until most recently."

In Tokyo a large Japanese family was sitting in their sparsely furnished living room watching the broadcast. It was early morning, and the sleepy-eyed children were still dressed in their nightclothes. As the salesman continued, the members of the family listened attentively.

"By choosing the planet of a mid-cycle star, and given the evolutionary pressures already at work, we could ascertain that in time, as your sun slowly dies out, this humanoid form would evolve into a more perfect expression of spirit and be capable of spontaneously energizing the body physical and ascending. It was our safety valve, as you would say. Of course, any totally awakened soul has the same power, but for the race as a whole, there had to be an open pathway back. Now that avenue is being threatened, and my race, our race, faces eternal banishment in matter."

At a missionary hospital in Kenya, the doctors and nurses were sitting on the porch watching the broadcast. Several Masai warriors of the region were standing behind them talking among themselves. One of the doctors turned to a native colleague. "What are they going on about?"

The man shook his head in astonishment. "That the white man in the picture speaks perfect Masai."

"That's ridiculous, he's speaking in English," the doctor insisted.

"No," a nurse spoke out, "it's in French."

When they realized they were all hearing the man speak in their native tongue, everybody turned back to the broadcast with renewed interest.

The salesman paused, and looking straight into the camera, turned his head from side to side as if he were viewing a crowded scene. "Recently your scientists have begun to tamper with the genetic makeup of your species with the hope of one day improving it. Now to correct a defect is one thing, but to attempt to remake the species using any limited program will rob the gene pool of its great variability, and with that its ability to adapt to changing conditions within and without. In time, after each succeeding generation programs its own biased direction, the species will have lost its natural responsiveness. It will have fallen out of sync with the evolution of the planet and the solar system at large. And the soul will have lost its vehicle back to the stars."

At the White House in Washington, the President sat in the Oval Office with a hastily gathered assembly of his top advisors. They were watching the broadcast on a big-screen television with heightened concern. Behind them, speaking in a low voice, the Secretary of Defense was talking over the phone with the Joint Chiefs of Staff at the Pentagon about the military options open to them.

The salesman was now heard saying, "Use the knowledge gleaned from our experiment to alleviate pain and suffering for those afflicted with treatable defects. But don't presume to remake your species, when you know so little about the dangers involved and have so little understanding or appreciation for your real heritage and future possibilities."

The Secretary of Commerce now turned to the President. "Sir, may I suggest we quickly confiscate all this scientific data for. . .careful evaluation."

The President said, "This should give us a real jump on the Japanese." Everybody in the inner circle nodded their heads in agreement. They turned back to the broadcast.

In San Martin, Jerome Hall had finally reached the Governor and was talking with him on the radio phone. The soldiers at their sergeant's command had re-formed the barricade line and were nervously awaiting orders to take direct action against the transees. Hall now turned to Sergeant Miers some fifteen feet away and held the phone receiver in the air. "Sergeant, the Governor of the good state of California would like to talk with you."

Miers shook his head in abject defeat and reluctantly walked over to receive his orders. But, one of his men, supposedly startled by a tank starting up its engine, turned sharply with his drawn bayonet and cut off the jeep's antenna. The Sergeant took the phone, but all he could hear was static coming from the other end. Grinning broadly, he handed the receiver back to Hall and walked away.

On the steps of the hospital, the salesman continued, "In the last six months, we have conducted an experiment here in San Martin, and as you can see from my little friends, quite successfully. But, contrary to popular belief, they were not transformed by the genius of an advanced science, but by the force of an awakened soul. And it was not only the patients but the townspeople, the doctors and scientists, everyone here who has responded to this crisis with love and not fear, hate, or ignorance, who has awakened this force within themselves and fed the completion of this process."

The salesman paused as he again looked out as if viewing all of humanity in one sweep of his head. "Some have asked why we have chosen this time to make our presence known, when it is obvious to all that we have been here observing you for a very long time. Well, not long ago the five billionth human child was born. Another way of looking at it, is that many souls are now incarnate here. And that is the critical mass needed for planetary transformation."

An army helicopter now flew into sight and momentarily hovered over the town square. Everybody looked up at it before it sped away. The salesman waited until he had their attention again. "The time grows short, but before my friends retire to the mountain caves behind this town, hopefully to complete the final stage of their transformation, I would like to demonstrate the possibilities open to all willing to call forth from its long slumber that greater part of themselves. For this I will now transform by the gentleman's consent the body I inhabit. This unassuming salesman, this peddler of trinkets, has shown the faith needed to reach out and embrace his future." The man now stepped clear of the others and stretched his arms out to the crowd and the viewing audience in a gesture of welcome. "COME JOIN US NOW!"

Suddenly the tips of his fingers began to shine with a bluish, white light. That radiant glow moved down his fingers, across his open hands and up his arms, leaving a vaporish trail in its wake. When it reached the trunk of the body, the light split in two, moving at once up the neck and down the chest. Soon the entire body was set ablaze by the burning of the light. Reflected through the rising vapor, a rainbow-colored halo now appeared around the transformed body, giving form to the luminosity. Then, without warning, it shot upward and arced across the now-darkening sky to the cheers of those below, and then it swung back and hovered over the square. The soldiers, at Miers's command, now escorted the transees through the crowd and loaded them onto transport vehicles for a short ride to the mountains behind the town.

## San Martin, California
## January 31

### 6.

As the helicopter swooped in low over the mountain range, the huge granite block hanging beneath it dipped down and clipped the tops off a row of pine trees. The pilot looked out and could see several hikers scrambling to avoid the falling timber. He turned to his co-pilot and gave him a thumbs-up signal, then pulled the helicopter up as they approached the mountain. At the entrance to the cave, a unit of the Army Corp of Engineers was waiting to put the granite block in place. The helicopter now came in and hovered overhead, slowly lowering its load. The engineers grabbed hold of the block from either side and guided it into the steel frame built around the entrance. They now secured it with huge metal clamps on both sides, then signaled for the pilot to drop his line. A moment later the block hit the floor of the cave with a resounding thud. The helicopter lifted off and then joined the others spotting hikers for the ground troops, who were trying to gather up the remaining trespassers before their five o'clock deadline.

In town a caravan of cars pulling U-hauls and open trailers stacked high with furniture slowly moved down Alameda heading for the highway out of town. They passed by an army bus with barred windows parked in front of the Sheriff's office. It was half-filled with disgruntled townspeople who had refused to leave town and tried to evade the Army's last-minute evacuation sweep. A jeep now pulled up with an elderly couple sitting in the backseat.

"But what about our belongings?" asked the man.

"Sorry folks, but you've had ample time to gather them up," Lieutenant Dodge said. "But don't worry, Uncle Sam will replace everything you've left behind."

The old man shook his head in disgust. How could money replace fifty years of memories, and how could he explain that to this child? He took his wife by the arm, and they slowly walked over to the bus.

Captain Thomas Baer, in charge of the Army's evacuation, now stepped out of the Sheriff's office and looked up and down Alameda at the long line of cars. He shook his head; it was moving much slower than anticipated. He now walked over to Lieutenant Dodge. "Lieutenant, how's the roundup proceeding?"

"Sir, there're still twenty-five people unaccounted for."

"Well, keep looking, but at four o'clock I want you back here," Baer said. "We're going to start pulling people out of their cars at that point and fly them out of here."

The Lieutenant nodded his head in beleaguered acknowledgment, got back in his jeep, turned it around and drove up the street in the opposite direction of the outgoing traffic.

At the roadblock outside town, both lanes of traffic were now open heading north along the coastal highway. On the side of the road, the CBS camera crew was set up, filming a report by Leslie Howell with the line of cars moving behind her in the background. Suddenly, there was a five-second earthquake tremor. Everybody stood still for a moment, and the cars came to a stop. An avalanche of small rocks slid down the roadside cliff and swept up against the inside row of cars. And then it was over.

Fifty yards up the highway, two hikers, apparently dislodged by the tremor, tumbled out of the underbrush onto the road.

Soldiers raced up the road to place them under arrest. Bart Travis, the CBS director, stepped in front of Leslie Howell and stopped the report. He now turned to his cameraman. "Hank, take the portable unit and follow Leslie." He turned to his commentator, but she had already taken off after the soldiers.

When Hank caught up with her, Howell had talked the soldiers into letting her interview the two hikers. She now turned to the camera. "And even now, as the last of the residents are being evacuated from San Martin, thousands of others, disregarding earthquake warnings and risking life and limb, are streaming into the surrounding mountains."

Leslie Howell now turned to a bearded young man in his early twenties, wearing a T-shirt that read: DON'T NUKE THE SPOOKS. "Tell me, were you planning to go on despite the severity of this last tremor?"

"Tremor my ass, that's the Army setting off charges to scare everybody away."

"Do you have any proof of that?" Howell asked excitedly.

Before he could answer the question, the two soldiers grabbed the boy by the arm and started dragging him, fighting and kicking, back to the troop carrier filled with the other interlopers. They left his companion, a young girl in her late teens, a glassy-eyed "space cadet," behind. Howell walked up to her, and she could not help but smile at the slogan on the girl's T-shirt: TAKE ME WITH YOU. "Would you really go through with it?" she asked her. "Let them actually transform you like the others?"

With an insolent toss of her head, she looked up at the commentator. "As long as they didn't turn me into a news hound."

With flushed cheeks, Howell turned back to the camera for her summation. "Well, there you have it: two rugged young individuals, defying a county-wide quarantine, here with thousands of others, to protect what they consider the latest endangered species. This is Leslie Howell for CBS News in San Martin, California."

She now turned to the director to ask about cutting the girl's comment, when another earthquake tremor hit. There was no mistaking it for an explosive charge, as the ground rose beneath them before dropping back down, knocking everybody off their feet. When they stood up and brushed themselves off, Bart Travis turned to his crew and told them to pack up their gear because they were heading home.

In the cave for the past week, the transees under Asawa's guidance had prepared themselves for their ascension. The process was essentially to recognize that the ability to ascend, to transmute the physical body into energy and then solidify it at some distant point, was a long dormant faculty, a part of their totality, that could be called upon once they assumed its ownership again. What had heretofore blocked it out was the overriding belief in their present identity, no matter how elevated or inclusive that description.

The major lesson was for them to realize that there was no time-space. The supposed distance between objects in the physical world, or between points in time was merely a mental configuration. Like all physical manifestation, it was based on a mass belief, and one that could be altered by the individual. Next came exercises on how to move the body from one place to another as you would move an object within the mind. Since all objects including the body were part of the mind, part of the spirit, the I AM essence of each of them, such movement did occur solely in the mind directed by one's thoughts.

As such one would not catapult across space to arrive at a distant point. One simply would leave here and arrive there simultaneously. Also, since the body would be a mass of particles, it could also be transmuted into other forms during this transition. By breaking down their belief systems on the size limitations of the body, this method had once been used to enlarge the body and create a race of giants. The body could also be condensed to a smaller size, redesigned if desired, rejuvenated if needed, or even made immortal. All this and much more could be attained simply by breaking down old, outmoded belief systems and by replacing them with new systems that reclaimed for the individual lost parts of themselves. And they could also see that they, like other aspects of themselves, were part of a much greater whole. They sensed, felt deeply, overwhelmingly, the oneness and unity of all life. And now they were ready to harness the power of this totality, their overriding identity, to raise themselves along with it to a higher vibratory rate of pure and absolute love.

Across the country and around the world, people were following the events in San Martin with keen interest. And every thought, every feeling directed toward the transees sealed off in a mountain cave and under direct military threat, was feeding the process of their final transformation. But, as planned from the beginning, the process worked both ways. It was also drawing forth from each and every concerned human being that long-buried part of themselves that saw in the transees' struggle its own hope for survival. Like a slumbering giant, the human race was finally waking up.

As the final hours approached, the transees linked together in a circle. With outstretched hands inches apart, they looked up into the face of the image engraved on the slanted temple wall to seek communion with it. The image itself had changed from that seen earlier to a more beatific visage, transformed by their receptive hearts. They had come to realize that this image was a collective archetype from a racial memory that went back long before their current sojourn on this planet. And as they opened themselves to its transformative energies, they had turned aside its dark destructive face and now looked upon one of love and light.

Now the final channeling of energy began, but this time the energies flowed in not only from above but from within the collective body of the race itself. From around the globe a planetary link-up of an awakening humanity fed its vital energies into the transformation of this core group and were in turn fed by the powerful energies channeling through it. An integrated structure of five billion points, like neurons in a global brain connected and braided together, was formed by the flow of this energy. And it was slowly moving to that singular moment in time of maximum instability before it would either disintegrate or reorder itself at a higher level and transform the entire planet in the process. The catalyst was always one singular point, like the spark that kindles a forest fire. And the catalyst was ready.

## Edwards Air Force Base
## Mojave Desert
## 3 PM

### 7.

In the main briefing room, Major Jonathan Batton was standing at the podium briefing the crew of the B-1 bomber for the night's top-secret mission. Behind him was a map of California with the flight plan laid out in dashes. It started at the base, went south into Mexico, then across the Baja Peninsula out into the Pacific, arced north staying two hundred miles off the coast, then turned back over Northern California, south over the Sierra Nevadas, to Death Valley and then back to their base in the Mojave Desert.

Major Batton paused after the crew heard their destination and let this knowledge settle in for a moment before proceeding. "Because we've been unable to clear the area, we've changed our strategy from dropping a load of two-thousand-pounders to hitting the mountain with a single missile." There was a note of excitement in his voice as he described the missile. "It's right out of advanced research. And all I can say is that you can't see it, hear it, smell it, or track it. With the fake tremors as cover, a hit by this missile, shot by an aircraft on a routine mission two hundred miles away, will knock the top off this mountain and send these 'things' back where they belong. And the best part is that it'll end up looking like another Mt. St. Helen." He leaned over the podium and poked it hard with his forefinger for emphasis. "Anybody close enough to know differently won't be around to dispute that claim. I guarantee it."

Major Batton looked out at the four-man crew sitting in the front row of the huge hall. "Are there any questions?" The men showed little of the Major's enthusiasm for this mission, and they shook their heads no.

At the hangar the maintenance crew for the B-1 bomber had just finished its final check-out. While the crew chief double-checked their work, the men stood around the portable television set, sitting on the top of an overturned oil drum, and watched a live broadcast from San Martin without the sound. After Leslie Howell signed off, the network played back a brief recapitulation of the day's events. Here they saw shots of the mountain cave being sealed, an aerial shot of the surrounding mountains teeming with hikers, and the line of cars on main street heading out of town.

The pilot, Major Gary Fitzpatrick, now walked into the hangar followed by his downcast crew. He went over to the television set and watched it in silence, as they concluded this segment of their coverage with a replay of the salesman's transformation on the hospital steps. The crew chief, Master Sergeant Michael North, stepped over and watched it with him.

Fitzpatrick now turned to him, while nodding his head at the bomber. "She ready for a little spin?"

"She'll get you across the street and back," he said, chewing down on his tobacco wad.

"And our 'special package'?" Fitzpatrick asked.

"Oh, it'll be just fine," North said, smiling broadly. The two men turned back to the television set in time to watch the shooting star streak across the night sky.

In San Martin, a line of soldiers were carrying boxes filled with files and computer readouts down the steps of the hospital and stacking them in the back of an army troop carrier. Guy Joyner now walked out of the hospital with the last of the five patients who had refused to participate in the final experiment. By now they were being kept alive solely by artificial means, and they did not have very long to live. He watched from the porch as the two orderlies loaded the stretcher into the ambulance, got in and closed the door behind them, and drove away. When Joyner turned to go back inside, Captain Baer was standing in the doorway watching him. The man now walked over.

"Well, that looks like everything," Baer said as he studied Joyner's reaction. The Captain felt that Dr. Joyner's part in this sorry affair was downright treasonous, and if he had been military, Baer would have had him locked up and charged.

"I haven't been back there, but did you get the freezer with all the tissue samples?" Joyner asked in apparent concern.

The captain nodded his head, taken aback momentarily. "Is there any danger in handling this material?" he asked in a more conciliatory tone.

"Not from these samples; the only danger would be exposure to the live virus, and I believe you've already destroyed them," Joyner said with equal suspicion.

It was now Baer's turn to squirm uncomfortably, but he got the doctor's message. It left him with a grudging respect for the man. A jeep now pulled up in front of the hospital, and the driver beeped his horn several times. "Well, I'm going doctor, and I would strongly advise you to leave immediately. And I mean... now." Baer turned and hurried down the steps.

After the jeep had left, Joyner looked out at the now deserted streets of this town where so much had already happened and then up at the darkening sky, and he wondered what the coming night would hold in store for them.

Andrea Hunter now stepped out onto the porch and came over to him. "Ken called from San Diego and said he sent out the last set of disks to the University of Stockholm this morning."

"Along with the others, that should get it out there." Dr.

Joyner now turned to his assistant and asked her with some concern, "Are you sure about staying? We don't know what's going to happen?"

"I wouldn't miss it for anything," Dr. Hunter said adamantly.

At the grade school across town, the back door to the boiler room now opened, and Paul Jordan stuck his head out into the alley. He looked both ways and watched for traffic on the crossing streets, and when no cars had passed by for five mintues, Jordan stepped out and walked down the alley. At a good pace he reached Alameda in fifteen minutes, as the twilight became night. Walking down the center of the street, he met up with Hugh Clarke and his wife Naomi coming out of their store; they picked up Reverend Taylor and his wife at the next corner, and to everybody's surprise, Sheriff Howser and his young deputy Marty Keller were waiting for them in front of the jail.

When they reached the town square, they found a crowd of about fifty people there including Guy Joyner, Andrea Hunter, Barry Hamilton, a few people from the hospital, Sergeant Miers and one of his men, and some hikers who had come down out of the hills. Nobody knew exactly why they were here. They suspected it was dangerous, that the military had evacuated the town to blow up the mountain. But, despite this bleak outlook, they were all filled with high expectations and great hope for the transees, a hope that somehow disaster would be averted and the promise of their transformation fulfilled.

Major Fitzpatrick received the new route coordinates from his navigator and called in the change in his direction. "This is Zeta 5. I am now turning east on new coordinates. Estimated time of drop: fifteen minutes."

"Zeta 5, I read you. And have further instructions. Increased seismic activity at target, and that's the real stuff, boys, means you'll have to fly by at fifty thousand feet. Do not, and I repeat, do not descend below this altitude. Who knows, maybe this thing will blow on its own, and save Uncle Sam some money."

"Yeah," Fitzpatrick replied gruffly and flipped off his radio.

He would now observe radio silence for the remainder of the mission. He turned and looked out the cockpit window. It was dark now; the last rays of the sun, lasting longer at this altitude than at ground level, had finally died out. In the distance he could see the California coast outlined in flickering lights coming up fast. As they quietly slipped through the night approaching their target, the other crew members became increasingly nervous. Fitzpatrick could hear it in their voices, see it in his co-pilot's drumming fingers. Nobody liked the nature of this mission. When the call went out earlier in the week, everyone knew what the unspecified target would be, and there were no volunteers. Finally, after added pressure, Fitzpatrick came forward and put this crew together. From the start they sensed a strange commitment from him, as if he were on a private mission. They knew if anybody would stand up and defy these orders, he was their man. But now, as they closed in on their target, the others began to wonder.

"Major," his navigator said, "we are within range of the target."

"Okay, Pierce," Fitzpatrick said to his weapons officer, "start the firing sequence."

Lieutenant Pierce reached over and flipped on a row of switches. He waited for ten seconds until the red firing light flashed on, and then he pushed the button beneath it. "Firing."

The light continued flashing. He waited a moment before saying, "We have a malfunction. Am checking it out." Fifteen seconds later, Pierce said, "The release mechanism is stuck. Looks like the main hydraulic line has burst. Switching to backup." There was a moment of silence before he came back on the line. "Major, the backup line is frozen solid," he said in a voice mixed with surprise and elation.

Fitzpatrick flipped his radio back on. "This is Zeta 5 at site. System's problem prevents delivery of package at this time. Am turning around and heading back to base."

The plane was now buffeted by a strong shock wave. "Holy shit, look out the window, Fitz," yelled his co-pilot, Lieutenant

Howard.

The Major turned and saw the top of a mountain in the range up ahead exploding in a stream of bright light, forming a crater at its top. Out of the light shooting stars now flared out and arced across the night sky. The Major smiled knowingly, turned his plane southeast, straightened it out on a heading for their home base, and put the controls on automatic pilot.

A moment later, when a flash of light illuminated the cockpit, the co-pilot turned away from the window expecting to find the instrument panel on fire. To his great astonishment, he discovered that Major Fitzpatrick had disappeared, leaving scorch marks on his seat.

In the cave the final note had been struck, and the illuminate beings gathered there were now reduced to a billion particles of light, each particle singing its own individual song, yet each harmonically blended with the others, until they converged into a single all-pervading note of incredible power. As the beings coalesced into monads of light, the sound vibration blew the top off the mountain and sent their souls hurrying home.

In the town square the explosion shattered store windows around the block. At first, due to the extraordinary brightness of the light given off, people feared it was an atomic blast. If so, they soon realized that, at this distance, they would have been instantly vaporized. And then they saw the first of the shooting stars rising skyward. A roaring cheer went up from the crowd gathered here. As more of the shooting stars shot across the night sky, these people, who had fed the process with their faith and love, were now overcome with such joy that it set them ablaze. One after another of the witnesses were transformed. Some of them shooting skyward, while the others remained behind in their former bodies but now illuminated selves.

Lieutenant Howard was ordered to swing the bomber back around the target area and photograph the occurrence below.

With all the streaking lights flying past them, he thought they were being shot at and even armed his plane's remaining weapons. But these were no guided missiles. It took the flyers a moment to realize that these lights were the transformed patients returning, as the salesman had urged them, to their home among the stars. The spectacle moved everybody greatly. From this altitude they could see half the California coast, and what they now saw were lights blazing up everywhere. From the east, across the Sierra Nevadas, more lights were streaking across the night sky. The world was on fire, and the flame reached up and touched them all.

When the wreckage of the B-1 bomber was discovered in the mountains three days later, none of the four crew members were aboard, and it was unlikely anybody could have survived the crash.

# ACKNOWLEDGMENT

I would like to thank several people whose efforts have contributed, in one way or another, to the writing of this book: Brock Hood, who channeled a series of tapes from Raphael on ascension, from which I have drawn when describing this process; Tom Brennan, Ph.D., who looked over the final manuscript and caught a few scientific bloopers; and finally to Marilyn Ferguson, whose book *The Aquarian Conspiracy* first introduced me to Ilya Prigogine's theory of "Dissipative Structures" and to Gould and Eldredge's evolutionary theory of "Punctuated Equilibrium," which have so informed this work.

## AUTHOR'S AFTERWORD

The story for *Transformations* came to me in late 1984, while I was suffering from a bad case of Candidiasis. I began turning the story into a screenplay, since I lacked the concentration at that point to write prose. The screenplay was finished in late 1985. When my treatment of the subject proved too "heavy" for most producers, and after another year of research I decided, with my publisher's encouragement, to take the basic concept and write a full-length novel based on it.

Now, this story was written well before the current medical crisis with AIDS was upon us, and it was never intended, or at least not consciously so, as comment on the progress of that disease and the social reaction to it. Faced with my own, if somewhat less intense, medical crisis, I was seeking through my art a way out of this jungle of misinformed doctors and wrong-headed therapies, which were worse than the illness itself. I found that for me the only solution was meditating long and hard until I finally began to piece together, from a variety of sources, a program of therapy that led to my recovery.

With this biological sketch as a background, the reader is free to draw from the metaphorical content of my novel, which admittedly is more inconclusive than its source-material, whatever conclusions these symbols call forth. It could be that I was responding to an outcry from the collective consciousness of the race, but if so, I make no claim to have set out at the beginning to address such issues.

## ABOUT THE AUTHOR

John Nelson has been a serious student of metaphysics for over 20 years. He has worked in advertising as a writer and in the film business as a writer/director. Mr. Nelson now makes his home in Virginia Beach, Virginia where he is presently working on another novel.